Nigerian parents. She holds a PhD in English and is a professor of creative writing and literature at the University of Buffalo. She has written more than a dozen books for children, young adults and adults. Her first novel *Zahrah the Windseeker* won the Wole Soyinka Prize for African Literature (2008) and was shortlisted for the CBS Parallax Award and the Kindred Award in 2010. In 2011, her novel, *Who Fears Death* won the World Fantasy Award and was nominated for the Nebula Awards. In 2015, her novel *Lagoon* was nominated for the British Science Fiction Association award for Best Novel and The Kitschies Red Tentacle Award for Best Novel. Her adult novel *The Book of Phoenix* was a finalist for the Arthur C. Clarke Award (2016) and her latest Sci-Fi novella *Binti* was the winner of the 2016 Nebula Award for Best Novella. You can find Nnedi on Twitter (@Nnedi), Facebook and Instagram (@nnediokorafor). For more information, visit her website: www.nnedi.com.

WHAT SUNNY SAW IN THE FLAMES

Nnedi Okorafor

Abuja – London

Copyright © Nnedi Okorafor 2016

First published by Viking, an imprint of Penguin Random House, 2011.

First reprint, 2021

A CIP catalogue record for this book is available from the British Library.

ISBN (UK) 978-1-911115-10-6
ISBN (Nigeria) 978-978502-385-5
eISBN 978-1-911115-11-3

Printed and bound in Great Britain by Bell & Bain Ltd, Glasgow.
Distributed in the UK by Central Books Ltd.

Stay up to date with the latest books, special offers and exclusive content with our monthly newsletter. Sign up on our website:
www.cassavarepublic.biz

Twitter: @cassavarepublic
Instagram: @cassavarepublicpress
Facebook: facebook.com/CassavaRepublic

To my mother,
who was terrified of masquerades as a
kid and still is.

This book dances with them. Enjoy.

You need imagination in order to imagine a future that doesn't exist.

Azar Nafisi, Iranian writer

Contents

1

PROLOGUE
THE CANDLE

I've always been fascinated by candles. Looking into the flame calms me down. NEPA is always taking the light, so I keep them in my room. Candles and matches don't run out of batteries the way a torch does.

One night, after the power went out, I lit a candle as usual. Then, also as usual, I got down on the floor and just gazed at its flame.

My candle was white and thick. It reminded me of the ones they use in church. I lay on my belly and just stared and stared into it. So orange, like the abdomen of a firefly. It was nice and soothing until...it started flickering.

Then, I thought I saw something. Something serious and big and scary. I moved closer.

The candle just flickered like any other flame. I moved even closer, until the flame was an inch from my eyes. I could see something. I moved closer still. I was almost there. I was just starting to understand what I saw when the flame kissed something above my head. Then the smell reached my nose and the room was suddenly bright yellow orange. My hair was on fire!

I screamed and smacked my head as hard as I could. My burning hair singed my hand. Next thing I knew, my mother was there. She tore off her wrapper and threw it over my head.

The electricity suddenly came back on. My brothers ran in, then my father. The room smelled awful. My hair was half burned away and my hands were tender.

That night, my mother cut my hair. Seventy percent of my lovely long hair, gone. But it was what I saw in that candle that stayed with me most. I'd seen the end of the world in its flame. Raging fires, boiling oceans, toppled fallen skyscrapers, ruptured land, dead and dying people. It was horrible. And it was coming.

My name is Sunny Nkeiruka Nwazue and I confuse people.

I have two older brothers. Like my parents, my brothers were both born here in Nigeria. Then my family moved to America, where I was born in the city of New York. When I was nine, we returned to Nigeria, near the town of Aba. My parents felt it would be a better place to raise my brothers and me. They wanted us to know who we were and where we came from – at least that's what my mom says. We're Igbo, so that makes me American and Igbo, I guess. Igbo-American? Nigerian-American? American-Nigerian? Naijamerican? Whatever.

You see why I confuse people? I'm Nigerian by blood, American by birth, and Nigerian again because I've lived here for years now. Yes, I speak Igbo. I have West African features, like my mother, but while the rest of my family is dark brown, I've got light yellow hair, skin the colour of 'sour milk' (or so stupid rude people like to tell me), and hazel eyes that look like God ran out of the right colour. I'm albino.

Being albino made the sun my enemy; my skin burned so easily that I felt nearly flammable. That's why, though I was really good at soccer, I couldn't join the boys when they played after school. They wouldn't have let me anyway, me being a girl. Very narrow-minded. I had to play at night, with my brothers, when they felt like it.

Of course, this was all before that afternoon with Chichi and Orlu, when everything changed.

I look back now and see that there were signs of what was to come.

When I was two, during a brief visit to Nigeria with my family, I contracted malaria. It was a bad case and I almost died from it when I got back to the States. I remember. My brothers used to tell me that I was a freak because I could remember so far back.

I was really hot, absolutely burning up with fever. My mother stood over my bed, crying. I don't remember my father being there much. My brothers would come in once in a while and pat my forehead or kiss my cheeks.

I was like that for days. Then a light came to me, like a tiny yellow flame or sun. It was laughing and warm—but a nice kind of warm, like bathwater that has been sitting for a few minutes. Maybe this is why I like candles so much. It floated just above me for a long time. I think it was watching over me. It was summer in New York at the time and I remember that sometimes mosquitoes would fly into the strange light and get vaporised.

It must have decided that I wasn't going to die, because eventually it went away and I got better. So it's not as if strange things haven't happened to me before.

I knew I looked like a ghost. All pale-skinned. And I was good at being ghost-quiet. When I was younger, if my father was in the main room drinking his beer and reading his paper, I used to sneak in. I could move like a mosquito when I wanted. Not the American ones that buzz in your ear—the Nigerian ones that are silent like the dead.

I'd creep up on my father, stand right beside him, and wait. It was amazing how he wouldn't see me. I'd just stand there grinning and waiting. Then he'd glance to the side and see me and nearly jump to the ceiling.

"Stupid, stupid girl!" he'd shout, because I'd really scared him—and because he wanted to hurt me because he knew that I knew he was scared. Sometimes I hated my father. Sometimes I felt he hated me, too. I couldn't help that I wasn't the son he wanted or the pretty daughter he'd have accepted instead. But I couldn't not see what I saw in that candle. And I couldn't help what I eventually became.

WHAT IS A LEOPARD PERSON?

A Leopard person goes by many names around the world. The term 'Leopard Person' is a West African coinage, derived from the Efik term 'ekpe,' or 'leopard.' All people of true mystical ability are Leopard People. And as humankind has evolved, so have Leopard folk around the world organised. Two thousand years ago there was a great massacre of Leopard People worldwide. It was first sparked in the Middle East after the murder of Jesus Christ (this is dealt with in Chapter Seven: A Brief Ancient Historical Account). The killing rippled out all over the world. Nowhere was safe. The massacre is known as the Great Attempt. However, we are invincible, I tell you, and so we have since revived. Obviously, juju was used to cover up the fact of the Great Attempt, very strong juju. By whom? There are many speculations, but nothing solid (see Chapter Seven).

from Fast Facts for Free Agents by Isong Abong Effiong Isong

CHAPTER ONE
ORLU

The moment Sunny walked into the schoolyard, people started pointing. Girls started snickering, too, including the girls she usually hung with, her so-called friends. Idiots, Sunny thought. Nevertheless, could she really blame any of them? Her woolly blonde hair, whose length so many had envied, was gone. Now she had a puffy medium-length Afro. She eyed at her friends and hissed loudly. She felt like punching them each in the mouth.

"What happened?" Chelu asked. She didn't even have the courtesy to keep the stupid grin off her face.

"I needed a change," Sunny said and walked away. Behind her, she still heard them laughing.

"Now she's really ugly," she heard Chelu say.

"She should wear some bigger earrings or something," Buchi added. Sunny's ex-friends laughed even harder. *If you only knew that your days were numbered*, she thought. She shivered, pushing away the images of what she'd seen in the candle.

Her day grew even worse when her literature and writing teacher handed back the latest class assignment. The instructions were to write a four-page narrative essay about a relative. Sunny had written about her arrogant oldest brother, Chukwu, who believed he was God's gift to women, though he wasn't. Of course, it didn't help that his name meant 'Supreme Being.'

"Sunny's essay received the highest mark," Miss Tate announced, ignoring the class's sneers and scoffs. Miss Tate was a volunteer from London through the Volunteer Service Overseas. She'd been teaching at Sunny's school for three years. She was the only white teacher in the school. "Not only was it nicely written, but it was engaging and humorous," Miss Tate added.

Sunny bit the inside of her cheek and gave a feeble smile. She hadn't meant the essay to be funny at all. She'd been serious. Her brother truly was an arrogant *nyash*. To make things worse, her classmates had all scored terribly. Out of ten points, most received threes and fours.

"It's a waste of time trying to teach you all proper English," Miss Tate shouted at the rest of the class. She snatched an essay from the pile and read it aloud: 'My sister always beg even though she make good money. Na true talk o. She have but she no dey give. She no go change.'" Miss Tate slammed the essay back onto the boy's desk.

"But Miss Tate, you said that we should write 'casually', as if we were having a conversation at home," her classmate Jibaku insisted. "Sunny is American. She doesn't—"

Miss Tate's eyes looked as if they would pop out. "When I said 'casual' I did NOT mean deteriorated! Do I need to explain every single detail to you people?" She paused as the class stared back at her. "And you were all so timid in what you wrote. Who wants to hear, 'My mother is very nice' or 'My auntie is poor'?

And in Pidgin English, at that! This is why I had you write about a relative. This was supposed to be an easy exercise in narrative!"

As she spoke, she stomped and clomped about the classroom, her face growing redder and redder. She stepped in front of Sunny's desk. "Stand, please."

Sunny looked around at her classmates. Everyone just stared back at her, with slack faces and angry eyes. Slowly, she stood up and straightened her navy blue uniform skirt.

Miss Tate left her standing as she went to her desk in front of the class. She opened a drawer and brought out her yellow wooden koboko. Sunny's mouth dropped open. *I'm about to be flogged*, she thought. *Ah ah, what did I do?* She wondered if it was because she was twelve, the youngest in the class. "Come," Miss Tate said.

"But—"

"Now," she said more firmly.

Sunny slowly walked to the front of the class, aware of her classmates' eyes boring into her back. She let out a shallow breath as she stood before her teacher.

"Hold out your hand." Miss Tate, already bloated with anger, had the *koboko* ready. Sunny shut her eyes and braced herself for the stinging pain. But no sting came. Instead, she felt the *koboko* placed in her hand. She quickly opened her eyes.

Miss Tate looked to the class. "Each of you will come up and Sunny will give you three strikes on the left hand." She smiled wryly. "Maybe she can beat some of her sense into you."

Sunny's stomach sank as her classmates lined up before her. They all looked so angry. And not the red kind of anger that burns out quickly—but the black kind, the kind that is carried outside of class.

Orlu was the first in line. He was the closest to her age, just a year older. They'd never spoken much, but he seemed nice. He liked to build things. She'd seen him during lunch hour—his friends would be blabbing away and he'd be to the side making towers and what looked like little people out of Coca-Cola and Fanta caps and candy wrappers. She certainly didn't want to bruise his hands.

He stood there just looking at her, waiting. He didn't seem angry, like everyone else, but he looked nervous. If he had spoken, Miss Tate would have boxed his head.

By this time, Sunny was crying. She felt a flare of hatred for She felt a flare of hatred for Miss Tate, who up to this day had been her favourite teacher. *The woman's lost her mind*, she thought miserably. *Maybe I should smack her instead.*

Sunny stood there carrying on the way she knew her mother hated her to do. It was pathetic and childish. She knew her pale face was flushed red. She sobbed hard and then threw the cane on the floor. This made Miss Tate even angrier. She pushed Sunny aside. "Sit," Miss Tate shouted.

Sunny covered her face with her hands, but she cringed with each slap of the *koboko*. And then the person would hiss or squeak or gasp or whatever suited his or her pain. She could hear the desks around her filling up as people were punished and then sat down. Someone behind her kicked her chair. It was Jibaku, the girl who'd tried to explain to the teacher that many of them had misunderstood the assignment. "Stupid albino akata bitch!" she growled. "Your hours are numbered!" she added in Igbo.

Sunny shut her eyes tight and gulped down a sob. She hated the word 'akata' more than the word 'bitch'. It meant, 'bush animal' but its implication was heavier than its meaning. The word was used to refer to and, more often, degrade black Americans or foreign-born blacks. It was a hurtful word.

After school, Sunny tried to escape the schoolyard. She made it just far enough for no teachers to see her get jumped. Jibaku, the girl who'd threatened her, led the mob. Right there on the far side of the school schoolyard, three girls and four of the boys beat Sunny as they shouted taunts and insults. She wanted to fight back, but she knew better. There were too many of them.

It was a schoolyard thrashing and not one of her ex-friends came to her rescue. They just stood and watched. Even if they wanted to, they were no match for Jibaku, the richest, tallest, toughest, and most popular girl in school.

It was Orlu who finally put an end to it. He'd been yelling for everyone to stop since it started. "Why don't we let her speak?" Orlu shouted.

Maybe it was because they needed to catch their breath or maybe they truly were curious, but they all paused. Sunny was dirty and bruised, but what could she say? Jibaku spoke up instead—Jibaku, who had slapped Sunny in the face hard enough to make her lip bleed. Sunny glared at her.

"Why didn't you just do it yourself?" The sun bore down on Sunny, making her sensitive skin itch. All she wanted to do was get in the shade. "You could have pretended to be weak. It wouldn't have pained us!" Jibaku shouted. She switched to Igbo. "Or did you enjoy seeing that white woman flog us like that? Did it make you feel big because you're white, too?"

"I'm not white!" Sunny shouted back in English, finding her voice again.

"My eyes tell me different," a plump boy named Periwinkle said. He was called this because he liked the soup with the periwinkle snails in it.

Sunny wiped the blood from her lip and said, "Shut up, snail-sucker! I'm albino!"

"'Albino' is a synonym for 'ugly,'" he retorted.

"Oooh, big words now. Maybe you should have used some of those on your stupid essay! Ignorant idiot!" Some of the others laughed. Sunny could always make them laugh, even when she herself felt like crying. "You think I can go around flogging my own classmates?" she said, snatching up her black umbrella. She held it over herself and instantly felt better. "You wouldn't have done it, either." She hissed and switched to Igbo, "Or maybe you would have, Jibaku."

She watched them grumble to each other. Some of them even turned and started walking home. Sunny clenched her umbrella handle. She'd had enough. If those who remained came at her again she decided that she'd swing at them with it.

There was a long pause. Jibaku hissed loudly, looking Sunny up and down with disgust. "Stupid *oyibo akata* witch," she spat. She motioned to the others. "Let's go."

Sunny and Orlu watched them leave. Their eyes met, and Sunny quickly looked away. When she turned back, Orlu was still watching her. She forced herself to keep her eyes on him, to really see him. He had slanted, almost catlike eyes and high cheekbones. He was kind of pretty, even if he didn't talk much. She bent down to pick up her books.

"Are...are you all right?" he asked, as he helped.

She frowned. "I'm fine. No thanks to you."

"Your face looks..."

"I don't care," she said, putting the last book in her satchel.

"Your mother will care," he said.

Sunny leapt over an open gutter, leaving the school grounds. Orlu followed. The road was clogged with *okadas* and they stuck to the far side of the dirt path for safety. Sunny paused and looked back angrily at Orlu. "Why didn't you stop them?" she shouted over the noise of the *okadas* and cars. She slung the satchel over her shoulder and continued walking.

Orlu followed. "I tried!"

She laughed angrily, leaping over a large pothole as they quickly crossed a side street. "No you didn't," she said over her shoulder.

They passed a few shops, an unfinished house and a dilapidated office building and made the turn into their quiet neighbourhood. Sunny ran a hand over the smooth trunk of the palm tree growing on the corner of the street. She did this every day.

"I did try to help, Sunny," Orlu insisted. "You didn't see Periwinkle and Calculus do this?" He turned his head so she could see his swollen cheek.

"Oh," she said, instantly ashamed. "I'm sorry."

"No shaking," he said, smiling. "Periwinkle's chin is probably even worse right now."

Sunny laughed. "Good."

By the time they got to the intersection where their paths home diverged, she felt a little better. It seemed she and Orlu had a lot in common. He agreed Miss Tate's actions were way out of line, he liked reading books for fun, and he too noticed the weaver birds that lived in the tree beside the school.

"I live just down this road," Orlu said.

"I know," she said, looking up the paved road. Like hers, his house was white with a modest wall surrounding it. Her eye settled on the mud hut with the water-damaged walls next door. She'd always wondered about it. Such homes were never in neighbourhoods like this and she wondered why anyone tolerated it. Whenever she asked her mother about it, her mother would get annoyed and tell her to stop being nosy. She didn't bother asking her father.

"Do you know the woman who lives there?" she asked Orlu.

There was smoke coming from the back. Probably from a cooking fire, she thought. She had only seen the woman who lived in it once, about two years ago. She'd had smooth brown skin tinted slightly red from the palm oil she rubbed into it. Some of her ex-friends believed the woman was some sort of witch, but they didn't really know anything concrete. *They think anyone who is different is a witch*, Sunny thought.

"That's Nimm's house," Orlu said. "She lives there with her daughter."

"Daughter?" she asked. She'd assumed the woman lived alone.

"Hey!" someone yelled from behind them. "Orlu! Who is this *onyocha*?"

"My God," Orlu groaned. "Will this drama never end?"

Sunny whirled around. "Don't call me that," she said before she got a good look at the girl. She switched to Igbo. "Do I look like a European?" she hissed. "You don't even know me!"

"I have seen you around here," the girl said, now speaking in Igbo, too. She was fine-boned, dark brown, and elfin, but her voice was loud and strong and arrogant. So was her smile. She wore an old-looking red, yellow, and blue dress and no shoes. She swaggered over to Sunny and they stood there, sizing each other up.

"Who are you?" Sunny finally asked.

"Who are *you*?" the girl retorted. She motioned to Sunny's dirty clothes. "Have you been rolling around in the dirt?"

Orlu sighed loudly, rolling his eyes. "Sunny, this is Chichi, my neighbour. Chichi, this is Sunny, my classmate."

"How come I've never seen you at school?" Sunny asked, still irritated. She dusted off her hopelessly dirty clothes. "You look around our age, even if you are kind of...small."

"I don't need your silly school," Chichi said.

She and Orlu exchanged a look. Sunny frowned. *What was that about?* she wondered.

"And I could be older or younger than you," Chichi continued. "You'll never know, even if you *are* a ghost." She smirked, looking Sunny up and down, obviously itching for a fight. "Even when you speak Igbo you don't sound Igbo."

"That's my accent. I'm American," Sunny said through gritted teeth. "I spent most my life there. I can't help the way I speak."

Chichi put her hand up in mock defence. "Oh, did I offend you? Sorry o." She laughed.

Sunny could have slapped her. At this point, another fight wouldn't have made much difference.

"Come," Orlu quickly said, stepping between them, "let's take it easy."

"You live there?" Sunny asked in English, leaning around Orlu and motioning towards the hut.

"Yes," Chichi said in Igbo. "My mother and I don't need much."

"Why?" Sunny asked in Igbo.

Orlu stepped back, looking perplexed.

"I'll never tell you," Chichi said with a sly grin. She switched to English. "There's more to the world than big houses, money and material nonsense." She chuckled, turning away. "Have a nice evening, Orlu. See you around, Sunny."

"Yeah, if I don't step on you first," Sunny replied in English.

"That's if I can even see you coming, you ghost," Chichi shot back over her shoulder.

Orlu only shook his head.

HOME

Home will never be the same once you know what you are. Your whole life will change. Nigeria is already full of groups, circles, cultures. We have many ways. You are Yoruba, Hausa, Ibibio, Fulani, Ogoni, Tiv, Nupe, Kanuri, Ijaw, Annang, and so on. You add being a Leopard person to that and your groups split into a thousand more groups. The world becomes much more complicated. Travel overseas and it's even more complex. Plus, you are a Leopard person living in a world of idiot Lambs, so that doesn't help. You are fortunate because being a free agent puts you (though uncomfortably) with the rest of us Leopard folk, and comfortably with Lambs. Your ignorance will smooth out the edges of your dealings with the world you used to be a part of.

from Fast Facts for Free Agents by Isong Abong Effiong Isong

CHAPTER TWO
CHICHI

Over the next two weeks, Orlu and Sunny made a habit of walking home together. A friendship was sprouting between them. For Sunny, this was a nice distraction from what she'd seen in the candle. But there was another reason for walking home together these days, too.

That reason's name was Black Hat Otokoto. He was a ritual killer, and he was on the loose. The local newspapers were constantly running terrifying stories about him with headlines like: **Black Hat Otokoto Claims Another Victim**; **Killer Kills Calm Yet Again**; and **Fresh Ritual Killings In Owerri**.

Black Hat's targets were always children.

"Make sure you and that boy Orlu walk home together," Sunny's mother insisted. Her mother had liked Orlu since the day Sunny came home all bruised up and Sunny had told her that Orlu had stopped the fight.

Almost every day after school, Chichi was there at the crossroads to greet them and Sunny began to grow used to her. Chichi said she spent most of her time helping her mother around their hut. When she wasn't helping, she did what she called 'travelling,' walking to the market, the river, kilometres and kilometres all over the countryside. Sunny wasn't sure if she believed Chichi's story of walking the fifty-five kilometres all the way to Owerri and back in an afternoon.

"I got this wrapper from the market there," she said, holding up a colourful cut of cloth.

It was indeed very fine. "Looks expensive," Sunny said.

"Yes o," Chichi said, grinning. "Maybe I stole it." She winked and laughed at the disgust on Sunny's face.

Chichi loved bombast and trickery, too. She bragged that she sometimes approached strange men and told them how lovely they were, just to see their reactions. If they were too friendly, she would scold them for being nasty and perverted, reminding them that she was only ten or thirteen years old—whatever age she felt like using at the time. Then she would run off, laughing.

Sunny had never met anyone like Chichi—not in Nigeria, and not in America, either. Chichi didn't know where her father was, and that was all she would say. But Orlu told Sunny that Chichi's father was a musician who used to be Chichi's mother's best friend.

"They were never married," he said.

"When he got famous, he left to pursue his career."

Sunny almost spontaneously combusted when he told her it was Nyanga Tolotolo. "He's my father's favourite musician!" Sunny exclaimed. "I hear him on the radio all the time!"

When she confronted Chichi about this, Chichi merely shrugged. "And so what?" she said. "All I have from him are three old CDs of his music and a scratched-up DVD of his videos that he sent a long time ago. He's never given us any money; he has never visited us or done anything for us. The man is useless."

After a while, Sunny decided that Chichi wasn't so bad. She was certainly more interesting than any of Sunny's ex-friends.

One day, Sunny found herself walking home alone. Orlu had some place to go right after school. "I'll see you tomorrow," was all he said as he ran to shove his way onto a crowded bus. *If he's not going to tell me where he's going, I won't ask*, she thought. Thankfully, Jibaku and company only sneered and snickered at her as she left the schoolyard.

Without Orlu to talk to, she kept looking around for Black Hat Otokoto. She was looking so hard for him that she nearly sprained her ankle in the pothole she usually leapt over. There were people everywhere and the streets were busy with cars and *okadas*, but would anyone notice if she were snatched into a car or pulled down into a gutter or an alley? Then her thoughts moved to even darker territory, to what she'd seen in the candle—the end of the world. Yet another day had passed, bringing it closer. She shivered and walked faster, she was almost home.

"Come, what's your problem?"

She turned around to face Chichi, her face already prepared to look annoyed. "Why are you so rude?" Sunny groaned. But she was secretly pleased.

"I speak my mind. That doesn't make me rude," Chichi said with a grin, giving Sunny a friendship handshake. Today, she wore a battered green dress and, as usual, no shoes.

"In your case, it does," Sunny said, laughing.

"Wharreva," Chichi drawled. "Are you going home?"

"Yeah. I've got some homework."

Chichi bit her lower lip and made an arc in the dirt with her toe. "So you and Orlu are close friends, now?"

Sunny shrugged.

"Well," Chichi said, "if you're going to be good friends with Orlu, then you have to be friends with me, too."

Sunny frowned. She'd thought she and Chichi were friends, sort of. "Why's that?"

"Because you're his in-school friend and I'm his out-of-school friend."

Sunny laughed and shook her head. "I'm not his girlfriend."

"Oh, neither am I. We're just friends."

"Okay," Sunny said, frowning. "Uh...well, then...well, okay."

"I don't know you enough to say we're friends," Chichi said. She cocked her head and switched to Igbo. "But I can see that there's more to you."

"What do you mean, 'more'?"

Chichi smiled mysteriously. "People say things about people like you. That you're a ghost, or a half-and-half who has one foot in this world and one foot in another." She paused. "That you can...see things."

Sunny rolled her eyes. *Not this again*, she thought. *So cliché. Everyone thinks the old old woman, the hunchback, the local crazy man, and the albino have magical evil powers.* "Whatever," she grumbled. She didn't want to think about the candle.

Chichi laughed. "You're right, those are silly stereotypes about albinos. But in your case, I think there is something to it." She paused, as if about to say something very important. "You know, Orlu can take things apart—undo bad things."

Sunny frowned. "I see him messing around all the time, fixing radios and stuff like that. So?"

"So, it is not what you think."

"What's your point, Chichi?"

"Well, if you're going to be Orlu's friend, you should know the real story."

They were standing by the side of the road. A car zoomed by, leaving them in a cloud of red dust. "Tell me something secret about yourself," Chichi suddenly said. "That will bond our friendship, I think."

"You tell me a secret first," Sunny said, playing along. This was one weird game.

Chichi frowned and bit her lip again.

"Must you go home right now? Can you come with me for a few minutes?"

Sunny considered. It was Friday, so it would probably be ok. She called her mother on her mobile phone and told her she was with Chichi. After a long pause, her mother said it was all right to stay until six o'clock.

"Come," Chichi said, taking her hand.

"Let's go to my house."

Chichi's hut looked as if it would melt into the ground come rainy season. The warped walls were made of red mud, and the vines, trees, and bushes around it crept in too close. The front entrance was doorless, covered by a simple blue cloth. Sunny's nose was assaulted with the smell of flowers and incense as soon as she entered. She sneezed as she glanced around.

The only sources of light were three kerosene lamps, one hanging from the low ceiling and two others on stacks of books. The place was full of books—on a small table in the middle of the room, packed under the bed, stacked against the wall all the way up to the ceiling. The corners of the ceiling were clotted with webs inhabited by large spiders. A wall gecko scurried behind a book stack. She sneezed again and sniffed.

"Sorry o," Chichi said, patting her shoulder. "I suppose it's a little dusty in here."

Sunny shrugged. "It's okay. My room's the same way."

It wasn't as bad as Chichi's hut, but it was getting there. Sunny had run out of shelf space, so she had started keeping books under the bed. Most were cheap paperbacks her mother had found at the market, but she had been able to bring a few over from the United States, including her two favourites—Virginia Hamilton's *Her Stories*, and *The Witches* by Roald Dahl.

The books here looked older, thicker, and probably weren't novels. Chichi's mother was perched on top of a stack of books, reading. She looked up and saw them, and used a leaf to hold her place. The first thing Sunny noticed was that Chichi's mother had the longest, thickest, coarsest hair she had ever seen. It was well past her waist.

"Good afternoon, Nimm," Chichi said. "This is Sunny."

Sunny stood there staring. *That's what she calls her mother?* "Good afternoon," she finally croaked.

"I'm happy to hear that you have a voice," Chichi's mother said, not unkindly.

"I—I have a voice..." Sunny managed.

Chichi's mother chuckled. "Do you want some tea?"

Sunny hesitated. Where would Chichi's mother warm up the water? Would she have to go outside and make a fire? But it was also rude to act as if there was nowhere to do it. "Um, yes, please," she said.

Chichi's mother picked up a tea kettle and left the hut.

"Sit on this," Chichi said, pointing at a large thick book. "We've both read it so many times we really don't need it anymore."

Sunny couldn't see the title on the spine. "Okay."

Chichi sat beside her on the dirt floor and grinned. "So this is where I live," she said.

"So many books. What about when it rains?"

Chichi laughed hard at this. "Don't worry. I have lived here all my life and I have never seen a book come to harm."

They were quiet for a moment, the only sound the whistle of the tea kettle outside. That was fast, Sunny thought. Must be a fire out back. But she didn't recall seeing any smoke before they went in.

"So your mother has read all these?" she asked.

"Not all," Chichi said. "Most of them. I've read a lot of them, too. We bring in new books and trade back the ones that we are tired of."

"So this is what you do instead of school."

"And when I'm not travelling."

Sunny fidgeted. It was getting late. "Um...what secret are you going to tell me?" Before Chichi could answer, her mother came with the tea. Sunny took one of the porcelain cups. Its rim was chipped and the handle was broken off. The other two cups didn't look much better.

"Thank you," she said politely. She took a sip and smiled. It was Lipton, only slightly sweetened, just the way she liked it.

"You are Ezekiel Nwazue's daughter, aren't you?" Chichi's mother asked, sitting back down on her book stack.

"Yes," she said. "You know my father?"

"And your mother," she said. "And I know of you. I have seen you here and there."

"It's hard not to notice her," Chichi said. But she was smiling.

"So what are you reading?" Sunny asked.

"This dried-up old book?" Chichi's mother answered. "It's one of the few that I've read many, many times and will never trade back."

"Why?"

"It carries too many secrets yet to be unlocked. Who would have expected this would be the case with a book written by a white man, eh?"

"What's it called?"

"*In the Shadow of the Bush* by P. Amaury Talbot. 1912. Shadows, bushes, jungles, the 'Dark Continent'. Sounds so stereotypical, but there's plenty of knowledge in this old thing. The man who wrote it managed to preserve some important information—unbeknownst to him."

Sunny wanted to ask more, but something else was nagging at her. Her father believed that all one needed to succeed in life was an education. He had gone to school for many years to become a barrister, and then had gone on to be the most successful child in his family. Sunny's mother was a medical doctor, and often talked about how excelling in school had opened her to opportunities which only two decades before girls didn't normally get. So Sunny believed in education. But here was Chichi's mother, surrounded by the hundreds of books she'd read, living in a decrepit old mud hut with her daughter.

They sipped their tea and talked about nothing in particular. After a little while, Chichi's mother got up and said she had to go run some errands.

"Thanks for the tea, Mrs. ..." Sunny trailed off, embarrassed. She didn't know whether Chichi's mother went by Chichi's father's name or not. She didn't even know Chichi's last name.

"Call me Miss Nimm," Chichi's mother said. "Or you can call me Asuquo—that's my first name."

Sunny realised something once Chichi's mother had left. "Your mother's name—she's Efik?"

"Yes. My father is Igbo, like you."

There was an awkward silence. "How long have you known Orlu?" Sunny finally said.

"Oh, since we were about four. We—"

As if the mention of his name summoned him, they heard the gate to Orlu's house creak open. Chichi grinned, got up, and went out. "Orlu," she called after a moment. "Come here."

Chichi had barely sat back down when Orlu pushed the cloth aside and peeked in. "Chichi, I just got—oh, Sunny," he said, frowning at her. "What are you doing here?" He stepped inside.

"I guess Chichi has let me into her secret club," she said.

"Club?" he asked, frowning very deeply at Chichi.

"Do want some tea?" Chichi quickly asked.

"Sure," he said, slowly sitting on a stack of books.

She went out to the back, leaving Sunny and Orlu to just look at each other. Sunny wanted to break the awkward silence so she said the first thing that popped into her head. "Orlu, can you really 'undo things'?"

Without hesitation, Orlu turned to the back door and shouted, "Chichi!"

"Eh?" she shouted back.

"Come here," he said.

"What?" Sunny asked. "Did I say something—"

Chichi came stomping in. "Don't speak to me like that, Orlu."

"*Ah-ah*, why is your mouth so big?" Orlu shouted. "Can't you..." He pressed his lips together. "Is your mother home?"

"No," she said, looking at her feet. Sunny frowned. It was a rare thing for Chichi to not yell back at someone.

The three of them were silent. Sunny looked uncomfortably from Orlu to Chichi and back to Orlu. Orlu glared at Chichi and Chichi looked at the ceiling. Then Orlu slapped his knee hard and said, "Explain, Chichi! Why?"

"No," Sunny screeched. "You explain, Orlu! We're supposed to be friends. Tell me and then you can tell her off!"

"It's none of your—" He turned back to Chichi. "Are you stupid? Just because you're alone with your thousand and one secrets doesn't mean we all have to be like that! *I* chose not to be that! *I* know how to keep secrets!"

"We won't lose Sunny as a friend. Trust me. Let her in," Chichi said. "Look at her!"

"So? Her being albino doesn't mean anything! It's just her medical condition. Everyone has their own physical things!"

"This is different," Chichi retorted. "Even my mom thinks so."

"Wait!" Sunny yelled loudly enough that they both jumped. "Shut up and wait! What is going on?!"

Orlu and Chichi looked at each other for a long moment. Then Orlu sighed and said, "Fine." He pulled a piece of white chalk from his pocket. "Only this way," he said when Chichi started to protest. "No other way. We have to be sure."

Chichi hissed loudly and looked away. "You should tell her first. If she's such a good friend, you should trust her."

"This isn't about trust," he said, as he picked up book after book. He chose one that was bound in leather. On the back, he used the chalk to draw:

Oddly, the chalk drew clearly on the book's smooth leather surface. He muttered something and shaded in the centre of the circle. Around the circle and lines he quickly scribbled a series of symbols that looked like the kind of things Americans would get tattooed on their biceps and ankles.

"That's really good," Chichi said, impressed.

"Mark it," he grumbled, ignoring her.

Chichi pressed her thumb to the shaded circle. When she brought her thumb up, it was coated with white chalk.

"You do the same thing, Sunny," Orlu said, his voice softening.

"What is it?" she asked.

"If you want to know anything, you have to do this first."

Sunny had never seen juju performed but she knew it when she saw it.

"My mother says this kind of thing is evil," she quietly said. "It's the work of the devil."

"Look, no disrespect, but your mother doesn't know anything about juju," Orlu replied. "Trust me."

Still, she hesitated. In the end, her curiosity got the better of her, the way it always did—especially after what she had seen in the candle flame. Quickly, before she could think too hard about it, she pressed her thumb to the same place Chichi had pressed hers. Orlu did the same. Then he took out a blade the size of his hand. Chichi hissed. "Is this necessary?" she asked, irritated.

"I want it to be strong," he said.

"You barely know how," Chichi said.

He ignored her and touched the knife to his tongue. He winced, but that was it. Carefully, he handed the knife to Chichi. She paused, pursing her lips. Then she did the same and handed the knife to Sunny.

"Handle it with care," Orlu said.

"You want me to..." There was blood on the knife. Thoughts of AIDS, hepatitis, and every other disease she'd learned about in school and from her mother rushed through her head. She barely knew Chichi, or Orlu, really.

"Yes," he said. "But once you do it, you can't turn back."

"From what?"

"You can't know unless you do it," Chichi said with a smirk.

Sunny couldn't take it anymore. She looked at the knife. She took a deep breath. "Okay."

She cut with the part of the blade that was free of blood. The knife was so sharp! She barely had to touch the thing to her tongue. But, goodness, it stung! She wondered if it was coated with some kind of chemical because suddenly everything around her looked funny.

"I hope you know what you're doing," she heard Chichi tell Orlu.

"We'll see," Orlu mumbled. They both looked intently at Sunny.

"What's happening?" she whispered.

Nothing was changing—but everything was. The room was as it was, the books, Orlu and Chichi, her schoolbag beside her. Outside she could hear a car passing by. But everything was... different. It was like reality was blossoming, opening and then opening some more. More of everything, but all was the same.

"You...you see it?" Orlu said, his eyes wide.

"Make it stop," Sunny said.

"See!" Chichi said. "I was right!"

"*Abeg*," Orlu snapped. "You can't be sure. She could just be sensitive."

But Chichi looked very smug.

"Do you solemnly swear on the people you hold dearest, on the things dearest to you, that you will never speak of what I am about to tell you to anyone on the outside?" Orlu asked.

"Outside of what?" Sunny shrieked. She just wanted it to stop.

"Just swear," he said.

She'd have sworn anything. "I swear." Before she could get the second word out of her mouth, it all stopped, settled, grew still, normal.

Chichi got up, took the empty cups of tea, and walked out. Sunny looked down at the book. The markings had disappeared. She could still taste blood in her mouth.

"Okay, so ask and I'll tell you whatever you want to know," Orlu said.

A thousand things were flying through Sunny's head. "Just tell me."

"Tell you what?"

She groaned, exasperated. "What'd we just do?"

"We gave our word," he said. "That was a trust knot. It will prevent you from telling anyone about any of this, not even your family. I couldn't tell you anything if we didn't make one."

"Chichi would have," she said.

"Well, I'm glad you didn't ask her. She's careless and thinks nothing can ever happen to people like us. She acts like there are no crazy people who do violent, crazy things." He paused and then added. "Plus, we would have all been in terrible trouble if you let anything slip after she told you."

"Let *what* slip?"

41

Orlu clasped his hands together. "Chichi and I," he began, "and our parents are—"

"Don't tell her like that," Chichi said, coming back in. She was carrying a tray with three fresh cups of tea on it. "She's ignorant."

"Hey, no I'm not."

"Plus, she understands better when you show her," Chichi said. "I know her a little."

Orlu shook his head. "No, too early."

"Not really," Chichi said. "But tell her about what you can do, first."

Orlu looked at Sunny, then looked down and sighed.

"I can't believe this." He seemed to gather himself together "It's hard to explain," he said. "I can undo bad things, bad...juju. It's like an instinct. I didn't have to learn how."

"Isn't all juju bad?" she asked.

"No," her friends both said.

"It is like anything else, some of it is good, some of it is bad, some of it is just there," Chichi said.

"So you all are—witches, or something?"

They laughed. "I guess," Orlu said. "In this country, we call ourselves Leopard People. Long ago, there were powerful groups called the *Ekpe*, or Leopard Societies and that was how the name just stuck."

Sunny couldn't deny what she'd seen. The world had done a weird blossoming thing and though it had stopped, she still felt it with her. She knew it could happen again. And what about the candle?

"Chichi can remember things if she sees them," Orlu said, "so her head is full of all sorts of juju. See all these books? Just ask her to recite a paragraph from a certain page and she can."

Sunny slowly got up.

"Are you all right?" Orlu asked.

"This is—I don't—I…I think I need to go home," she said. She felt ill.

"Are you doing anything this weekend?" Chichi quickly asked.

Sunny slowly shook her head as she picked up her schoolbag.

"Tomorrow is Saturday," Chichi said. "Come here in the morning, around nine. You should allow for the whole day."

"To…to do what?" Sunny asked, clutching her schoolbag. She stepped towards the door.

"Just come," Chichi said.

Sunny nodded, and got out of there as fast as she could.

WHAT IS CHITTIM?

Chittim is the currency of Leopard People. Chittim are always made of metal (copper, bronze, silver, and gold) and always shaped like curved rods. The most valuable are the large copper ones, which are about the size of an orange and thick as an adult's thumb. The smallest ones are the size of a dove's egg. Least valuable are chittim made of gold.

When chittim fall, they never do harm. So one can stand in a rain of chittim, and never get hit. There is only one way to earn chittim: by gaining knowledge and wisdom. The smarter you become, the better you process knowledge into wisdom, the more chittim will fall and thus the richer you will be. As a free agent, don't expect to get rich.

from Fast Facts for Free Agents by Isong Abong Effiong Isong

CHAPTER THREE
INITIATIVE

When Sunny got home, everything seemed normal. She kicked a soccer ball around with her brothers. She easily stole the ball and wove between them with her fast feet and because they found this annoying, they talked rubbish about how she looked like a white girl. Her mother, who was home early, made stew with chicken. Her father came home late and ate alone as he read his newspaper. Not once did the world bloom or shift.

But goodness, she was tired. Exhausted. She tried to read a few pages of *Cloth Girl*, a book she'd begged her mother to buy, but soon she fell asleep. She slept like the dead. When morning came, she felt better. She lay there thinking about what happened yesterday. Whatever Chichi and Orlu had done to her, she would open her mind to it, she decided. Why not?

She quickly dressed in jeans, a yellow T-shirt, leather sandals, and her favourite gold necklace. It was the only costly gift her father had ever given her.

"Be home by four o'clock," her mother said during breakfast. Sunny was surprised that her mother hadn't asked a whole bunch of questions. She quickly got up before her luck changed.

"Where are you going?" her brother Chukwu asked.

"Out," she said. "Bye."

In one hand, she carried her black umbrella. In the other was her blue purse with a stick of lip gloss, some sunscreen, a washcloth, a mango, her mobile phone, and enough money for lunch and a little whatever.

"Sunny!" Chichi yelled when she saw her coming up the street. Chichi was dressed up, at least by Chichi's standards. She wore a green wrapper with yellow circles on it and a white T-shirt. She was wearing sandals, too. Sunny raised a tentative hand in greeting.

"Stop that now," Chichi chided gently. "Relax." She linked her arm in Sunny's and they walked toward Orlu's house. He stood at the gate.

"Good morning," she said.

"Nice shoes," Chichi said, looking at Orlu's brand-new red Chuck Taylors.

"My uncle is visiting from London," he said. "He brought them for me."

"So where are we going?" Sunny asked.

Chichi and Orlu exchanged a look.

"Did you tell your parents you will be back around three?" Orlu asked her.

"Four," she said proudly.

"Well done," Chichi said, grinning.

"I asked my mother about this," Orlu said to Chichi. "She was really angry with me for making that trust knot with Sunny."

Here we go again, thought Sunny. More things I don't know. More of them not telling me anything.

"Sunny has to be involved," Chichi said, looking annoyed. "I told you what my mother said."

"Well," Orlu said slowly. "I asked my parents. She can't set foot in Leopard Knocks...unless she's fully initiated." Chichi tried to hide a smile. "Chichi, you knew this was the rule!"

"I did," she said, laughing. "What better way to get her initiated?"

"But..." Orlu tapered off, looking very angry.

Sunny had had enough. "All right, start explaining. Trust knot? Leopard Knocks? Initiation? What's going on?"

Orlu only shook his head. Chichi took Sunny's arm again. "Just come and see for yourself."

"As if she has a choice now," Orlu snapped. "As if any of us have a choice now."

"Orlu, I believe she's one of us," Chichi said. "My mother does, too."

"Would you want to go through something like this without knowing anything?" he asked Chichi.

Chichi only shrugged. "It's the only way."

Sunny groaned. "Please quit talking as if I'm not right here."

Chichi lowered her voice. "The worst that can happen is—"

"Is what?" Sunny shouted.

"We can never talk to you again and you can never speak of any of this."

They started walking away without her. For a moment, Sunny just stood there, watching them go. Then she collected herself and followed.

"Where're we going?" she asked after several minutes. "Just tell me that, if nothing else."

"To the hut of Anatov, Defender of Frogs and All Things Natural," Chichi said.

As they passed the palm tree at their neighbourhood's entrance, Sunny ran her hand across its smooth trunk as she always did. She hoped this wasn't the last time she did so.

They flagged down a taxi on the main street, squeezing in with four other people. Chichi sat on Sunny's lap and Orlu squeezed in beside them.

"We are dropping at Ariaria Market," Orlu said, handing the man some naira. Orlu waved Sunny off when she tried to offer some money. "No, don't worry."

The cab reeked of dried fish, egusi, and exhaust. There were big holes in the floor. After the cab dropped off his four other passengers, stopping at four different places, the three of them finally got out at the market. But they didn't go in. Instead, they crossed the busy street and went in the opposite direction. They walked for a while, passing buildings and avoiding hawkers selling cashew fruits, suya, phone cards, mobile phone accessories, and plantain chips.

They turned a corner and walked, turned another corner and walked. Sunny knew the area, but now she felt lost. They stopped at a small path that led into a patch of lush bush. A group of older men were just emerging. Some of them wore old jeans and shirts, others wore colourful wrappers and T-shirts.

"Good morning," Orlu, Chichi, and Sunny said together.

The men looked each of them in the eye and nodded. "Good morning, children."

"Do you know where you're going?" one of them asked.

"Yes, sir," Orlu said.

"No, I mean her," the man said, pointing at Sunny. She felt her face grow warm.

"She's with us," Chichi said.

This seemed to satisfy him, and he moved on with the others.

"Where are we going?" Sunny asked as they walked down the shaded path. The bush seemed to close in around them. Where it had been hot, it was now sweltering.

"I told you," Chichi said. "To see Anatov."

"Yeah, but who is he?" She stopped walking. "Chichi, Orlu, stop." She hoisted up her purse, her closed umbrella under her arm. "What's going on? Where are we going? What's happening?"

They both looked uncomfortable.

"Anatov will explain, Sunny," Orlu finally said.

"It's easier that way," Chichi said. "Just trust us."

"Why?"

"Because we're your friends," Orlu said.

"And we've changed your life...maybe," Chichi said. Then she looked away. "Just allow Anatov to explain."

They started walking again.

"Is he mean?" Sunny asked. The path had narrowed and they were walking single file, Sunny last. She heard Orlu laugh to himself.

"Anatov is Anatov," Chichi said, turning around and grinning.

Great, Sunny thought. Some friends. Not telling me a thing. For all she knew, they could have been accomplices working with Black Hat Otokoto. Anything is possible. Even the worst is possible. The candle showed me so. The worst was more than possible. The worst was inevitable. But she was in too deep now. Her parents didn't know where she was—she didn't even know where she was! She slapped at a mosquito on her arm.

Sunny heard it before she saw it. At first, it sounded like a bunch of people softly whispering, yet she saw nothing but forest. Minutes later, the noise grew to the sound of crashing water. It was a river so angry that its churning waters threw up a white mist. Never heard of this river, she thought. Stretching across it was a thin, slippery-looking wooden bridge. There were no handrails.

"How is anyone supposed to cross that?" she asked, horrified.

"You just do it," Orlu said, stepping up to a large rock that sat in front of the bridge. He rubbed its smooth black surface with the palm of his hand. "Beyond the mist is the entrance to Leopard Knocks."

She waited for him to go on.

"The full name is Ngbe Abum Obbaw, that's Efik for 'Leopard Knocks His Foot,'" Chichi explained. "Long ago, some Efik woman created a juju that stopped a leopard from attacking her. It made the leopard stub its foot on something hard, and the pain scared it away. The builders named Leopard Knocks His Foot after her strong juju. The Efik people have the strongest juju in the world."

"In whose opinion? Not the Igbos'," Orlu said irritably. "Sunny, there are Leopard people all over the world from every tribe, race, whatever. No one of them is better than the other."

"Abeg, be realistic," Chichi said, rolling her eyes.

But Sunny wasn't really listening. She couldn't take her eyes off of that narrow bridge. The wild waters beneath it boiled and churned.

"Only truth will allow you across," Orlu said.

"Every time," Chichi added.

"So you've crossed that?" Sunny cried. "It's so flimsy! The thing doesn't even look like it's—" She stopped talking and just stared at it.

"No shaking," Chichi said, putting her arm around Sunny. "We're not going over the bridge right now. We're going that way." She pointed to a small path that ran to the right, beside the river. She pulled Sunny along.

"I don't like this," Sunny said.

"You're just not used to it," Orlu said.

"No," she said, shaking her head. "I don't like this. You're both crazy."

Chichi giggled.

Anatov's hut was much bigger than Chichi's. It was long with a thatch roof. The red walls were decorated with white symbols and caricatures of people. The wooden front doors were waist-high, and looked as if they swung in and out like the doors of a saloon in an American Western. They were painted with black and white squares. In swooping white letters, one door was labeled IN, the other OUT. She noticed that they entered through the OUT door.

Inside, the air was heavy with incense so strong that it made her slightly ill. She waved her hand in front of her face. Through her watery eyes she saw that the hut's inner walls were also decorated with white chalk artwork.

A man sat in a throne-like chair on the far side of the room. When he stood up, she gasped. He was the tallest man she had ever seen—taller than any Maasai or American basketball player. He was light-skinned with short brown bushy dreadlocks and a small gold ring in his left nostril.

Sunny was trying to be polite when she stifled her sneeze, but the sneeze was so hard that she blew snot into her hands instead. Great first impression, she thought. Her face and hands were a mess.

"This girl isn't proper," Anatov told Chichi. He spoke in English and had an American accent. He turned to Orlu and looked down his nose at him. "Explain. I can barely stand to have so many Ekpiri in here. Clutters up the vibe, know what I'm sayin'? But you bring an improper, at that? Y'all don't think."

"Oga Anatov, this is Sunny Nwazue," Chichi quickly said. "We're sorry... Are you busy?"

Suddenly, Anatov strode over to Sunny, who was still holding her face. He frowned at her. "What's wrong with you?" he asked switching to Igbo.

"I need—I need a tissue."

He pulled a handkerchief from his pocket and thrust it at her. To her further embarrassment, he watched intently as she wiped the snot from her hands and face and blew her nose.

"Yellow," he said, when she was finally done. "On all levels, she's yellow."

"I know I'm yellow," she snapped. "I'm albino! Haven't you ever seen an—"

"Quiet," Anatov said. "Sit down or I'll throw you out and make your life more miserable than it is. You have no idea what you've gotten yourself into."

"Sunny, sit," Chichi whispered.

"Fine!" she said, sitting.

"Good," Anatov said. He walked a circle around her. "Okay," he mumbled. He reached into his pocket and brought out a handful of white powder and started sifting it from his hand as he circled her again. This time he moved slowly. When he'd completed the powder circle, he brought out a knife. It had a handle with red jewels. The blade was shiny and very sharp looking.

Sunny glanced at Orlu, who gave a small smile of encouragement. All she could think about was Black Hat. Anatov was too close for her to make a run for the door.

"Excuse me," she stammered. "What are you..."

"You'll remember this for a long time," Anatov said with a chuckle as he raised the sharp, shiny knife. She leaned away from him, her hand up as a shield. She braced herself. But no blow came. He seemed to be drawing in the air. A soft red symbol—a circle with a cross in the centre—floated above her head like smoke. Slowly, it descended on her.

"Hold your breath," Chichi said just as it touched her upturned face. But before she could, she was pulled down. Yanked like a rag doll. First through the hut's dirt floor and then into sweet-smelling earth.

As she was pulled downward, Sunny's mouth filled with earth. She couldn't scream! The earth was pushing its way down her throat, pulling up her eyelids, scratching her eyeballs, grating her clothes away, and pressing at her skin.

It got worse.

Her skin went from cold to hot and then cold again, as if she were passing through various living and dead parts of the earth.

Finally, she stopped descending and started moving slowly up. All was dark. She was glad. She didn't want to see where she was. Her entire body screamed with pain. How was she still alive? How she was still breathing?

As she ascended, she heard a mulching low wet grumble. It grew louder. Suddenly, she burst into water. It had to be that terrible river. It was cold and turbulent, threatening to rip her apart, but she was moving too fast, dragged up through whipping river debris and bubbles and underwater noise and currents.

Then, just as suddenly as she was taken—splat!—she was back in the hut. She inhaled incense-tinged air. She sneezed, but at least now she could breathe. She tasted gritty mud on her breath and it coated her lips, throat, and nostrils. Several small but heavy things were dropping around her. They hit each other with a metallic chink chink chink chink.

"No. Step back," she heard Anatov say. He whispered a phrase, and then she felt something rough wrap itself around her body.

"Who'd have thought?" she heard Chichi whisper.

Sunny decided to open her eyes. Her face felt tight and tingly. When she looked around everything looked deep, colourful, and almost too alive, like when they'd made the trust knot.

"What happened?" she mumbled, and froze. Her voice was deep and throaty, like some sultry, glamorous woman who smoked too many cigarettes. When she got up, her movements felt effortless, amazing, full of poise and grace.

She stood up, her shoulders back and her head held straight and high. When she touched her face, it was with gently held arms and softly curved hands and lightly parted fingers, like a ballet dancer.

"Look at her," she heard Orlu sigh. "I've never seen that kind before."

"Eh? And how many 'kinds' have you seen?" she heard Chichi snap. "Why don't you have some decency and turn away?" When Sunny looked at them, she saw that Chichi, who was looking away, had pink sparks jumping off of her and Orlu was dripping with almost invisible blue water. She didn't look at Anatov.

"Okay," she whispered. "Enough. Can this stop now?" She felt whatever was holding her up shrink into her, like it was a genie and she was the bottle. She staggered and sat down heavily on the floor. When she looked down, she was wearing some kind of dress made of light brown raffia. She touched her neck and was relieved to find that at least her gold necklace was still there. Her sandals were still on her feet, too.

"You passed! I knew it," Chichi said, throwing her arms around Sunny and pulling her up. "I knew I was right."

"My clothes!" At least her voice was normal again. "Where—?"

"Forget your clothes," Chichi said. "You passed!"

Anatov came toward them, a woven cane chair following of its own volition, like a faithful dog. He sat down. "Orlu," Anatov said, "put the *chittims* in her purse."

She stared as Orlu took her purse and scooped the handfuls of fist-size horseshoe-shaped copper rods into it.

"Rare," Anatov said, still looking at her. "Just as it's rare for a pure Igbo girl to have skin and hair the colour of washed-out paper, so it is for one to be a free agent. Neither of your parents, I assume?"

"What?" she asked.

"Are Leopard people."

"I—I guess not," she said. "Not that I know of."

"If you don't know, then they aren't. No mysterious aunts, uncles, grandparents?"

"Well," she said. Her throat was sore and she wanted to get the taste of dirt out of her mouth. "My—my grandmother on my mother's side was...a little strange, I think. Maybe she was mentally ill. My mother won't talk about her much."

"Ah," he said. "And let me guess, she's passed on."

She nodded. "Some years ago."

"She look like you?"

"No."

"Do you know her name? Her true name, the name before she was married?"

She shook her head.

"Hmm," he said. "In any case, you're what we call a free agent Leopard person. You're in a Leopard spirit line...somehow. It's not a blood thing. Leopard ability doesn't travel in the physical. Though blood is familiar with spirit.

"It may have been through your grandmother or she may have just been crazy, who knows. It's known to happen once in a while, but rarely. Most Leopard people are like your friends here, born to two sorcerer parents—strong ancestor connections. They are the most powerful, usually. Those born to one parent can't do much of anything unless they have an especially expensive juju knife or something like that or if they come from an especially adept mother. It travels strongest from woman to child, since she's the one who has the closest spiritual bond with the developing foetus.

"And to tell you what's just happened—you've been initiated." He paused. "Do you use computers?"

She blinked at the odd question. Then she nodded.

"Of course you do," he said. "Imagine that you are a computer that came with programs and applications already installed. In order to use them, they have to be activated; you have to, in a sense, wake it up. That's what initiation is. You were probably ready for initiation around when these two were, two years ago. You have anything odd happen to you recently?"

Sunny's mouth went dry.

"What happened?" he asked more intently.

It was a relief to tell him about what she had seen in the candle flame. But when she finished, she didn't like the look on Anatov's face. "Are you sure this is what you saw?" he asked quietly. She nodded. "Hmm. That's...interesting."

"Oga, please start from the beginning." Orlu said. "You are just confusing her."

"That's your job," Anatov said, annoyed. "Teach her the rules, too. I expect you all back here in four nights. Twelve midnight, sharp."

"What?" Sunny said. "I can't—"

"You're now a Leopard girl," Anatov said, getting up. "Find a way." Business completed, he turned to Orlu and grinned. "Guess who arrived today?"

Orlu groaned. "Already? Abeg!"

"Your mother didn't remind you?" Anatov said with a laugh. "She, his mother Keisha, and I have been talking about it for a week. Maybe your mother wanted to surprise you."

"I hate surprises," Orlu mumbled.

Chichi laughed. "And we didn't even plan to come today."

"Things have a way of working themselves out," Anatov said. "It's as I taught you: the world is bigger and more important than you."

Orlu grunted.

"So," Chichi asked looking around, "where is he?"

"Who?" Sunny asked, rubbing her forehead. She had a headache.

"Sasha!" Anatov called. A voice responded from somewhere outside. Anatov hissed, irritated. "What are you doing? Get over here," he said in his American-accented English.

"Sasha?" Chichi whispered to Sunny in Igbo. "What kind of name is that for a boy?"

58

Sunny was tired and confused, but she couldn't help but giggle. It was a girly name. Still, the boy who entered the hut wasn't girly at all.

"What took you so long?" Anatov asked sternly.

"I was taking a nap," Sasha said, blinking and rubbing his eyes. He, too, spoke with a strong American accent. "Still got jetlag, man." He wiped his face with his hand.

"Sasha, meet Orlu, Sunny, and Chichi," Anatov said formally.

"Hey," Sasha said coolly, thrusting his hands in his pockets. "'S up?"

Everything about him said 'America.' His baggy jeans, his white T-shirt with a logo on the chest, and his super-white Nike sneakers. He was tall and lanky like Sunny and he had tightly cornrowed hair that extended into long braids that went past his neck, and he wore a thick gold necklace.

"Good afternoon," the three friends said together in English.

His eyes fell on Sunny.

"Sasha's from Chicago," Anatov said. "He's been sent here to... cool down. In the meantime, he'll also be taught by and going through Mbawkwa with me."

"Did you just arrive?" Chichi asked.

"Yeah, three days ago," Sasha said. "My first time on a plane. Can't wait till I pass Ndibu, so I'll never have to use a goddamn plane again."

"And what makes you so sure you'll pass Ndibu?" Chichi said.

"Watch me," he said.

Chichi seemed to like this response. "How do you like it in Nigeria?"

He shrugged and smiled. "It's cool." He laughed to himself. "No, it's hot, damn hot. But it's cool. I dig Leopard Knocks. Wish we had a community central space like that in Chicago. Most of us are in what I consider hiding."

"We hide here, too," Chichi said. "But we find a way."

"Orlu, Sasha's things are already on their way to your parents'. You're all free to go," he said, shooing them out. "I've got things to do. I'll see y'all in four nights." He paused and looked at Sunny. Then he smirked. "And take care of her."

"We will," Orlu said.

"Of course," Chichi added.

Before Sunny knew it, Anatov had pushed them out through the IN door.

"What's wrong with that guy?" She went to lean against a nearby tree, feeling nauseous, tired, and irritable. Not a good combination. "And why does he have those 'in' and 'out' signs if no one uses them?"

"To him, his hut is outside the rubbish-filled world," Orlu said, looking back. "He only leaves with reluctance."

"Here," Sasha said reaching into his pocket and bringing out what looked like a fresh chewing stick. "Chew on this for a while. You'll feel better."

It was minty. She did feel better. "Thanks," she said.

"Yeah," Sasha said. "Man, I wish I'd have known. I've never seen an Ekpiri initiation on a free agent. I was half asleep outside when I heard your return. Splat!" He laughed.

"It was loud like that?"

"Yep," Sasha said. "Like a pile of rotten guts dropping on the floor."

"How come I'm dry now?"

"That's the way it works."

Chichi looked at Orlu as if waiting for him to say something. When he didn't, she turned to Sasha and asked, "Are you ready to go?"

Sasha cocked his head. "Why doesn't he ask me?" he said, looking at Orlu. "He's the one I'll be living with."

"Because I don't speak to dangerous people," Orlu grumbled in Igbo.

"Yo, what is your problem?"

Orlu turned to Sasha. "I know about you," he said in English, scowling. "My parents told me everything. Why would I want to live with someone like you?"

"Orlu!" Chichi said.

Sunny leaned back against the tree, chewing the mint stick.

Orlu scoffed. "Why don't you tell them why you're here? Give them some of the details."

Sasha thrust his hands deeper into his pockets. "Self-righteous African. So holier-than-thou," he mumbled.

"Trouble-making American," Orlu spat. "Akata criminal."

"Hey!" Sunny said.

"As if I don't know what that means," Sasha said, looking mildly annoyed.

"Do I care?" Orlu said.

"Abeg! Shut up, both of you," Chichi said. "Sasha, what's your story? Just tell us."

"Why should I?" Sasha said.

"Because we asked," Sunny said quietly, sitting down at the foot of the tree.

Sasha paused, then sighed.

"So you know," she continued, "I was born in the States, too. I came back with my parents when I was nine. That's only three years ago." She paused and looked meaningfully at Orlu. "I may not talk about it much, but most days I feel very much like an…akata."

Orlu looked at his feet, obviously ashamed. Serves him right for being so thoughtless, Sunny thought.

Sasha seemed a little calmer.

"Fine. Okay. Like it matters." He ran his hand over his cornrows. "I got into one too many fights at school. My parents were stupid enough to move into a neighbourhood that was not only all white but all Lambs."

"Lambs?" she asked.

"Folks with no juju," he said. "There wasn't a sorcerer, healer, or seer, for miles and miles. Anyway, so yeah, because of all that and because I don't take crap from anybody, I got into a lot of fights. And," he added quickly, "maybe I worked some stuff on some kids who were giving me trouble."

Orlu laughed scornfully. "He set a masquerade on three boys in his class!"

"What?" Chichi exclaimed.

"They talked smack about my parents and were harassing my sisters!" Sasha shouted.

"You can do that?" Chichi asked, impressed. "That's Ndibu level juju!"

"Who cares what level it's on?" Orlu said. "He's Ekpiri just like us."

"Man, there are books and I read them," Sasha said. "Plus, it was only a minor masquerade."

"So what?" Orlu cried. "There are rules! And two of those boys are mentally messed up because of what you did. I heard my father talking to your father on the phone just after it happened."

"Oh, well," Sasha said with a shrug. "Shouldn't have disrespected my parents or touched my sisters."

"Sasha hasn't mentioned that he also switched the minds of two police officers," Orlu added.

"They were harassing me and my friends," Sasha said. "They were pushing around this girl I know. And they were just...they were abusing the power they were given! Y'all don't know what it's like to be a black man in the States, ok. And y'all certainly don't know Chicago cops on the South Side. Here everyone's black, so you don't have—"

"Abeg, don't give me that nonsense!" Orlu said. "You are just making excuses for everything. That's why your parents sent you here."

"Enough," Sunny said. "How are you two supposed to live together? Sasha, try and turn over a new leaf or something. It'll be easier if you and Orlu try and be friends."

Sasha and Orlu looked at each other and then away.

"You'll feel better if you walk around some," Chichi said, helping Sunny up. "Let's take her to Leopard Knocks."

"What?" Sunny said, nearly sinking down again.

"Relax," Chichi said. "You'll be ok."

Orlu chuckled.

"I checked it out yesterday," Sasha said, brightening up. "My parents would love that place."

Chichi smiled. "Let's go, then. While we get lunch, we can explain more things to Sunny."

Sunny tried to stand up straight and stumbled to the side. "No way! I'm not crossing that—"

"Here," Chichi quickly said, pushing it into her hands. "Take your purse."

"Ah-ah!" Sunny exclaimed. "It's so heavy!"

"You have at least a hundred *chittims* in there. Maybe more," Orlu said.

"What's *chittim*?" she asked.

"Currency," Orlu said. "You earn it when you learn something. The bigger the knowledge, the more *chittim*. I didn't receive half as many *chittims* when I went through Ekpiri!"

"Ekpiri is level one," Chichi explained. She turned to Orlu. "That's because you always knew what you were. Sunny's a free agent. She didn't know anything."

Even Sunny couldn't argue with that.

WHAT ARE MASQUERADES?

Up to now you've known masquerades to be mere symbolic manifestations of the ancestors or spirits. Men and boys dress up in elaborate cloth and raffia costumes and dance, jeer, or joke depending on who they are manifesting. Up to now, you've believed masquerades to be nothing more than myth, folklore, theatrics, and tradition. Now that you are a Leopard person, know that your world has just become more real. Creatures are real. Ghosts, witches, demons, shape-shifters, and masquerades, all real. And masquerades are always dangerous. They can kill, steal your soul, take your mind, take your past, rewrite your future, bring the end of the world, even. As a free agent you will have nothing to do with the real thing, otherwise you face certain death. If you are smart you will leave true masquerades up to those who know what to do with juju.

from Fast Facts for Free Agents by Isong Abong Effiong Isong

CHAPTER FOUR
LEOPARD KNOCKS HIS FOOT

"I thought today was supposed to be fun," Sunny mumbled when they got to the bridge. She tugged at her raffia dress. "This is so scratchy."

"Would you prefer to have fun or would you rather discover the meaning of your life?" Chichi asked.

"There's no 'meaning' to any of this."

"Let me carry that for you," Orlu said, taking Sunny's heavy purse.

"Thanks."

Orlu rubbed the smooth black stone buried at the bridge's beginning in a way that reminded Sunny of how she ran her hand across the trunk of the palm tree back home. Then he stepped onto the bridge. As he walked, Sunny could have sworn that she saw something weird happen to his head. Her entire body went cold. Walking easily along the super-narrow bridge, strolling casually, he soon disappeared in the mist.

As Sasha followed Orlu across the bridge, Chichi turned Sunny's head to her. "Focus on me," she said.

"What happens when you cross?" Sunny was glad Chichi wouldn't let her look. She suspected that if she watched Sasha, she'd see the weird thing happen to his head, too.

"To cross the bridge…you need to know some things," Chichi said. "We'll tell you everything once we get to Leopard Knocks."

More things that I don't know. Great, Sunny thought.

But to her surprise, Chichi began giving her answers. "Okay, as they said, Lambs are people who have no juju. You were never a Lamb, but you have to be initiated to become a functioning Leopard person. That dress you're wearing is a dress for new initiates."

"Did you have to be initiated?" Sunny asked.

"Yes, two years ago. But I've always known of my Leopard inheritance and I've always been able to do small things like, eh, make mosquitoes stay away, or warm my bathing water, things like that. Initiation meant something different to me than to you. It's more like a mark of beginning my life's journey. Yours was, too—but it was also the beginning of your true Self.

"Every Leopard person has two faces—a human face and a spirit face. I have always known my human and my spirit face. When I was born, I wore my spirit face for the first week of my life. My parents didn't know what my human face looked like until I was seven days old." She paused, looking at Sunny's shocked face.

"*Haba*, relax," she snapped. "It was the same with Orlu and Sasha — in fact, all Leopard people with pure inheritance. Anyway, the spirit face is more of who you are than your physical face, it stays with you, it doesn't age, and you can control it as it controls you. But it's very rude to show it in public. It's like being naked. I think it's because in this form, you cannot lie or hide anything. Lies are a thing of the physical world. They can't exist in the spirit world."

Sunny thought it all sounded like something a crazy old man would say. Imagine some inebriated old man shambling down the street, a bottle of palm wine in his hand, shouting, *"My face is no longer of this world o!"* Maybe Chichi, Orlu, and Sasha were all on drugs.

Chichi went on. "The bridge is a 'link.' It's a piece of the spirit world that exists in the physical world. That's why Leopard Knocks was built here. Leopard Knocks is on an island conjured by the ancestors..." She shook her head. "Is any of this making sense to you?"

"Sort of." Actually, Sunny thought Chichi was utterly insane.

Chichi smiled. "So, to cross you have to call up your spirit face." She looked around. Sunny looked around, too. They were alone.

"I'll show you mine," Chichi whispered.

"Okay," Sunny said, though she wasn't sure if she wanted to see it, especially if it was supposed to be like being naked.

"And don't think that I will ever do this for you again," Chichi said. "And if you ever dare tell Sasha or Orlu what it looks like..."

Sunny considered giving an even more cutting response, but then she realised that Chichi was dead serious. "Okay," she said again.

Chichi stepped back. Right before Sunny's eyes, Chichi's face melted, shifted, and morphed into something inhuman. Sunny stifled a scream.

Chichi's spirit face looked like a perfectly carved ceremonial mask.

It was long, about the length of her forearm, and made of a hard marble-like periwinkle substance. The two eyes were square indentations coloured in with what looked like blue paint. Two white lines ran from the eyes to the sides of a pointy chin. The nose was long and outlined in white. The mouth was a large black grin. And it wasn't just her face that had changed. Her body language changed, too. She was suddenly quick and precise.

"I am Igri," Chichi said in a deep male voice. She laughed, doing a back flip. Sunny stumbled away, startled by Chichi's sudden flexibility and agility. Chichi was always quick and on point, but now those qualities were exaggerated. The oddest thing was that Chichi's spirit face still somehow looked like Chichi. She did have a pointy chin and a long face. She changed herself back, and for a moment the girls just stared at each other.

"What's Igri?" Sunny asked.

"My spirit name."

"So I have my own spirit face, too?"

"Yeah."

Sunny held the chewing stick Sasha had given her, and though it was all frayed, she put it in her mouth. She was glad it was still minty. "So, how do I—"

"Do you remember how you felt when Anatov brought you back?"

"Yeah," she said. "Like the greatest ballet dancer on Earth."

Chichi smiled. "Wait a minute, you and Orlu—and Anatov—"

"Yes, we all saw you," she said, looking guilty. "But I only saw you for one second before I turned away."

"But you said it's like being naked."

Chichi smiled sheepishly.

"Oh my goodness! I'm so embarrassed!"

"We're all your friends, Sunny. It's not..."

"Look at all the stuff you said before you would even give me a peek of your spirit face! Yet, there I was for everyone to see! It's like my butt was exposed!"

"That is different now," she said with a laugh. "Anyway, your spirit face is nothing like your *nyash*."

"At least Sasha wasn't there," she mumbled. "So...what did I look like?"

Chichi gestured at Sunny's umbrella. "It's funny. You know how you told me that you need this for the sun? Well, your spirit face looked...you looked like the sun!"

Sunny shrank back. "What?"

Chichi just shrugged. "So you felt like a ballerina?"

Sunny blinked and then nodded. "Yeah. All graceful and..." she tapered off. "I've always loved ballet but I can't do it."

"Okay, well—Take." Chichi reached into her pocket and took out a knife with a jade handle and a bronzed blade. She cut the air in front of Sunny and spoke some words. Sunny didn't understand, but she recognised them as Efik. Suddenly, classical music began playing. Right above Sunny's head, to her left, to her right, she couldn't tell where it was coming from.

Sunny had always felt a strange, sometimes painful, pull whenever she heard classical music. It was part of the reason she liked ballet so much. Now that feeling was stronger than ever.

"Concentrate on the ballet music and cross the bridge," Chichi said quickly. "Your grace will protect you from falling...I hope."

"You hope?" she asked. But something was taking her over. She could feel that tightening sensation on her face. A languidness in her body. She strode onto the bridge, disregarding its narrowness.

She felt so good and confident that she laughed, thinking, *Man, this is going to be easy.* With her peripheral vision she could see golden points radiating from her face. Her spirit face had sun rays, too! She laughed again, feeling a wave of pleasure as the classical music hit a crescendo. She danced over the narrow bridge on her sandaled toes, once in a while doing leaps that took her dangerously close to the edge. She felt not an ounce of fear.

Beneath, the water swirled, pounded, gushed, and thrashed. She watched it as she danced, glimpsing an enormous dark, round face under the water. Whatever the creature was, the river's strength was nothing to it. It was watching her. She did a leap for the monster, a *chaîné* turn, and then a pirouette. She looked it in the eye, another laugh in her throat. Only a few feet away, the white mist swirled and gave way to the end of the bridge and whatever lay beyond it.

Suddenly, her confidence wavered.

The wind blew harder and Leopard Knocks opened up before her like the New York skyline. It was nowhere near as big, but it was grand. Huts stacked upon huts like hats at a hat shop. Not a European-style building in sight. All this was African.

She quickly walked to the end of the bridge. When she got there, something possessed her to stretch herself into an arabesque. The music abruptly stopped. She felt her spirit face pull in and she gasped, teetering on the bridge's slippery wood. Directly below, she saw something undulate. The river creature! She thrust out her arms to keep her balance.

"Ah!" she shouted as she fell. Something tugged hard at her neck. Sasha had her by her gold necklace. He pulled her forward and she stumbled into his arms. As he held her, she looked back, tears in her eyes.

"Here," Sasha said, helping her to a nearby picnic table under a large iroko tree. "Sit."

"Are you okay?" Orlu said, running over.

She nodded. "Thanks, Sasha."

"You should thank your necklace," he said.

"What happened?" Chichi said a minute later, after emerging from the mist.

"What do you think happened?" Orlu said.

"Oh," she said. "The juju should have lasted longer than—"

"Please, the river beast can easily break that," Orlu said. "It probably waited until she was almost safe to make her fall more dramatic."

"One day, someone is going to kill that thing," Chichi said, kneeling before Sunny.

Sasha laughed and said, "Girl, please. Anatov told me that monster is older than time. It'll be here messing with shit long after we're all gone."

Sunny shivered, knowing they'd have to go back over the bridge to get home. It was already noon. *I'll cross that bridge when I get to it*, she thought drily.

As her heart beat slowed, she took in her surroundings.

So this was Leopard Knocks. The entrance was flanked by two tall iroko trees. They were slowly shedding a constant shower of leaves, though their tops remained healthy and bushy. At the foot of each tree were small piles of leaves. Beyond was the strangest place Sunny had ever seen.

She was from New York and she'd been to a handful of other American cities. She'd been to the Bahamas and Mexico, too. Since moving to Nigeria, she'd been to Lagos and Jos to visit relatives, and to Abuja. But this place was something else entirely.

The buildings were made of thick grey clay and red mud with thatch roofs. They reminded her of Chichi's house, but more sophisticated. Almost all of them were quite large. Many had more than one storey; several had three or four. How clay and mud could stand up to this kind of use was beyond her. Every building was full of windows of various shapes and sizes. Large squares, circles, triangles—one building had a window shaped like a giant heart. All were decorated with white intricate drawings—snakes, squiggles, cattle, stars, circles, people, faces, fish. The list of things was infinite. Pink smoke billowed from the centre of a large one-storey hut.

The buildings were crowded tightly together. Still, tall palm trees and bushes managed to grow between them, and a dirt road packed with people wound among the buildings. From somewhere nearby, up-tempo highlife music played. She turned around and saw more people emerging from the mist. She stepped closer to Chichi, feeling like an intruder. "Maybe I should just go home," she whispered. She thought about the monster again and cursed.

"Eh? Why?" Chichi said looking surprised.

"I'm not supposed to be here."

Chichi laughed. "You have more than a hundred *chittim* in your purse! Trust me, you're very welcome here!"

She took Sunny's hand and they followed Orlu and Sasha. There were a few people ahead of them. She stopped. Iroko leaves were falling around her, and as she watched, one of the leaf piles took a humanoid shape. It sloppily cartwheeled over to a man and fell apart, burying the man in its green leaves. As the leaves covered him, the man looked more annoyed than afraid. When the leaf thing took a humanoid shape again, a gun was disappearing into its chest.

"*Biko*, please!" the man begged, holding his hands up and smiling, embarrassed. "I forgot I was carrying that."

The leaf person cartwheeled back to its place in front of the tree and was motionless again. Orlu and Chichi were snickering.

"Dumbass," Sasha said in a low voice. "What's he packing for? I've got more powerful juju in one finger. Dude probably didn't even make *Mbawkwa*."

Sunny looked closely at the leaf person on her left as she passed it. Even up close it was just a bunch of leaves.

"This is the forefront," Chichi told her. She waved at a boy passing by and slapped hands with him. He wore baggy jeans and sneakers like Sasha, but she could tell he was Nigerian.

Something about the way he wore his American-style clothes, but he looked Nigerian, too. Probably Yoruba.

"Friend of mine," Chichi said.

"Heh, Chichi has a lot of friends," Orlu said.

"Sharrap," Chichi said coyly. "Anyway, most of these places are shops. That's Sweet Plumes, it's a juju powder shop."

Sweet Plumes was one of the first buildings, a two-storey red mud hut decorated with thousands of tiny white circles that gave it an almost reptilian look. The front door was round and covered with a silver cloth that moved in and out as if the building itself was breathing. As they passed it, she smelled a sulphuric odour, like rotten eggs.

"Their products are good unless you are trying to do very, very advanced juju. But that's normal," Chichi added. "By the time you have reached that stage, you should just grind your own."

They passed more shops. Many of them sold normal stuff like clothes, jewellery, computer software, and mobile phone accessories. They stopped outside a place called Bola's Store for Books.

"We'll be fast," Chichi said, when Orlu gave her a look. They were all hungry. Chichi took Sunny's heavy purse. "Sunny, come with me."

It was large and cool inside. In the centre, woven cane chairs were set up around a wicker coffee table. A woman wearing a big metallic blue headtie, an expensive-looking *buba* and matching wrapper was reading a dusty book. When she turned a page, she ground the book's filth into her lovely clothes a little more. Her hands were covered with the book's dust, too. *What book is that interesting?* Sunny wondered. She wanted to see, but Chichi led her in a different direction.

There were books written in Hausa, Urdu, Yoruba, Arabic, Efik, German, Igbo, Egyptian hieroglyphs, Sanskrit, even one written in a language Chichi called Nsibidi. "Can you read N—Nsibidi?" Sunny asked with a laugh, picking up the book. What kind of name was that? It sounded like a stifled sneeze.

"Later, Sunny," Chichi said, taking the book from her and putting it back. "We have to be fast. I want to go eat."

All the people in the store were quiet, reading and browsing with such intensity that she ached to look at some of the books, too. They passed an empty section with a warning posted above it saying, **Enter and Buy at Your Own Risk**.

"Here it is," Chichi said. They stopped at a shelf marked, **intros/ outed/eyes opened**. She picked up a slim green paperback titled *Fast Facts For Free Agents*. "*Oya, oya*, let's go," she said. "Orlu's going to catch fire if we don't hurry."

Sunny held her heavy purse as Chichi fished out a copper chittim and handed it to the old man behind the table. He looked at the *chittim*, reached into his pocket, brought out a pinch of what looked like sand, and rubbed it against the *chittim*. There was an instant burst of wet mist. It smelled like roses. The man smiled and rubbed his hands in the mist. Chichi did the same. Sunny imitated her and found that her hands came away smelling like roses, too.

"I am just making sure," the man said.

"After so many years, you still don't trust me?" Chichi asked.

"All you Efik women and girls are crafty," he said.

Chichi laughed. "*Haba*, Mohammed, my father is Igbo, have you forgotten?"

"Eh," the man said handing her the book and five shiny silver *chittim*. To Sunny, these looked much more valuable than the dull copper ones. "Daughters are their mother's children now." He motioned to Sunny. "Is the book for her?"

"Yes. This is Sunny," Chichi said, handing the book to Sunny. She put the *chittim* and the book in her purse and waved shyly at the man.

He looked at Sunny for a long time and then said, "You should take her to my second wife for a divination reading."

"I know," Chichi said. "But not today. Tell your wife that we will come another time."

"Don't worry, she probably already knows when you'll be coming."

They were starving and it was nearly two o'clock, so Sasha suggested that they go to Mama Put's Putting Place. The small outdoor restaurant was quick. It was run by a fat woman who preferred to be called Mama Put. She stood behind a counter collecting money and barking out orders to her employees. Sunny ordered a large plate of *jollof* rice and roasted spicy chicken and a bottle of Fanta. She paid with one silver *chittim* and Mama Put gave her back six small gold ones.

They sat at a table in the shadiest part of the restaurant. The rice was nicely spicy, the chicken savoury. As soon as her stomach was calmed, she said, "Okay, talk. I don't care if you spit food or choke while you do it. Just keep explaining."

"Ahh!" Sasha exclaimed, his mouth hanging open. He'd just tasted his pepper soup. "Woohoo! That's hot! That's *hot!*" He swallowed, and then used his napkin to blow his nose. "Damn!"

"But do you like it?" Orlu asked.

"Oh, yeah. Real good!" He coughed. "Wow. Gotta get used to the food here. Not even good soul food has anything on this!"

"Mama Put uses tainted peppers," Orlu said.

"Those are peppers that grow near spill sites—places where they dump out used magical brews," Chichi explained to Sunny. "They're popular in Africa and India."

"Definitely not America," Sasha added.

Sunny filed this information away.

"Okay. Well, come on. Tell me what you know."

Orlu stuffed a large chunk of palm oil-soaked yam into his mouth, then took a bite of his large butter cookie. Sasha, now sweating profusely, dove back into his pepper soup.

"Ok, I'll tell you," Chichi said, annoyed. "After all, I'm the most knowledgeable." Neither boy argued with her. "Let's start from the beginning: There are Leopard People. We have always existed all over the world. In some countries, we're called witches, or sorcerers, shamans, wizards, things like that. So it's not just Africans."

Sunny took a deep breath. "Okay, I have to ask—do you all have anything to do with...the witches I always hear about? Like those child witches?" She shuddered.

Sunny often heard her mother talking to her auntie in America about this, so she knew plenty about it. There were many churches coming up which practised a fanatical Protestantism that combined itself with bits of traditional spirituality. These churches were always shouting about 'spiritual attacks,' 'demonic enemies' and 'witches and wizards.' They were even known to torture and kill women and children accused of witchcraft. Even in civil society, people accused of being witches could be evicted from their homes, fired from their jobs and driven out of their communities.

Children marked as 'witches' were then blamed for anything that went wrong, from illnesses to accidents to death. Eventually, the community would rise up and administer all kinds of punishments on these poor children in order to get rid of their 'evil magical powers.' It was the worst kind of child abuse. Sunny had even seen documentaries and movies on child witches.

"No," Orlu firmly said. "We have absolutely nothing to do with any of that. That one is just twisted Lamb religion and superstition. Those victims are just normal innocent non-magical people being scapegoated. That's part of the reason why we made that trust knot. It's the easiest way to keep knowledge of us away from those paranoid churches."

Sunny breathed a sigh of relief.

"Anyway, being a Leopard person is not genetic," Chichi continued. "It is spiritual. The spiritual affects the physical... It's complicated. All you need to know is that Leopard people tend to stay within their families, but sometimes it jumps, like in you. I think maybe your grandmother was of Leopard spirit. But anyway, all this is in that book I just helped you buy. So make sure you read it."

"Oh, I plan to. Go on."

"So Leopard Knocks is the main West African headquarters," she said. "Sasha, where is the headquarters in the United States?"

Sasha smirked. "New York, of course. But I don't consider that place the head of anything. It doesn't represent black folks. We are a minority, I guess. As a matter of fact—everything's biased toward European juju. The African American headquarters is on the Gullah Islands in South Carolina. We call it Tar Nation."

Sunny laughed. "I like that name."

"We try," Sasha said proudly.

"So, you know the way you had to be initiated before you could come here?" Chichi asked.

"Yeah."

"Well, because we have Leopard parents, Orlu and I knew our spirit faces, so we have always been able to come here. We both went through the first level, the initiation, two years ago. It's called *Ekpiri*," she said. "Most Leopard people go through it at around fourteen or fifteen."

"But I'm twelve," Sunny said.

"Yes, you are early," Chichi said. "So was Orlu."

"So was I," Sasha said. "I went through it last year. I'm thirteen."

"How old were you, Chichi?" Sunny asked.

She only smiled. Yet again, she managed to keep her age hidden. "The second level is *Mbawkwa*—you go through that at around sixteen or seventeen. That's when you start learning serious juju. You have to pass all these tough tests to get to that level."

"I can pass all that right now," Sasha boasted.

"Me, too," Chichi boasted back. "It's very easy."

Orlu scoffed. "Well, the rules say that you cannot take the test yet."

"Screw rules," Sasha said. "They're made to be broken."

"But only when you've mastered them," Orlu said quietly.

"Anyway, the third level is one that very, very, very few people ever pass, that's *Ndibu*. It's like getting a PhD. To pass it you have to attend a masquerade meeting and get a real masquerade's consent. A real masquerade, not these men and boys who dress up for festivals."

"A real one?" Sunny asked quietly, as if to speak of them too loudly would call the spirits from their dwelling place in the other world.

"Yes," Chichi said. "And that means you have to die in some way. I don't really understand it."

"So what's the last grade?" Sunny asked.

"*Oku Akama*. No one knows how to get there. In Nigeria, only eight living people have reached it. Four live around Leopard Knocks. Anatov is one—he is the 'scholar on the outside.'"

"But he's not that old," Sunny said.

"No, he isn't. He's only fifty-something, I think."

Sunny hissed. "How can such a mean guy be so important?"

"Sometimes too much knowledge can make you like that. You know too much," Chichi said.

Orlu loudly hissed. "You always make excuses for him. Teacher's pet."

"And so? I'm sure you wish you were," Chichi said, looking smug. "Anyway, Kehinde and Taiwo are twins who passed the last grade and they went on to become the 'scholars of the links.'

An old woman named Sugar Cream is the fourth, the 'scholar on the inside.' She lives in the Obi Library most of the time. She's the oldest and most respected. She's the Head Librarian."

Sunny frowned. "Librarian? Why is that such a big—"

"Let me tell you something that Chichi and Sasha don't respect," Orlu said, putting his fork down. "Leopard people— all of our kind all over the world—are not like Lambs. Lambs think money and material things are the most important things in the world. You can cheat, lie, steal, kill, and be seriously dense but if you can brag of having money and lots of things, and your bragging is true, that bypasses everything. Money and material things make you king or queen of the Lamb world. You can do no wrong, you can do anything.

"Leopard people are different. The only way you can earn *chittim* is by learning. The more you learn, the more *chittim* you earn. Knowledge is the centre of all things. The Head Librarian of the Obi Library of Leopard Knocks is the keeper of the greatest stock of knowledge in West Africa." Orlu sat back. "One day, we'll take you to the Obi Library and you will see."

"Wow," Sunny said. "I like that."

Orlu smiled and nodded. "It's great, isn't it?"

"People *are* too focused on money," Sunny said. "Yes it's supposed to be a tool, not the prize to be won."

"Spoken like an upward-standing Leopard person," Chichi said mockingly. "No wonder my mother likes you so much."

Now Sunny understood why Chichi and her mother lived the way they did. "Your mother doesn't care for material things, does she?"

"No, and neither do I," Chichi said. "My mother has reached every grade except the last. And people think that one day she will."

"Chichi's mother is a Nimm priestess," Orlu explained. "One of the last princesses in the Queen Nsedu spiritline."

Before Sunny could ask what that was, Sasha said,

"Not all Leopard people live by the Leopard philosophy."

Orlu nodded.

"Just like in any other place, there are killers—even here in Leopard Knocks. There are people who only want power and money, who don't earn any *chittim* at all and would rather steal what they want. Then there are some people who are rich in *chittim*, yet they still want Lamb power and wealth. I think those ones are the most dangerous."

It made sense. There were flavours of 'Leopard-dom,' too, they explained. For example, Orlu's parents owned a fairly large home and another home in Owerri. Unlike Chichi's mother, they liked nice things.

Sasha frowned and looked at Chichi. "You know what? We're an *Oha* coven, aren't we?"

Orlu hissed. "Nonsense. We're too young," he said just as Chichi smiled at Sasha and said, "You think so, too?"

"Think about it," Sasha said. "First, there are four of us. There aren't any more in our group, right?"

"No," Chichi said.

"Right. Second, one of us is an outsider—me, being from a different country, a descendent of slaves and such. Right, Orlu?"

Orlu shrugged, refusing to respond.

Sasha chuckled. "And one of us is outside in." He gestured at Sunny. "Black on the inside but white on the outside."

Sunny hissed but said nothing.

"Just telling it like it is," Sasha said lightly.

"And two of us are girls and two of us are boys," Chichi added. Then together, Chichi and Sasha said, "Balance."

"Whatever," Sunny grumbled. "What's an Oho coven?"

"*Oha,*" Sasha corrected. "An *Oha* coven. It's a group of mystical combination, set up to defend against something bad."

"So, what does that have to do with us?" she asked. "What bad thing are we—"

Suddenly, they all looked above her head. Sasha cursed loudly. Sunny looked up just as whatever it was exploded. Warm, wet air that smelled like rotten meat enveloped her. She threw her arms over her head and ducked to the side, falling off her chair. Things hit her head and arms and dropped on the table. She heard Sasha spit several more curses as white chips rained down, clicking and clacking. Something black fell lightly onto the table as well.

Sunny quickly got up and looked. "What is—is that hair?"

There were tufts of it all over the table. It looked like the floor of a barber shop. "And—and what the hell is that?" She pointed to red chunks of raw meat among the hair tufts. She felt her gorge rise.

"Don't worry," Chichi said. "Just relax."

"In a restaurant?" Orlu said. "*Kai,* filthy!"

"Come on, the place is open," Sasha said. "It's not like we're indoors."

Sunny looked at the table a little more closely and screeched. The white chips were teeth!

Mama Put came bustling from behind her counter, all apologies. She shouted orders at one of her employees to clean up the mess immediately.

"It's ok. It wasn't any one's fault," Chichi told the woman.

"It's the goddamn *tungwa's* fault," Sasha said, brushing a tuft of hair off his shoulder. "Damn it. Anatov told me about these. Disgusting!" Sunny wanted to burst out laughing at the nastiness and absurdity of it all and at their nonchalance. Every time she thought she had reached the threshold of weirdness...

"*Tungwas* are just things that dwell at Leopard Knocks," Orlu explained. "Floating bags of teeth, bone, meat, and hair. They explode when they're ready." He shrugged. "Don't know what they are. Might be creatures that just don't develop right. We deal with them like we deal with mosquitoes, flies, and cockroaches."

Sunny shuddered. Mama Put gave them each a free bag of chin-chin. Sunny gave hers to Sasha. As they walked back, she looked at the time on her mobile phone and gasped. "It's three-thirty! I'm going to be late!"

She speed-dialed her home number and held the phone to her ear, her heart pounding. It was best to warn her mother. That way, things wouldn't be as bad when she got home. The call wouldn't go through. She redialed. Again, it didn't go through. There was no signal.

"Don't mobile phones work here?" she asked Chichi.

"I don't know. I don't have a mobile phone."

"My mother's going to kill me," she said, putting the phone back into her purse. It clinked against all the *chittim*.

Crossing the bridge was much easier the second time, once Sunny managed to call up her spirit face. It took ten minutes, and Chichi had to conjure up classical music three times before Sunny felt her body go languid and her face tighten. Apparently, it was harder to bring forth one's spirit face when one was tired.

But once she changed, she found she didn't need the music at all. And when she looked down at the roiling creature below, she laughed loudly and blew it a kiss. Not far behind, she heard Chichi laugh. "Move faster!" she shouted through the mist.

Sunny didn't want to zip about like Chichi; she wanted to dawdle and dance. Nevertheless, she moved along, thoughts of her mother's angry face enough to keep her focused, even with her spirit face on.

"You won't sleep well tonight," Chichi said. They stood outside Sunny's house. Sasha and Orlu had already said goodbye. They had to go straight to Orlu's so that Sasha could officially greet Mr. and Mrs. Ezulike.

"Why?"

"You've been initiated today. You're more awake than you've ever been."

"Is it going to be—"

"It's different for everyone. I just wanted to warn you."

As Sunny entered her compound, she remembered that they were to meet with Anatov in four nights. At midnight. How was she was going to pull that off?

She unlocked the door.

"*Sunny, is that you?*" her mother shouted from the kitchen.

"Yes, Mama," she said. "Sorry I'm late."

She glanced at her watch. It was six o'clock. She was two hours late. As she walked in, she remembered the raffia dress she wore. Before she could think of a possible excuse, her mother came hurrying from the kitchen, her father behind her.

"Mama, I—"

Slap!

"Why didn't you call, eh?!!" her mother yelled. She had tears in her eyes.

"I—I tried!" Sunny stammered. "The phone wouldn't work! I tried, I swear!"

"Where were you?" her father demanded.

"With Orlu, Chichi, and Sasha—he's Orlu's family friend who just came from America," she said quickly. She flinched as her father moved toward her. His hand was always heavier than her mother's and far less predictable.

"Did you know your mother has been worried?" he bellowed. "She was sure you were been taken by that Black Hat criminal! How dare you cause her that kind of stress, stupid girl. If you ever return home late again, she won't be able to hold me back! I will flog you tirelessly!"

"I'm sorry," Sunny said quietly, her head down.

She knew she wasn't out of danger yet.

"It just got late and..." She rubbed her stinging cheek.

Her mother sniffled and wiped her face. She glanced at Sunny's raffia dress, but said nothing. She pulled Sunny into a hug. Only then did Sunny know that she was safe. In that moment Sunny hated her father more than she'd ever hated him before. *As if he really cares about me*, she thought. "Your mother's been worried," he'd said. Obviously, he wasn't. *As far as he's concerned, Black Hat can have me.*

Her brothers had never been slapped for coming home late. They didn't even have a curfew, not even when they were her age. It was only her mother who yelled and scolded them. Her father would only laugh and say that 'boys should be boys.' Sunny didn't ever want to be a boy—but she didn't want a father who hated her, either.

Her mother let go of her and pushed her toward her room.

"Go and bathe," she said in a low voice. "And change your clothes."

WHAT IS IT?
That clear green substance

One of the most perplexing materials you can (but probably will never) encounter as a Leopard person is a rare substance that is more 'unbreakable' than diamond. When it is found, it is most often embedded in ceremonial rings. However, once in a while, this material is found as the blade of a juju knife. Whomever is chosen by such a knife begs the question of 'What have you done in your past life to require such durability?' This hard, clear, green substance is so rare that it has no name and no one knows its origins. Some speculate that it was brought from a mysterious forest only accessed in the middle of the Sahara Desert and that it comes from the molted eye cuticle of a car-sized beetle that lives in this forest.

from Fast Facts for Free Agents by Isong Abong Effiong Isong

CHAPTER FIVE
SUNNY DAY

As she bathed from the bucket, every drop of water that touched her skin tickled. And not in a playful way. Sunny's body felt alert, like she was full of excitable bees.

When she returned to her room, the front page of the newspaper was on her bed. The headline was circled: **Black Hat Otokoto Kills Again**. She locked her door and sat on her bed to read it. A five-year-old child had been found dead in the bush yesterday with no eyes or nose. A black hat had been drawn on his arm in permanent marker. She shivered. *No wonder Mama was going crazy*, she thought.

She considered going to her mother and trying to explain that she wasn't stupid and that she knew how to stay away from trouble, but it wouldn't do any good. That wasn't the only thing not worth discussing with her parents.

She could never tell them about being a Leopard person. Her mother was a devout Catholic. She'd have screamed and accused Sunny of running about with 'idol-worshippers.' She'd never let Sunny see Chichi or Orlu again. And who knew what her bull of a father would do—something bad, for sure. She didn't even consider telling her brothers. On top of it all, she'd made a trust knot, and probably couldn't even talk about it if she tried.

She would have to deal with whatever was going to happen alone.

When Sunny tried to sleep, her head buzzed. Her hands shook and itched. She sweated through her sheets. When she closed her eyes, she saw crumbly brown dirt. She could taste and smell it, too. She felt as if she was sinking into and through her bed, her body trying to return to the earth. So she kept her eyes open.

By 3am, Sunny was weeping. She didn't know what to do or how to stop it, and there was no one to turn to for help. Around four, her body started shifting. Her face would become her spirit face and then it would go back to normal, then it would become her spirit face again.

Once, when her spirit face came forward, she got up and looked at herself in the mirror. She nearly screamed. Then she just stared. It was her, but it felt as if it had its own separate identity, too. Her spirit face was the sun, all shiny gold and glowing with pointy rays. It was hard to the touch, but she could feel her touch. She knocked on it and it made a hollow sound.

Her spirit face was smiling. Still, somehow she knew it could be angry if it had to be. Her eyes were carved slits, yet she could see perfectly. The nose was shaped like her nose. As she stood there, she watched herself change back, her human face sucking her spirit face in.

She was scared, but she was excited, too. Her spirit face was beautiful. And it was utterly crazy-looking. And it was hers.

All through the night, she battled herself. Or battled to know herself. She fell apart and then put herself back together and then she fell apart again and put herself back together, over and over.

Finally, she pushed aside the mosquito net, opened her window wider and stuck her head outside for several minutes. Her room was on the second floor of the house, so the mosquitoes weren't so bad. At least that's what she told herself. She'd have told herself anything—the fresh air felt wonderful. She eventually fell asleep right there, beside her window.

Red. A river at sunrise. She was swimming in it and through the water she could see the wavy red sky above. A new day. She laughed and did a somersault. Then she looked down and met the two large eyes of the river beast deep below her, just close enough to catch the glint of red sunshine from above.

When Sunny awoke, the sun was shining directly on her face. She'd been sleeping in it for hours. She gasped and quickly moved out of the raw bright sunshine. Her face was almost certainly badly burned.

She tentatively touched her cheek. She froze. She touched her cheek again. Then she got up and ran to her mirror. Her face looked fine! She grinned. Then she laughed out loud, and rushed to stand in the sunshine again. She closed her eyes and soaked in the warm light. She didn't need to stand in there for an hour to know—she knew deep in her skin. The sunshine felt like a warm friend, not an angry enemy. She didn't need her umbrella anymore.

"Oh good," she whispered. "I can play soccer!"

Realising what she was was the beginning of something, all right...but it was also the end of something else.

WHAT IS A FREE AGENT?

A free agent is one who isn't privileged with even one pure Leopard spiritline from the survivors of the Great Attempt. She or he is a random of nature, a result of mixed up and confused spiritual genetics. Free agents are the hardest to understand, predict, or explain. Learning will not come easy to you. You are a Leopard person only by the will of the Supreme Creator and, as we all know, She isn't very concerned with Her own creations.

After your initiation, make sure that someone is there to help you, for you will not be able to help yourself, so new the world will be to you and so fragile your ego. You're like an infant. You will be dumbfounded and disoriented. What's most important is—

CHAPTER SIX
THE SKULL

Sunny threw the book across the room. *How am I supposed to read this?* she thought. *What a pompous discriminating idiot of an author. If they have racism in the Leopard world, this book is so 'racist' against free agents!*

She sighed. The last thing she wanted was to return to Anatov still ignorant and prove the author right. As she grudgingly got up to get the book, something began to happen to it. Tiny black legs sprouted from the spine. Sunny fought hard not to flee. The legs suctioned themselves to the floor and pulled the book up, pages facing the ceiling.

Sunny scrambled to the other side of the room as the book walked back to her bed, climbed up the side, and plopped itself near her pillows. The legs retreated back into the book's spine with a soft slurping sound. Sunny didn't move, staring at the book, waiting for it to do something. When nothing did, she crept towards it.

Once at her bed, she slowly reached forward, planning to grab the book and fling it back across the room. When she was within an inch of it, the book flew open. She leaped back. The pages leafed this way and that. They stopped and the book opened and stretched out so flat that she could hear its spine crack. She leaned just close enough to see what it had opened to. *Chapter Four: Your Abilities.*

After a few minutes, she sat beside it, ready to run away if the book so much as shivered. She began to read.

Chapter 4: Your Abilities

This will be new to you, since you are fresh from Lamb country and have just entered the high society of Leopards. Lambs are on a constant, unrealistic, irrational, and unnatural quest for perfection. They seek to have bodies with no blemishes or disease; that do not age; that have perfect eyes, noses, and lips all in the right place; that are thin like fashion models' or muscular like athletes'; that are tall; lacking warts, extra fingers, pimples, scars; that always smell fresh like flowers; etc. There are no Lamb cultures where people do not strive for this inferior thing called perfection, no matter their definition of it.

> WE LEOPARD FOLK ARE NOTHING LIKE THIS.
> We embrace those things that make us unique or odd. For only in these things can we locate and then develop our most individual abilities. Even you, free agent, have an ability given to you by the omnipotent distracted Supreme Creator.
>
> HOW TO DISCOVER YOUR ABILITY:
> It's doubtful that you have the intelligence to figure out something so important. But here is something to think about: one's ability lies with those

things that mark him or her. They can
be talents, like an affinity towards
gardening or being able to play the
guitar well. Often they are things that
Lambs make fun of, imperfections. They
can be physical, psychological, behavioural.
And I do not mean things that are a
result of your actions, like being fat
because you eat too much and sit and
play video games all day.

Usually someone of pure spirit will
have to help you figure it out. But once
you discover it, you will have to find a
dedicated and patient pure spirit who
is willing to help someone as needy and
ignorant as you.

Once Sunny got past the book's rude, condescending tone, she found it had plenty to teach her. She also found that the book itself was eager to be read. It made sure that it was always nearby. Sometimes it actually crawled onto her lap! The strange black legs were actually soft as mushroom stems and were careful to tread lightly.

Over the next few days, when she wasn't in school or doing homework, she was reading *Fast Facts*. No time for television. She focused most on *Chapter 8: Very Basic Beginner Juju*. It was the juju called '*Etuk Nwan*' that most interested her. If she could get it to work, she would be able to leave the house for Saturday night's meeting with Anatov. There were only four ingredients and most of them were easy enough to collect: camomile leaves, palm oil, some rainwater. It was the fourth that she was worried about.

The day before the big night, she stood in the sunny market with her black umbrella. She no longer needed it, but she didn't want to draw the wrong kind of attention. The meat seller's section always smelled rancid with fresh and drying blood and cracked bone. Each table displayed piles of various types of meat, stringy purple entrails, hooves and horns.

Sunny stopped at a table with a heap of sheep heads. Rivulets of blood ran down the side of the table, hinting that the heads were fresh. "Excuse me, Miss," Sunny said to the meat seller. "I'd like—I'd like to buy a sheep's head."

Her father was very fond of *nkowbi*, which was stew made with goat's brain. Plenty of people were, so she wasn't doing anything unusual. And she had enough money saved up. The woman put the black sheep's head on a piece of newspaper and wrapped it up with more newspaper. Then she put it into a black plastic bag.

Sunny couldn't think of any other way to ask, so she just asked. "Is that...my, uh, father told me to make sure it was an *ebett,* a—a 'sleeping antelope sheep.'" She knew her face was red with embarrassment.

"Eh?" the woman said frowning. "What are you talking about?"

Suddenly, Sunny was very aware of her albinism. What must she have looked like, all bleached-looking and asking for something that sounded straight out of a black magic cookbook? "Oh, nothing," she said, deciding not to bother with haggling. "This—this is fine." She hoped it would be.

She got home before her parents. She had to move fast. They'd be home within the hour. Her brothers were out playing soccer.

Thank goodness, she thought. She ran to the kitchen with her package and placed it on the kitchen counter.

"Just do it," she said to herself, rubbing her hands nervously against her shorts. "The faster, the less time to think about it."

Easier said than done. The mere thought of the sheep's head nauseated her. She didn't know how her father could eat goat brains or how her mother could prepare them. She took a deep breath, then, as fast as she could, unwrapped the package.

The head was black, the wool on its face a deeper black. It looked like one of her mother's wigs. She felt another wave of nausea. Even worse, its eyes were glassy and dry. Its mouth was open, its pink purple tongue lolling out to the side. Its yellow teeth would never chew grass again; its mouth would never be warmed by its breath.

This couldn't be a 'sleeping antelope sheep.' In the book, it said the face of a 'sleeping antelope sheep' would look peacefully asleep in death. This one looked as if it had died in horror.

"Well," she breathed. "Work with what you have."

She had no idea how she would get out of the house if the juju didn't work. Her brothers tended to play video games or watch movies until well past midnight, even on school nights. The slightest noise brought her mother peeking into her room. If she were caught, her father would happily flog her; he'd certainly been looking for a reason lately. She needed this juju to work.

She grabbed a paring knife, paused, then gritted her teeth. She started scraping and cutting and gouging. The book said to use the skull, nothing else. She had to remove all the meat on and inside the skull.

Biology, she thought as she worked, breathing through her mouth. She didn't want to smell the raw flesh. *Think of biology class*. She enjoyed biology, eagerly taking in the readings about microorganisms, animal systems, vertebrates, and invertebrates. Still, at the moment, she found that the less she thought about the fact that this had been a living, breathing, pooing, baaing, eating thing, the better.

It took her half an hour to remove all the hair, skin, brains, and muscle. All she needed now was to rinse it well and let it dry until nighttime. She heard her brothers outside. She cursed. The counter was a mess.

She quickly rewrapped the skull. Any moment, her brothers would burst in looking for something to eat. It was always the first thing they did when they came in. She grabbed a bunch of greens, onions, tomatoes, peppers, and spices from the fridge and threw them on the counter in front of the pile of flesh. She was taking out some dried fish when they entered.

"Hello," Chukwu muttered, pushing her aside. Ugonna punched her shoulder. Neither even glanced at the counter. She smiled. Her dumb brothers never cooked. She didn't think they even knew how! A human being who needs food to live but cannot prepare that food to eat? Pathetic. In this case, it was an advantage. They weren't interested in any food until it had been cooked for them.

"Were you playing soccer?" she asked. They took out bottles of Fanta and a bag of chin-chin.

"*Football*, American girl," Chukwu said wiping sweat from his face.

Sunny rolled her eyes. She'd been calling it soccer all her life, she wasn't going to change that.

"We won," Ugonna said.

"That's good," she said, leaning against the counter, shielding the wrapped skull and mess.

"Have you heard the latest news?" Ugonna asked. She frowned, and shook her head. "Black Hat got some kid in Aba."

"What?" Aba was only a few minutes' walk away.

"Yeah," Chukwu said. "So don't go out alone. If you want to go to the market, let us know. We'll go with you."

After they left, as soon as she heard the sound of the television, she collected herself and rinsed off the skull. She was uneasy, but determined. What better time than now to learn the Leopard ways? Some self-defence would do her good.

As she ran up the stairs to her room, she saw something red out of the corner of her eye, something weird sitting on the banister. She didn't stop to check it out—she had to get the skull to her room. Once inside, she shut and locked the door, leaned against it, and let out a relieved breath.

The skull was still wet. It was five o'clock. Six hours and fifteen minutes before she had to meet Orlu, Sasha, and Chichi. She put the skull under her bed and picked up her purse full of *chittim*.

She dumped them out and counted. There were a hundred and twenty-five, including the bronze, gold, and silver ones. She put two copper and six bronze ones back into the purse and threw in her lip gloss, some tissues, a pack of biscuits, pen and paper, and a few naira notes. She piled the rest of the *chittim* in an old wrapper, tied it up, and pushed it far under her bed.

She grabbed the purse, opened the door, and peeked into the hallway. The coast was clear. She dashed outside and hid the purse behind a bush near the house gate. Then she returned to the kitchen, cleaned up the mess, and spent the next hour cooking up a spicy stew with chicken and bits of sheep brain for her parents and brothers. Full bellies meant heavy sleep.

After dinner—which everyone, even her father, said was delicious—she quickly bathed and dressed in a pair of shorts, T-shirt, and sneakers. At 10:30pm, NEPA took the light and her father turned on the generator. Twenty minutes later, her brothers were playing video games and her parents had gone to bed.

It had to be done at exactly eleven o'clock. Her book said this was the most powerful hour of the night. She went over the juju charm one last time:

Etuk Nwan is very simple juju. If you can't make this work, I feel sorry for you. Etuk Nwan will allow you to pass through standard locked doors. Make sure the door is locked.

Sunny checked her lock and brought out the sheep's skull. It was still a little damp. She sipped her cup of rainwater, rubbed her hands with the palm oil, opened a tea bag, and sprinkled her hands with the camomile. She sat on the floor, crossed her legs, and held the skull in her oily hands. Okay, she thought. *Now to empty my mind of all thought and focus on the skull.* She'd done this so often with candles that it was easy. Her watch beeped eleven o'clock. The skull was warm and heavy. Suddenly, it dropped right through her hands and clunked on the floor.

It had to be the palm oil. She tried to pick it up. The charm wouldn't work if she wasn't holding the skull. Her hands passed right through the skull again. She jumped up. "It worked!" she whispered, her voice echoing strangely about the room.

There was no weightless or insubstantial feeling. She felt quite normal. But when she looked in the mirror, she could see ever so slightly through her flesh. *If Mama and Dad come in right now, will they see me?* It didn't matter. She needed to get out in the next few minutes. She looked at the skull sitting on the floor.

"God, I hope they don't come in here." She went over to the locked door. Before she could wonder what to do next, she was yanked through the keyhole. The sensation was itchy and a little painful. She came out on the other side of the door. About twenty copper *chittim* loudly clinked at her feet. She froze. Everyone had to have heard the noise. No one came. She tried to pick up one of the *chittim*. Her hand passed through it.

"Move," she told herself. What else was she supposed to do?

She ran to the front door and passed through that keyhole, too. Then she ran to the locked gate and passed through its keyhole, too. When she emerged outside the compound, she felt the charm wear off. She could feel the warm air on her skin. The sound of night creatures grew louder, as if the volume around her was turned up. She snatched up her purse from behind the bush and started walking as fast as she could, pushing away thoughts of Black Hat and his minions being in every car that passed by.

She found Chichi outside her hut. When she saw Sunny, she smiled.

"Oh my God…I did it! I turned invisible!" Sunny exclaimed, jogging up to her. She started shaking uncontrollably. "I did something called *Etuk Nwan*." She laughed, tears falling from her eyes. Chichi took her hand and led her to the side of the road.

"Take a deep breath," she said, smiling.

Gradually, Sunny calmed down.

"How many *chittim* did you get?" Chichi asked.

"I don't know! I had to leave them in front of my bedroom door. Where does *chittim* come from anyway? And who drops it?"

"Me, what I wonder is where does it go? You know, after a period of time, all *chittim* returns to where it came from." She shrugged. "These are not our questions to ask, just facts to accept."

"You did it," Orlu said, coming out of the gate of his house.

Sunny smiled and nodded.

"Y'all ready?" Sasha said from right behind her. She yelped. Sasha laughed hard. He slapped hands with Chichi who said, "Nice one."

This time, they didn't take a taxi to Anatov's hut. Instead, they took the strangest vehicle Sunny had ever seen. It looked like a combination of a large semi-truck, a mammy wagon, and a bus. Its multi-coloured exterior was painted with abstract art that included loops, swirls, lines and dots. Chichi called the colourfully decorated thing a 'funky train,' and they caught it on the main street.

"Just ignore the smell," Chichi said, as they climbed on.

Inside everything was upholstered with plush cloth, from the floor to the seats. Of the rows and rows of beat-up seats, almost all were occupied. Sunny and Chichi sat on one side, while Sasha and Orlu sat closer to the front.

There was no roof, but when the vehicle moved, the smell of sweat, perfume, cologne, stock fish, and cooking oil hung in the air, thick and oppressive. The open top also didn't dilute the loud hip-hop music that played from huge speakers in the back, or the raucous laughter and conversation of the passengers, most of whom were their parents' age.

Then there was Sunny's sneezing. It started almost as soon as she sat down. And the sneezing came hard and consistent. She sneezed for the entire ride. When they finally got off, her eyes were red and her nose was sore from blowing. The driver felt so sorry for her that he only charged her one small gold *chittim* instead of two.

"You were also sneezing like that in Anatov's hut," Chichi said. "I think you're sensitive to juju powers. It is all over the train." Sunny's only response was to sneeze again.

She was still sniffling when they walked up to Anatov's hut. It was lit with bright halogen lamps that smoked with and smelled of burning insects. There were several sticks of incense burning, but this time she didn't sneeze. No juju power used in them this time, she guessed.

"Sit," Anatov said. Tonight, he wore a blue, green, and yellow dashiki and long jean shorts.

They sat in the woven cane chairs before his woven cane throne. Sunny honked one more time into her tissue, sighed, and sank tiredly into her chair. It was quite comfortable. She looked at the decorated walls and spotted something. She frowned and squinted. Her eyes widened and she grabbed Chichi's arm and pointed. "What the *hell* is that?" she asked. It looked like a red grasshopper the size of her hand.

"It's a ghost hopper," Orlu whispered. "Don't worry, they're harmless."

"You sure?" she asked. Then she blinked, realising something. "Those are all over my house!"

"It is probably only one," Orlu said. "It could be worse. Some people would love to have those instead of what they have."

"There are more, aren't there?" she said.

"More creatures I can see now?" A tiny bronze *chittim* fell into her lap. She picked it up and smiled.

"Millions," Orlu said.

"You should see the night birds in Chicago," Sasha said. "I went up to the Sears Tower one night, that's where you can see a lot of them. They look like small dragons."

"No way!" she said. She'd been to the top of the Sears Tower once. It was beautiful up there.

Anatov threw himself dramatically into his throne and looked at his students. "Welcome to Leopard School, Sunny," he said.

"Yes o, welcome," Orlu said.

"Welcome," Sasha said.

"It's more than time," Chichi said.

"Thank you," she said, blushing. "I'm glad to be here."

Anatov clapped his hands together and grinned devilishly. "So," he said, leaning back in his chair, "how did you do it?"

"Do what?"

"I met your parents," he said. "I stopped by and said hello to your mother in her office at the hospital and your father at his law firm."

"You went to see them?" She was horrified.

"Chatted with your father a bit, pretended to be one of your mother's old patients. Intelligent, hardworking folk. But strict. Especially your mother. So how did you get out?"

"I'm albino," she said with a sarcastic smirk. "I'm practically a ghost. What ghost can't sneak out of a house?"

Anatov laughed. "You don't know how close you are to the truth. At least in your very specific case. But really, how did you do it?"

"She worked an *Etuk Nwan*," Chichi burst out. "From her free agent book. Isn't that great?"

"The book said it was one of the easiest charms," Sunny said.

"Yeah, for someone with experience," Chichi added.

Anatov cocked his head. "What kind of sheep head did you use?"

"Well, the lady at the market looked at me like I was crazy when I asked about the *ebett*, the sleeping antelope. So I just got a regular sheep head."

Anatov laughed. Even Sasha and Chichi snickered.

"Yes, I strongly doubt you'll find an *ebett*'s head in your local Lamb market," Anatov said. "An *ebett* is an albino sheep that can sleep so deeply it becomes invisible. Its spirit goes to the spirit world until it wakes. You'd never find one in a Lamb market."

"So why'd the charm work, then?" she asked.

"You answered your own question," Anatov said. "You're albino. I thought you read that beginner book."

"I did. But it's fresh. I'm still processing—"

"Reread Chapter Four," he said. "The one about one's abilities." She nodded.

"I would ask these three to tell you about their abilities so you'll get it, but it's hard for people to talk about their own 'bad' qualities," Anatov said.

"But the book said Leopard people are proud of their imperfections," Sunny said, hoping to sound as if she knew something.

"Lesson One," Anatov said. "And this is for all of you. Learn how to learn. Read between the lines. Know what to take and what to discard. Sunny, we don't teach as the Lambs do. Books will be part of your learning but experience is important, too. You'll all be sent out to see for yourselves. So you have to know how to learn. For example, that book *Fast Facts For Free Agents.*" He spat the title as if he had little respect for it.

"It was written by a woman named Isong Abong Effiong Isong, one of the most knowledgeable Leopard people of all time, of the world. She passed the fourth level. The problem was, for her learning experiences, she chose to move to Europe and then America, where she thought the truly civilised ideas were being knitted."

Sasha scoffed.

Anatov nodded at him. "Exactly," Anatov said. "You know the deal. Anyway, while there, she developed the idea that free agents like you, Sunny, are the scourge of the Earth. She believed them ignorant and misguided. You can imagine what this African woman thought of us African Americans." He paused. "Prejudice begets prejudice, you see. Knowledge does not always evolve into wisdom.

"That said, when you read her books, you have to really read them. Be aware of her biases toward those not from her homeland and those who are not of traceable spirit."

"So, she'd probably want to kill me," Sunny mumbled. "I'm Nigerian, American, and a free agent."

"What a bitch," Chichi said.

"But useful," Anatov emphasised. "Sunny, wade through her vile way of speaking. You'll see that her book is good. She's the only scholar who took the time to write a book for free agents. Just know that most Leopards as a whole don't often consider your kind. Free agents are so rare."

"Now," he said slapping the arm of his chair, "the book spoke of Leopards as if we are the most confident beings on Earth and beyond. Don't get her wrong, we are a confident people. And we *do* embrace those things that make us unique. However, we have insecurities and problems like any other human.

"You all know why Sasha's parents got fed up and sent him here to live with Orlu's family," Anatov said. He glanced at Sasha, who looked at his hands. "A troublemaker through and through. Though he respects his parents, he has no respect for authority. I can tell you from personal experience, to be a young black man in America with a hatred for authority is a recipe for disaster.

"You see, Sasha can remember things," Anatov said. "He has what Lambs would call a photographic memory. He can read something and remember it word for word. On top of this, he has a lot of energy. You see the problem? He knows too much. He's always ahead. So how do you expect him to respect just anyone? How can you expect him to sit still? This young man is like a thousand volumes of juju.

"Chichi here, she is the same. It's rare to find two people so similar who come from different parents and countries. Chichi would never have survived at your Lamb school, Sunny. She'd have spent most of her time being punished for mouthing off. You know her; you must agree she has a big mouth."

They all snickered.

"But like her mother, like Sasha, she can read a thousand books and remember what's in all of them. Most people would dismiss Chichi and Sasha as disrespectful uncouth children who can't even get through a year of school. They'd insist they were destined to be criminals and streetwalkers. Doctors would prescribe Ritalin for their ADD and then throw their hands up, perplexed, when it didn't work. But as Leopard children, they're destined for great, great things. These two could probably pass their second and third levels if they were emotionally mature. Which they are *not*. Not even close."

Chichi frowned deeply at this and Sasha rolled his eyes.

"Now in Orlu's first few years of Lamb school, the teachers told his parents that he would never be able to read," Anatov said. "When Orlu tried, the pages looked like gibberish. When he tried to write, his hand wanted to write backward or combine the letters. They said he had a learning disorder called dyslexia."

Sunny glanced at Orlu, but he wouldn't meet her eyes.

"The moment the teachers told Orlu's parents this, they were elated. Orlu wasn't too happy. He was ashamed. The influence of Lamb society is strong. But his parents knew that this was the key to what their son would be. And to have such a serious 'disability' meant his talent would be amazing. And it is. Orlu can undo things. Throw a juju at him and he can undo it and make it harmless or useless without ever knowing what he's doing.

"Everyone can work juju charms, some of us better than others, but few can undo them on instinct. Once I started teaching Orlu how to hone this skill, his ability to read kicked in," Anatov said. "When I am through with this boy, no one will be able to harm him with any kind of juju.

"And that brings us to you, Sunny." He paused. Everyone looked at her and her skin prickled. "Your name reflects the sun, like the colour of your skin, no?" He grinned. "An ugly, sickly colour for a child of pure Nigerian blood. Everything about you is 'wrong'—your eyes, your hair, your skin. Otherworldly."

Sunny frowned but held Anatov's eyes.

"What has the Supreme Being endowed you with, eh?" he said. "They say your kind has one foot set in the physical world and one foot in the wilderness—that's what we call the spirit world. Do you believe you have that 'here and there' quality?"

"No," she said.

"Believe it. To be Leopard and albino is often a rare gift," he said. "Can any of you guess what she can do?"

"Of course," Chichi said. "She can make herself invisible."

"And why is that?"

"Because she has the natural ability to go into the wilderness anytime she wants. That is what makes her invisible."

"She can mess with time, too," Sasha added. "For the same reason. Time doesn't exist in the wilderness."

"Right, but that is a more difficult skill to harness. Sunny, all these things experienced Leopard sorcerers can do. But they will need their juju knives, powders, and other items to do it. You can do these things without any of that, once you learn how."

"*Oga*, don't forget the premonitions," Chichi added.

"Is that not what happened with the candle?"

"Right," Anatov said. "Because you can go into the wilderness, you are susceptible to wilderlings showing you things for whatever reason."

"Wilderlings?" she said. Her mouth went dry.

"Creatures, beasts, and beings from the wilderness," Anatov said.

"So, because I'm a Leopard albino, I can—"

"Yes. Certain attributes tend to yield certain talents. Very, very tall people tend to have the ability to predict the future through the stars. Very, very short people tend to make plants grow. Those with bad skin usually know and understand the weather. Abilities are things people are able to do without the use of a juju knife, powders, or other ingredients like the head of an *ebett*. They just come naturally.

"That's enough for now," Anatov said. "Orlu, Chichi, last lesson I had you go out to the street folk and talk to them. I wanted you to see them, to understand how it is they live. I had you go out with sacks of food. So?"

"We went out to the streets and helped some people," Orlu said. He looked at Sasha as he said it. "But two men tried to steal from us. Chichi blew lock-up powder on them. We left them on the side of the road groaning with cramped muscles. We were lucky; they only had knives."

"Knives?" Sunny cried.

"But most of the people we met were either homeless or too sad to go home or were trying to find their home. They were happy to see us," Orlu said. "Or maybe they were just happy to see the food we brought them."

"They thought we were angels," Chichi said.

"And did you sit and talk with them?" Anatov asked.

Orlu and Chichi nodded.

"What did you learn?"

"All those people...they have stories and lives and dreams," Orlu said.

"And sometimes right is wrong and wrong is right," Chichi added.

Anatov nodded, looking pleased.

"Sasha, from what I understand, the scholar you worked with in the United States, José Santos, sent you and his other students backpacking from San Francisco to some small town deep into Mexico?"

Sasha nodded. "For two months. I perfected my Spanish. We were robbed three times at gunpoint..." He laughed. "It was great."

"I met José once, years ago. I admire him," Anatov said. "Now, you two—you four—are my students. My job is to guide you." He looked mainly at Sunny as he said this. "You will learn about yourselves from me, you'll learn new and old juju, and I will help you, if I can, to pass your levels. And I'll send you out there into the world to catch your lessons. Fear? Get used to it. There will be danger; some of you may not live to complete your lessons. It's a risk you take. This world is bigger than you and it will go on, regardless."

What kind of thing is that to tell your students? Sunny wondered.

"Today's lesson is camaraderie," Anatov continued. "I want you to go and greet a friend of mine. Orlu, Chichi, you know of Kehinde."

"What?" Sasha exclaimed. "Even I know of him and I just got here. He's one of the most brilliant juju workers in the world. Isn't he practically a recluse?"

"Kehinde's a close friend of mine," Anatov said. "He's a recluse to folks he doesn't think are important. I was discussing you four with him yesterday. He wants to meet you."

"Why?" Sasha asked. "Why us?"

Orlu looked aghast. "Ah! We don't even...we can't go—"

"Kehinde wants to see you," Anatov repeated. "Figure out how to get to him. That's today's lesson, too. Oh, and beware of some of Kehinde's...friends. They're a bit possessive. Give him my regards. Peace out."

419 SCAMS AND LEOPARD PEOPLE

The 419 scam is an illegal practice that Nigeria has become known for all over the world because of a small group of internet-savvy criminals. It is a pox on this great nation's reputation; a symptom of its marrow-deep disease of corruption. If you use e-mail, you have to have seen the ones offering to pay you insane amounts of money if you help Chief or Prince So-and-So get his money out of the bank. That is an example of the billions of 419 scam e-mails sent out daily. In Nigeria, Leopard 419 scammers use a blend of internet technology and juju to make the target individual's electronic funds disappear and reappear elsewhere. Thankfully, even these people cannot tamper with whatever provides us with chittim. Still, Leopard 419 scammers can get up to some darker business in the Lamb world. It is believed that as we speak, some are using the Net to design a network of virus-driven juju-powered supercomputers so infectious that they could bring down the Lamb world's biggest economies with a few pecks on the keyboard. We will speak no more of this here. If you are approached by one of these criminals, decline involvement.

from Fast Facts for Free Agents by Isong Abong Effiong Isong

Again, they were hurried out of the hut. A little way down the path back toward Leopard Knocks, they stopped. Orlu, Sasha, and Chichi just stood there.

"What's the problem now?" Sunny asked. "Who is Kehinde?"

"Sunny, didn't you hear?" Chichi asked.

"Just tell me again. Unlike you, I don't have a photographic memory."

Chichi chuckled. "Okay o. There are eight living people in Nigeria who have passed the last level. Four of them are Anatov, Sugar Cream, and the twins named Taiwo and the one we're supposed to go and see, Kehinde. They are the scholars of Leopard Knocks; they are like our elders, but not all of them are old—only Sugar Cream. The problem with going to see Kehinde is that he lives in Night Runner Forest."

"Is that far away or something?" Sunny asked. She didn't want to take another funky train.

"Humph," Orlu said. "Now I know why he chose tonight instead of Saturday afternoon for this assignment. You can only enter Night Runner Forest at night."

Chichi cursed. "And it disappears in"—she grabbed Orlu's arm and looked at his watch—"four hours."

Sunny looked at her watch. It was 1am. Chichi was referring to sunrise. "We'll be back by then, right?" she asked.

"Let's go," Sasha said. "We use a *vévé* to get there, right?"

"Yes," Chichi said, looking intense. "But we have to work together."

Sasha knelt down, and took a small bag out of his pocket. He drew on the ground by making a fist and letting the powder sift out. "This," he said to Sunny, "is a *vévé*, a magical drawing. The faster you draw it the better. But you can't make a mistake."

"You memorise them?" she asked.

"Yeah."

"Is it hard?"

The drawing looked like a tree with a circle around it and four Xs around the circle.

"Not for me," he said.

"What will it—"

"Just watch." He brought a dagger from his pocket and stabbed into the centre of the *vévé*. "One of you has to say it," Sasha said. "I don't speak Igbo."

"Let Sunny," Chichi said.

Sunny shook her head, stepping back. "Let me just watch this first time."

"You learn faster by doing," Chichi said, pushing her towards the *vévé*. "Take a deep breath and loudly say, 'Night Runner Forest come,' in Igbo."

Sunny started sweating. Who knew what would happen if she messed up?

"Go on," Orlu said softly.

She spoke the words in Igbo, making sure they were loud and clear. Instantly, the *vévé* started to rotate in the dirt. It sounded almost solid as it pushed aside pebbles and scraped over the dirt. This magic was happening because of her own words! When it stopped, the top of the tree Sasha had drawn pointed off the path and into the forest, toward a new but darker path that hadn't been there before. Occasionally, a firefly flashed its tiny light.

"Orlu," Sasha said, "you first. You have the best defence."

Orlu stepped in front. "Okay," he said, looking around.

"Let's go." He brought out his juju knife, held it up, and moved it vertically before him.

"Bring light," he said in Igbo.

A firefly rushed to him and hovered before his face, flickering orange light every few seconds. "Tomorrow is a better day to find your mate," Orlu told it. "Tonight, please bring light for my friends and me."

For a moment longer, it hovered, still calling its mate. Then it must have decided that Orlu's cause was worthy, because it began to blaze the brightest light Sunny had ever seen come from an insect. She thought of the ghost hopper that lived in her house. Maybe this wasn't the usual type of firefly.

"That lightning bug has attitude," Sasha said. "For a second there, I thought she wasn't going to give us light."

Orlu shrugged. "It's her choice, isn't it? She has the right to think about it. Plus, the ones with attitude are the ones with the best light."

The firefly must have been listening because it burned brighter. Orlu chuckled. They started walking. As they moved along, the trees they passed were taller, wider, and closer to the path. "So does anyone know what Kehinde looks like?" Sunny asked, wanting to break the silence and focus on something other than the creepy forest around them.

"I hear he's very tall," Sasha said.

"I've heard he is very, very short," Chichi said.

"Well, that helps," Sunny said drily.

"It does not matter what he looks like," Orlu said. "This is Night Runner Forest. If he lives here, he is powerful. If he has passed the fourth level, he knows that the body is just the body. He could even be a shape-shifter."

"No," Chichi said. "He's not a shape-shifter. Kehinde was born physically perfect, no deformities or anything."

"Why does Anatov want us to meet him?" Sunny asked.

Suddenly, the forest heaved with life. Leaves shook. The ground hummed. Branches creaked. And a high-pitched chittering seemed to come from everywhere. "Get down!" Orlu shouted.

Sunny dropped to the ground, her hands over her head. Bats. Tons of them. She shut her eyes as the air grew very hot and then cool. Above the chittering noise, she heard the scuffle of feet.

"Chichi!" Orlu screamed. "Watch out!"

Sunny began to get up, but a bat smacked her in the side of her face. Then another. She dropped back down. "What do I do?" she shouted.

"I can't reach her," Sasha shouted, his voice cracking.

Chichi cried out. Now Sunny didn't care about being smacked or bitten by bats. She stood up. Around her was chaos. The night was full of bats. All she could see was Orlu's firefly still burning bright, the bats whipping and zooming around it. Orlu stood with Sasha only a few steps away. Where was Chichi? A bat snapped up the firefly and everything went dark.

"Everybody!" Orlu shouted. "Close your ears! Sasha, do it! Make it as high as possible! Bats can hear ultrasonic sound!"

Sunny clapped her hands over her ears, but not fast enough. For a moment, she heard a shrill noise so sharp she thought her head would explode. She pressed the heels of her hands to her ears as hard as she could. Gradually, the sound went so high she could no longer hear it. But the bats must have, because they fled. Some dropped to the ground, dead. The forest was silent, except for the sound of things falling. Seconds passed. *Chittim* clinked against each other.

"Bring light," Orlu said, out of breath. "For the sake of your mate who has been eaten!"

Immediately, a firefly came and shined a brilliant light. Sunny felt a twinge of sadness for the insect. All around them were dead bats. Piled around and on top of the dead bats were many copper *chittim*. Chichi sat nearby, holding her arm. A deep gash on her forearm was bleeding freely.

They all ran to her. "Are you all right?" Sunny asked.

She nodded.

Orlu was looking at Chichi with admiration. "Chichi, if it wasn't for you, we would all be dead," he said.

"Yeah," Sasha said. "That was good juju work. I didn't even see it."

"The bats were a diversion," Chichi said weakly.

"What?" Sunny asked, starting to cry. "What was it?"

"A bush soul," Chichi said. "Spirits, affinities, that live in forests like this. They attack people and steal their bodies. They always have the respect of animals that swarm or move in packs...like bats. Bush souls hide in them and use them to distract." She hissed as she looked at her arm. "I saw it in the swarm of bats. I slashed it with my juju knife. Sunny, when you hurt something with your knife, it's mirrored on your own body. But if I had not done it, we'd all be dead. It would have taken us all."

"We'd have arrived at Kehinde's hut as zombies," Sasha said.

"That looks really deep." Sunny winced, staring at Chichi's wound.

"Don't worry," Chichi said, slowly standing up. "Mirrored wounds heal in a few minutes...unless it is fatal."

As they waited for her to heal, Sunny stood watch. Orlu and Sasha picked up their *chittim*. "We got them for camaraderie, right?" Sasha said. "Teamwork."

"Yes," Orlu said. "We have learned our lesson."

"How many?" Chichi asked.

"Fifty," Sasha said.

"You can't divide that by four," Chichi said.

"Maybe you all earned more than me," Sunny said.

Orlu shook his head. "That is not the way it works. Why don't we add whatever we earn together?"

Sasha looked annoyed. "I know exactly what I want to buy with my share."

Sunny felt utterly useless and undeserving.

"Sasha, don't be greedy," Chichi said.

"Whatever."

"Let us take a vote," Chichi said. "All in favour of—"

"Naw, naw, forget it," Sasha said with a wave of his hand. "You're right. I'm being greedy. Sunny, put it all in your purse. It's probably best that you carry it. You keep it, too. I'm voting you as treasurer. All in favour?"

"Aye," Orlu and Chichi said.

"All against?"

Sunny laughed.

Once they got going, they moved faster than before. It was mainly Orlu who protected them, blocking and undoing. From left, right, forward, and behind, things came at them. Black-skinned fairies with the wings of flies and clothes made from spider webs threw poison spears at them. There were mosquitoes that weren't really mosquitoes. A three-foot tall masquerade in the bush just stood there, watching them pass. Something that looked like a giant wasp stung Sunny's leg. Immediately, both her legs went numb and she fell to the ground.

"It is only an insect spectre," Orlu said as he touched the sting with his knife. He made a popping sound with his lips.

"They are the result of insects that people kill. Most angry spirits come from deaths by acts of cruelty. If the insect is angry or vengeful, it will return as one of these." Slowly the feeling in her legs returned. The bruise on her hip from falling remained, though.

By the time they arrived at the tiny hut, Sunny was exhausted. The area around the hut was free of trees, bushes, even grass. It was as if the forest was afraid to get close. But they were too tired and had been through too much to be afraid. Even Sunny didn't think twice about stepping onto the barren, parched earth. The door of the hut was covered with a white cloth—at least it looked white in the firefly's light. There was one window, also covered by a white cloth.

"Good evening, *Oga* Kehinde," Chichi said loudly, "Sorry to disturb you, sir. We were sent by Anatov. We're his students."

A light went on inside the hut but there was no answer. Sunny frowned. There couldn't possibly be electricity here, in the middle of nowhere. She didn't even hear a generator. "*Oga* Kehinde?" Chichi said again. She turned to Sunny. "Ah-ah, I hope the man is around o."

"Which students are these?" an incredibly low voice asked in Igbo.

Sunny stepped back, sure that a giant was about to emerge. "What'd he say?" Sasha asked. She quickly translated.

Chichi spoke up. "My name is Chichi. And these are Sasha, Orlu, and Sunny. Please, speak English if you can. One of us doesn't know Igbo."

There was a pause as the door's curtain was pulled aside. "Ah, the princess, the American, the dyslexic, and the albino," the man said in perfect American English.

"What's he mean by 'princess'?" Sunny whispered to Orlu. He shushed her.

Kehinde wasn't a giant but he was pretty huge, taller than Anatov. Sasha glanced at Chichi, giving her an 'I told you so' smirk. Chichi made a face at him.

Kehinde wore only a long black wrapper with large white circles and squiggles. He looked a little older than Sunny's father but far more muscular, as if he spent all his time chopping wood. And he must have done it in the sun, for his skin was nearly black.

He had a braided goatee that nearly reached his waist. At its tip was a bronze band. Sunny would have thought he looked ridiculous if he didn't look so cool. He scrutinised them, a lit pipe in his mouth. First she had to put up with Anatov's incense addiction and now she'd have to try not to breathe in this man's disgusting smoke. "Sit," he said.

They sat down right there in the dirt. He held out his hand and pressed his fingers together. The dirt behind him began to build itself. Soon Kehinde had a chair made of dirt. He sat down and took a deep pull from his pipe. Slowly letting out the smoke, he said, "Bring light," in his thunderous voice.

Now his English was tinted with a Nigerian accent. Unlike Orlu, he didn't have to plead with the insects. Dozens of fireflies made the whole area brilliant with light.

"Hmm," Kehinde said, winding his beard around his long index finger. "Would you all like something to drink, you look...parched."

"Yes, please," they said.

A monkey about the size of a five-year-old child came running out. Its fur was light brown with hints of red, and it had a long strong-looking tail that swung in circles as it ran. It threw a bottle at Sunny. Thankfully, she was quick enough to catch it. The Fanta was ice cold. Orlu caught a malt, Sasha a Coke, and Chichi a bitter lemon. All were thrown with equally wild finesse. The caps popped off with a hiss.

"You made it," Kehinde said. "If you hadn't, you wouldn't have been worth my time."

Sunny frowned, irritated.

"What's that?" Kehinde asked her. "Speak up."

She glanced at Sasha, Chichi, and Orlu. They looked as angry as she felt.

"Why—I just—" she pressed her lips together and then shouted, "We could have all been killed!" She paused. "Honestly, what kind of 'teacher' does that to his students? We met with a bush soul! What if it had done us in? My parents don't even know I'm gone!"

"If you'd all perished, we'd have found you and your bodies would have been returned to your parents with...explanation," Kehinde said.

Sunny's mouth fell open. *What kind of barbaric cold-hearted man was this?*

"Come now," Kehinde said pulling out a newspaper. He shook it at them. "Have you seen the news lately? If you haven't noticed, a person's life, especially a young person's, isn't worth much these days. The world is much bigger than all of you. Chances have to be taken. But thankfully, here you are."

Sunny was about to say more but he held a hand up. "Shut up, now, Sunny," he said. "You've said enough."

"No," she snapped. "I—" The smack on the back of her head was hard enough to make her vision go blurry for a second. She turned to stare at Chichi, who'd hit her. "Shut up," she hissed. Sunny was so stunned that she did.

Kehinde smirked and nodded, satisfied. "I don't make it a habit of meeting Anatov's groups of students, but Anatov thinks you're useful—useful to the Leopard people as a whole, though all this might be harmful to you as individuals. But that's life, eh? We shall see. Sasha, stand up."

He stood.

"You like trouble?" Kehinde asked.

Sasha cocked his head and then said, "If I can find it."

Kehinde actually smirked. "I like this one," he said to himself. Orlu hissed with annoyance.

"Okay. Well, it grows late," Kehinde said, standing up. "I have other appointments, social occasions, places to visit, visitors to entertain."

That's it? Sunny wanted to shout. *All that and now he was going to send us right back into his crazy jungle?* Nevertheless, when she stood up, she felt refreshed, despite her annoyance and bruises. She looked back at the path. If they survived the walk back, it would then be the funky train home, most likely. What time was it? She didn't dare look at her watch.

The monkey came out again. "Ha, I am still drinking my own," Orlu snapped, as the monkey snatched his malt. It took all their drinks.

"Gotta be quick," Kehinde said. He shook each of their hands, patting Sasha on the back and whispering something in his ear, to which Sasha nodded and said, "Okay."

Then Kehinde pulled something small and shiny out of his goatee. He threw it toward the path, causing a small burst that sent creatures Sunny couldn't quite see scurrying in all directions. *They were all waiting for us,* she realised in horror. When the dust settled, the path was gone. In its place was a shorter path leading to Anatov's hut.

"You're lucky that I am a nice guy," Kehinde said with a wink.

"I'd have figured out how to do that," Sasha said. "Once I know the way back, I can do that."

"Not in the Night Runner Forest," Kehinde said, darkly. "This place would just laugh at you and then lead you toward more potential death. Eventually, Sasha, I'll show you how to do it. Till then, be on your way."

When Anatov saw them come in, a look of such relief passed over his face that Sunny understood then and there just how close they'd come to death. She felt a ticklish sensation in her belly. The feeling lasted through the smelly, sneezy, funky train ride back and her short walk home. Chichi came along to help her sneak inside.

"In your mind, imagine the skull and do the thing you did before," she said. "Remember, you have already done it before. You were the one who got yourself through the keyhole, not the skull."

Like her second time crossing the bridge, getting inside was wonderfully easy. In seconds, she materialised inside her room. She smiled when a bronze *chittim* fell at her feet. Quickly, she opened her bedroom door and looked in the hallway. The *chittim* that had fallen earlier were still there. She took them into her bedroom and softly shut the door. It was 5am. She had two hours until she had to get up for school.

COOKING AND RECIPES

If you are a girl and you are fortunate enough to marry a Leopard man when you grow up, you must not only know how to cook non-magical meals but the occasional magical one as well. Like any other Nigerian man, the way to a Leopard man's heart is through his stomach. A free agent woman who cannot cook Tainted Pepper Soup for her Leopard husband is done for. Thankfully, this recipe is very easy to follow, even for you. Practice and master making Tainted Pepper Soup now or you will be sorry later.

TAINTED PEPPER SOUP

Ingredients:

3-4 large tomatoes (Warning: If they are too small, the finished soup will explode within an hour!)

1-2 tainted peppers (Warning: Never ever use a tainted pepper that has turned orange or emits more than light wisps of smoke)

Meat (Warning: Do not use chicken. Chicken will cause the finished soup to explode within an hour!)

4 Maggi cubes (Warning: Do not use chicken Maggi cubes or the finished soup will explode within an hour!)

Palm oil

2 perfectly round onions (Warning: If they are not perfectly round, the finished soup will explode within an hour!)

Sea salt (Warning: Do not use table salt when using tainted peppers unless you plan to never have children)

50g / 2oz ground crayfish (Warning: make sure there is not one grain of sand in your ground crayfish or your soup will taste like glue)
Dry pepper
Water
Ice

Instructions:

Place the meat in a pot, add very little water (most meat produces water as it cooks), dice one onion in with the meat, add some sea salt, and cook the meat until it is almost tender.

Grind the tomatoes, the remaining onion, crayfish and tainted peppers together. Add ice to cool it all down (tainted peppers will make the blended mixture boil).

Pour the blended mixture into the pot with the meat. Also add the Maggi cubes. Then add palm oil, not too much, not too little (palm oil is extremely high in saturated fat).

Allow the soup to cook itself (the tainted peppers will cause it to boil) for about 20-30 minutes, stirring constantly. Do not use a metal spoon unless you want to poison your husband.

Add sea salt and dry pepper to his taste.

from Fast Facts for Free Agents by Isong Abong Effiong Isong

CHAPTER EIGHT
STEW AND RICE

Sunny could barely keep her eyes open at school. What kept her awake was the bruise on her hip, which throbbed miserably. To top things off, Jibaku was laying it on thick.

"Get out of my way," Jibaku snapped, shoving Sunny aside to get to her seat. Sunny nearly went flying into her desk. She glared back at Jibaku.

"You, what are you going to do?" Jibaku asked, returning her glare. Sunny could think of plenty of things to do. But all those things ended with a beating from her father after her parents found out. When she did nothing, Jibaku laughed loudly like the hyena she was.

"Don't mind her," Orlu whispered from two desks away as their maths teacher walked in.

Sunny sat down, yawning and rubbing her eyes. *Gotta get it together,* she thought. By lunchtime, she had a pounding headache. Everything around her seemed so normal—and strange. The other students, the walls, the floors, the smell of the hallways. Feeling out of place was nothing new to her, but now she felt even more removed. She'd barely stepped onto the school yard when Jibaku came up behind her and shoved her again.

"Excuse me, ugly girl," she said. Then two of her girlfriends pushed by. Sunny watched as they all met up with Periwinkle and Calculus and some other friends. Fatigue mixed with confusion, hunger and anger are a bad combination. She'd taken three angry steps toward the group when her mobile phone vibrated in her pocket.

She looked around for any teachers. If they caught her with her phone, they'd take it away. When she saw none, she took it out of her pocket. "Hello?" she said, through gritted teeth.

"Where are you?" It was Orlu.

"Good timing."

"I felt as if something was going to happen," he said.

"I'm at the door."

"Then I am behind you."

She turned to see him coming out of the classroom. "Can't we do something to her?" she whispered as they walked across the yard.

"Never use juju on Lambs for petty revenge," he said. "You'll find yourself standing in front the Library Council trying to defend yourself. That is not something you want."

"Have you told Sasha?"

Orlu laughed. "Don't worry, he knows. It's the same where he's from. He's been in front of the council before." He paused. "But you're right, he's in Nigeria now; punishment here is fast and painful, not verbal."

"I'm so tired," she moaned.

"You will get used to it."

She looked at him, shielding her face with her hand. Remembering, she opened her umbrella and held it over her head. "Orlu, how long have you and Chichi been going to see Anatov?"

Orlu shrugged. "A long time. Since I was two years old."

"But how...no wonder your grades were suffering," she said.

"No, I'm just not good at school," he said, with a chuckle. "Not this one, at least. You will get used to having less sleep. Just make sure you study earlier, so you can go to bed earlier. We have three days before we see Anatov again. You can work ahead."

"Three days? I didn't know that. Did he say?"

"We see him every Wednesday and Saturday." He stopped walking. "It is important that you keep your grades up. It is just as important as the other things."

"How am I supposed to do my homework when I feel like this?" she moaned.

"Just do it," Orlu said. "Do it and then sleep."

Easier said than done.

That evening, she felt as if she were fighting a silent tricky monster. Her eyes were heavy and her mind was muddled. *But I did it*, she thought as she finally put her pen down. She'd done a worksheet of maths, read for history and Igbo grammar, and written the draft of an essay due in two days. She went to the kitchen to get something to eat. Her mother was there cooking rice and stew.

"Good evening," Sunny said.

"Good evening, Sunny. Have you been home all this time?"

"Yeah, studying," she said.

"You look tired."

Sunny grabbed a mango and peeled it, aware that her mother was watching.

"Is everything all right?" her mother asked, the wooden spoon in her hand suspended above the pot of bubbling stew.

"Yes, Mama," Sunny said and smiled. "I'm just tired."

"Hm," she said. "You look..."

"I'm fine." She bit into the pulp of her mango. "Mama?"

"Mhm?" Her mother had turned back to the stew.

"What was your mother's maiden name?"

She stopped stirring, but just for a second. "Why?"

"Just wondering," Sunny carefully said. "You...you never really say much about her."

"Is Yaya not enough for you?"

Yaya was her grandmother from her father's side. Sunny got to see her on holidays. She liked her well enough.

"I only meant that—"

"Sunny, my mother has passed and that's the end of it."

"Okay," she said quickly.

"When you finish that mango, go and lie down," she said.

Sunny had always wondered about all the secrecy, and her mother's response never changed—cold and standoffish. That night, as she lay in bed, Sunny wondered even more.

Something landed on her bed. She jumped up and switched on the light. The red ghost hopper. It sat on her bed staring at her with its large orange compound eyes. Sunny wasn't afraid of grasshoppers, not even their strong flicking legs. But this creature was the size of an American football. It turned and, with a soft hum, hop-flew across the room, landing on the wall. Sunny stared at it for a moment and then just switched off the light.

Sleep came deliciously swift and easy, as it often does when it is well earned.

IMPORTANT NONHUMAN LEOPARD PEOPLE TO KNOW:

Udide is the ultimate artist, the Great Hairy Spider, brimming with venom, stories and ideas. Sometimes she is a he and sometimes he is a she; it depends on Udide's mood. Udide lives beneath the ground, where it is cool, dark, where she can put her eight legs to the dirt and know the earth's pulse. Some say Udide's lair is a great cave deep beneath the city of Lagos, where she delights in the noise of generators and fast life. Others believe his lair is beneath the country's capital of Abuja, not far from the Abuja National Mosque, where she starts her day by listening to the Morning Prayer. Still others think his home is in the swamps of the Niger Delta where he enjoys the sound of gunfire and sips the oily, polluted water like champagne. And there are a few who swear she lives just under the town of Asaba, for this was where one young Leopard woman found a copy of Udide's Book of Shadows, a book full of Udide's personal recipes, juju, stories and notes. This priceless tome has since been duplicated exactly three times, yet the whereabouts of these copies are unknown. Nevertheless, Udide revels in trickery. Udide obviously wanted the book to be found. Those who choose to use it are idiots.
from *Fast Facts for Free Agents* by Isong Abong Effiong Isong

CHAPTER NINE
TREETOP

Come Saturday morning, Sunny was up at 7am. She bathed, threw on some jeans, a T-shirt, and sneakers, and made a fast breakfast of fried plantain and egg stew. She poked her head into her parents' room and said a swift goodbye. They were half-asleep and barely muttered a sentence. Exactly as she planned. Then she was off.

Sasha, Chichi, and Orlu were outside Chichi's hut when she arrived. They were crowded around a newspaper. "See?" Orlu said. "She's on time."

"We were debating whether your parents would let you come," Chichi said. "I was saying that you'd come whether they let you or not, but you'd be late. Sasha didn't think you'd come."

"I left before they were really awake," Sunny said. "But I can't be late getting back this time."

"Or what?" Orlu asked.

"Or my dad will flog the hell out of me," she said. "And my mom will die of worry. Black Hat this, Black Hat that. Sheesh."

"Did you see the paper today?"

"No," she said, leaning forward to look. "How'd you guys get one so early? My dad usually brings it home in the afternoon."

"Sunny, Sunny," Chichi said, shaking her head. She laughed. "I'll sign you up for a *Leopard Knocks Daily* subscription. You'll get it nice and early each day."

BLACK HAT DOES IT AGAIN

Young Boy Found Wandering Market With Eyes Gouged Out

A seven-year-old boy from Aba who'd been kidnapped ten days ago was found wandering aimlessly through Ariaria market. Both of his eyes had been brutally removed. The wounds were cauterised. A black hat symbol was drawn on his right arm with a dye that doctors are finding impossible to remove. This is the known symbol of the ritual murderer Black Hat Otokoto. Ahmed Mohammed, 45, found the boy and immediately called the authorities and took him to the hospital.

"At first I was not sure if the boy was some sort of evil spirit," Mohammed said.

The boy is the seventeenth Black Hat victim. He is only the fourth to be found alive. All of Black Hat's victims have been children under the age of sixteen. Ritual sacrifices and occult activities have long been a problem in Nigeria, but never has Igboland had a ritual serial killer like this.

The Christian community condemns—

Sunny felt sick. "They have to catch this guy."

"I know," Chichi said, rolling up and squeezing the paper. "A seven-year-old! It's awful."

"It's shameful," Orlu said. "This is why I can't say that I don't believe in the penalty of death."

"Damn. They actually have serial killers here?" Sasha asked. "I thought that was an American thing. Ha."

"Oh, shut up," Chichi snapped. "There are serial killers everywhere."

When they arrived at Anatov's, he was playing one of Fela Kuti's half hour–long songs. Sunny loved Fela. This was one of the few things she and her father had in common.

"*Oga*, good morning," Chichi said.

"Chichi, it's good to see you."

She beamed.

Anatov held up a hand and the music lowered some. "My students," he said, "good morning."

As always, the hut smelled strongly of incense. Sunny's nose started to run.

"Sit, sit," he said. He lit yet another stick of incense and smiled devilishly at her. "Y'all really impressed Kehinde," he continued, sitting in his woven cane throne. "In particular, you, Sasha. He's agreed to be your mentor for your second level when the time comes. It's best to have a scholar as a mentor. Most are only able to get a father, mother, grandmother, family member. Kehinde was a troublemaker back in the day, too. You two will work well together. Watch for a letter from him, eh?"

Sasha looked ready to burst with pride and excitement. Sunny wanted to kick him. People only looked like that in cheesy Disney family movies. Orlu glanced at Sunny. She just shrugged. It seemed Anatov had chosen Chichi to mentor, and now Sasha, who had only just come to Nigeria, had been tapped by Kehinde. Sunny felt a little sorry for Orlu.

"Teamwork is the only reason you four lived to see Kehinde," Anatov said. "There are seriously unsafe places in Leopard Knocks. Places where people try to steal *chittim* instead of earning it. Where they have forgotten why they receive *chittim* in the first place. Knowledge is more valuable than the *chittim* it earns. You four please me. Even you Sunny, in all your shining blissful...ignorance."

Sunny found herself laughing with the others.

"Nonetheless, I had to risk losing you all." He paused. "You four have your work cut out for you. Help each other. You each know things the others do not. You each have talents that can keep the others safe. Sunny, Orlu, Chichi, teach Sasha to at least speak Igbo. Sasha, learn it and learn it fast. Then I'll teach you Yoruba."

"I can teach him Efik," Chichi volunteered.

"One at a time," Anatov said. "Sasha, do you speak any other languages?"

"French, a bit of Hausa; I'm pretty good with Arabic," Sasha said.

"Arabic?" Chichi said. "Really?"

"My father taught me," he said. "He's in the military. He was stationed in Iraq for four years."

"Can you write in it?" Chichi asked.

"Yep. Even better than I can speak it."

"That's impressive," Chichi said.

"Igbo shouldn't be hard for you to pick up," Anatov said. "You've learned a non-Romance language, you can learn more." He paused. "Okay, today's lesson: go and see another friend of mine."

They all groaned.

Anatov laughed. "No, no, it won't be as dangerous, unless you go down the wrong side road. Go and see Taiwo. Another scholar, yes. She lives in Leopard Knocks."

"Why are we meeting these...scholars?" Sunny asked.

"Don't question my teaching methods," he said, icily.

"I wasn't!" she stammered. "I...I was just..."

"Don't," Anatov said. "And get that hair reshaped. Your fro's been looking jacked up."

Sunny touched her hair, wishing there was a mirror nearby.

"Chichi," Anatov said, "give Taiwo this package." Whatever it was was tightly wrapped in newspaper.

Chichi took it and held it to her ear. "What's in it? Is it alive?"

"None of your business," Anatov said. "Taiwo lives at the end of the main street. On the way, I want you all to stop at Bola's Store for Books and buy two books each. *Advanced Juju Knife Jujus* by Victoria Ogunbanjo and a book of your choosing. Read them both and write a one-page report on each, due in three weeks, on the Saturday. See you Wednesday."

Sunny stood before the tree bridge to Leopard Knocks feeling sick. Sasha and Orlu had already gone ahead. "I'm going to show you how to call music," Chichi said.

"Okay," she said with a sigh.

"You don't have a juju knife yet, so just watch me." She brought out her knife, held it up and sliced the air. "It looks as if I'm cutting the air. That's the beginning of the juju." She flicked her wrist the slightest bit. "That creates a small juju bag for me to speak the words into." She held out her hand. "When you master it, you will do it so fast that you will be able to speak the words into it without catching it first. Once the words are inside, the juju lives and acts by itself. Bring your hand." She put the invisible juju pouch into Sunny's outstretched hand. It felt wet, soft, and cool.

"My first language was Efik, so I speak the activation words in Efik," she said. "Your first language was Igbo, so—"

"English," Sunny corrected.

"Eh?" Chichi said, cocking her head.

"Well, yeah."

"Okay, then your activation words will be in English."

"So what are the words?"

"Are you ready to cross?"

She hesitated. "Yes."

"Just say 'Bring music of my heart.' But I will say 'Bring music of Sunny's heart,' because this is for you. You should still try to bring forth your spirit face by yourself. Call it as if you were calling me or Orlu, as if it is a good friend." Chichi spoke the words in Efik and the music started.

Sunny looked out at the fast-moving river and the tree bridge. In her head, she said, *Come to me!* It came as if it had been waiting. From deep within, she heard a low voice whisper, "*Anyanwu.*" Anyanwu, that was her spirit face's name, her other name. In Igbo, Anyanwu meant 'eye of the sun.' It was a cool name. Definitely fitting. This time she walked in what she knew was a straight, regal manner. She inspected herself as she moved, for the rushing waters below didn't scare her.

"Hello?" she said testing out her voice. It sounded rich and a little lower. She considered herself, who she was, what she had learned in the last few days. She stopped and allowed herself to drop into that deep concentration she knew so well. With her spirit face, she was sure of what she was doing. It made sense.

She looked down. She couldn't see her feet. She laughed and rushed forth. She was wind, mist, air, partially here, but also there. The music was in her ears like the soundtrack of a dream, as she zoomed to the end of the bridge. She got there in seconds, the music still playing. She shot past Sasha and Orlu, behind a nearby tree. All she had to do was think it and she became visible again.

"Wow," she breathed, as she looked at her hands. Four large *chittim* fell at her feet. Copper ones, the most valuable kind. This was an important lesson to learn. She put them in her purse and went to the others.

"How did you get here so fast?" Chichi shouted, laughing.

"I did this invisibility thing! It was like flying without leaving the ground!" she said. And something else she couldn't quite describe. She looked at Orlu and Sasha. "I shot right past you guys."

"So the warm breeze we just felt, that was you," Orlu said.

"I thought it was someone else who didn't want to be seen," Sasha said.

"This is crazy." Sunny couldn't stop grinning. Life was getting weirder and weirder. But this weirdness she really liked. If she could do this at will, nothing could harm her. Not even her father when he was angry.

"It's not that amazing," Sasha said coolly. "I can do that with a little powder and a few words."

"Well, Sunny was able to do it from when she was born," Chichi said.

Sasha just scoffed and pursed his lips. Sunny was too excited to care that he was jealous.

"You should hope she does not treat you like that when you are learning Igbo, Sasha," Orlu said, as they started walking.

"I don't need my ass kissed to learn," Sasha grumbled.

They went right to Bola's Store of Books. Sasha headed straight to the section marked **Enter and Buy at Your Own Risk**. This time, two teenagers, an old man, and two women were perusing the section. Orlu went to a section marked **Books of Creatures and Beasts of The Mystic World**.

"What are you interested in?" Sunny asked Chichi.

She shrugged. "Don't worry, I will find something," she said over her shoulder, ambling away.

Sunny looked at all the categories: **Time Tweakers, Love Juju, Ability Honing for the Unblessed, Parenting, History, Leopard General Literature, Leopard Science Fiction**. Her eye fell on the same book that she had noticed last time. It was in a section labeled **Scripts, Alphabets, and Straight Juju**. She picked it up. *Nsibidi: The Magical Language of the Spirits.* When she opened it, all she saw were pictorial signs. The longer she looked, the more the signs began to pulse and migrate about the page. She held the book closer to her face and they moved about even more. On top of that, the book seemed to be whispering to her.

"Eh? What are you saying?" she whispered back. Someone tapped her on the shoulder and she jumped. It was the shop owner, Mohammed.

"Hi," she said, feeling her face grow hot. "I was—I was just..." She put the book down and smiled sheepishly. "Sorry. Was I not supposed to touch that?"

"Don't worry," he said. He picked up the book and put it back in her hands. "You are a free agent, aren't you?"

She nodded. A man browsing beside her hissed loudly and moved to another section.

"That's interesting," Mohammed said, ignoring the annoyed customer. "Did your instructor send all of you here to buy books?"

"Mhm. But I don't know anything, really."

"That is an understatement," he said, chuckling and patting her on the shoulder. "Did you see anything in that book that... moved a little bit?"

"Yeah. And I heard...whispering."

He nodded. "Few can see Nsibidi. Buy this book. It calls to you."

"What happens after they stop moving?" she asked.

"Eh," Mohammed said with a shrug. "Only people like you will know. But it is a book, so I'm sure you will learn something."

"Who's the author?" she asked.

"Sugar Cream."

She frowned. Where had she heard that name?

"She is one of the scholars," Mohammed said, laughing. "You are really fresh, aren't you? She's head of the Leopard Knocks Library Council."

She clutched the book to her chest. "Can you help me find one other book?"

"Of course."

"It's called *Advanced Juju Knife Jujus* by Victoria Ogunbanjo."

Now it was Mohammed's turn to frown. "For you?"

"Yeah."

"Hmm, okay o." But he looked unsure.

The book was small with leaf-thin pages. It had a picture of an ancient-looking juju knife on the front with blood dripping from its tip. Altogether, her books cost three copper *chittim*.

"That Nsibidi book is really expensive," Sasha said. "You can really see it move?"

"Yeah."

"What did you choose?" Chichi asked.

Sasha grinned. "*Udide's Book of Shadows*."

"What?" Orlu nearly shouted. "You're joking!"

"Who's Udide?" Sunny asked.

"The supreme artist," Chichi said. "A giant spider that lives underground. She's the most creative creature on earth. Did she actually write a book of shadows? *Na wa o*, that's a good find! What language is it in?"

"Arabic, for some reason. This thing cost me two copper *chittim*," he said.

"Are you sure that it isn't stolen?" Orlu asked. "You can never be sure at Bola's shop, especially in that section."

"Who cares?" Sasha said. He took Orlu's book. "*A Field Guide to the Night Runner Forest?*" He handed it back to Orlu. "Yo, it reeks of soil, wet leaves, and ant shit."

Chichi snorted a laugh. Sunny snickered, too.

"And what else is it supposed to smell like, eh?" snapped Orlu.

"What'd you get?" she asked Chichi.

"*Leo Frobenius: Atlantis Middleman or Sellout,*" she said. "My mother was just telling me about how Atlantis is located off Victoria Island, near Lagos. Of course, the Lambs think it is anywhere but off the coast of the so-called 'Dark Continent.' Frobenius was a Leopard man from Germany. The man was so in love with Atlantis that he lost his allegiance and wanted to tell the world what he knew. He almost told the secret to the Lambs."

Sunny had no idea what Chichi was talking about.

"My mother is going to want to steal this book from me," Chichi said, excitedly. "But I will be the first to read it."

"Y'all check out that other book Anatov had us buy?" Sasha asked.

"Oh my God, yes," Chichi said. "I hope he doesn't kill us with all of those things. Those are jujus for *Mbawkwa* and above." But she was smiling.

"That's second level, right?" Sunny asked.

"Yes."

"Well, isn't that illegal or something, since we haven't passed it yet?"

"Not for me," Sasha boasted.

"Working juju that is above your grade is not illegal," Orlu said. "It is just extremely dangerous. If you make a mistake, the consequences are often death." He looked at his watch and said. "Let's go. Taiwo lives at the end of this road. It is very far."

It took over two hours. And after the first hour, when there was still plenty of road in sight, Sunny began to wonder just how big Leopard Knocks was. According to Orlu, it was a chunk of land surrounded by the river, but she hadn't imagined that it was so huge. In the first hour, they passed shop after shop. From normal food stores to creepy huts painted black with black curtains over entrances that led into blackness.

"Those places either sell creatures sensitive to sunlight or items for riskier practices," Chichi said.

"But the most dangerous black juju shops are nearer to where Taiwo lives," Orlu said. "They call that place Leopard Spots Village. We are going east and Leopard Spots is southeast. With the amount of illegal juju that they do there, they might as well stamp that whole area as prohibited."

Sunny shivered at the idea of corrupt Leopard people.

"All places have a dark side as they have a light side. To get rid of Leopard Spots Village would cause chaos," Orlu added, seeming to read her thoughts.

The brightest part of Leopard Knocks was at its centre. She could see the enormous four-storey hut long before they got to it. The Obi Library. All around the red clay structure the grass grew wild, an occasional brightly coloured flower or aggressive-looking bush here and there. The library was wider than four mansions, and its floors were stacked crookedly on top of each other.

It looked as if it would fall over any minute. But through its many windows, each of which was placed almost at random, she could see people standing around, sitting, walking by or up some stairs. The Obi's outside walls were decorated with white drawings of battles, dances, forests, fields, city skylines, outer space, and creatures of all kinds. She could stand there all day and still see something new. It was as if the building was telling thousands of stories at once.

"They have a copy of every book, charm, and history in the world; oral, written, or thought," Orlu said. "They also write laws there." He looked at Sasha. "And punish law-breakers."

"Can just anyone go in?" she asked.

"Only to the ground floor," Orlu said. "The first and second floors are the university, for true scholars. Third levellers, *Ndibus*, who want to keep evolving."

"My mother goes there," Chichi said proudly. "She's one of the younger students, though."

"Younger?" Chichi's mother was about her mother's age.

"Here, it is not the same as with Lambs," Orlu said. "Age is one of the requirements to even start at the Obi University of Pre-Scholars. You have to be over forty-two."

"Sugar Cream lives inside there, too," Chichi said.

"Oh yeah, by the way, she's the one who wrote my book," Sunny said.

"Really?" Chichi said. Then she nodded. "That makes sense, somebody like her."

Like what? Sunny thought. She didn't feel like asking.

"For your information, *obi* means 'heart' in Igbo," Chichi told Sasha.

His nostrils flared but he said nothing.

"It can mean 'house' or 'soul,' too," Sunny added.

After the library, the land to the left of the road opened into a field of lush uniform farmland. To the right was a high wall. Both the farmlands and the wall ran as far as Sunny could see.

"A lot of the supplies sold in the shops are grown here," Orlu said. "The soil is strange and some of these things will not grow anywhere else. Like that flower over there." He pointed out a plain looking purple flower with a white centre. "It makes *vévé* dust." Sunny remembered how they had gotten to Night Runner Forest. "And that is the wall that protects the ideas of the idea brewers," he said. "Listen." He took her arm and stopped her. Sasha and Chichi kept going.

"What are we—"

"Shh, just listen," Orlu insisted.

She strained. Then…she could hear it! Whispering. Similar to her Nsibidi book, but more intense. Like thousands of people having a quiet, important conversation.

"Why didn't I hear that before?" she asked.

"You have to listen," he said. "On the other side of the wall there are dozens of people employed just to sit and make new juju charms."

"Isn't that something they'd do in the library?" she asked.

"Charm-making is like labour," he said. "It is just a matter of spending time and using the knowledge you already have. Most of the people there are first levellers. But the books put out by the idea brewery are useful."

An hour later, they finally arrived at the tall group of palm trees at the end of the main road. A hut was perched hundreds of feet up the tallest palm tree. Only three weeks ago, Sunny would have said this was impossible.

"Excuse me?" Chichi called up.

"Madam Taiwo? We were sent by *Oga* Anatov!"

No response.

"Your voice isn't going to reach all the way up there," Sasha said.

Minutes passed. Sasha grew annoyed and kicked the tree trunk. "We didn't come all the way out here to be ignored!" he shouted.

"*Haba*," Chichi said, "what kind of welcome is this?"

Sunny checked her watch. It was only a quarter to noon.

Sasha continued cursing at and kicking the tree. Chichi's voice grew hoarse from shouting at the hut. Finally, they sat with Orlu and Sunny at the base of the tree.

"She knows we're here," Orlu said.

"Oh, please," Sasha said, annoyed.

"It makes sense, if she's a scholar," Sunny said.

"She's probably not around," Chichi said.

"This is Anatov's way of teaching us to call before visiting," Sasha said.

"José, my teacher back home, did crap like this all the time."

Clack! It sounded like two giant sticks slamming together.

They looked up.

Sunny saw it first. "Hey," she said, pointing.

It was perched in the crown of one of the other trees. A bird the size of a horse! It was brown with strong bright blue feet. It clapped its long orange beak again. *Clack!*

"That is a Blue-Footed Miri Bird," Orlu exclaimed.

It jumped from the tree. For a moment, Sunny was sure it would land right on them. There was no way something that size could fly. It plummeted in a free fall and they scrambled away from the tree as fast as they could.

The bird was only playing. Swiftly it spread its enormous wings and flew into the sky. It hovered in midair before nose-diving right at them.

They flattened themselves to the ground, their hands over their heads. When it was five feet above, the enormous Miri Bird stopped itself and softly landed on the ground in front of them.

Sasha cursed and got up. "Goddamn *insane* bird," Sasha said, his voice shaking. "What kind of crap is that, man!" Chichi grumbled agreement as she dusted off her clothes.

The creature was magnificent, though. It clicked its beak, cocked its head and eyed them, as if it expected something.

"It's supposed to take us up," Orlu said, smiling at the bird.

"Please o! I am not getting on top of that flea-infested thing," Chichi said.

The Miri Bird loudly clicked its beak again and turned its backside toward Sasha and Chichi and pooed out an obscene amount of white and black droppings.

"Ugh!" Sasha exclaimed. "Oh my God. It's filthy!"

"I think it's angry," Sunny said. She would have done the same thing, if she were the Miri Bird. Sasha and Chichi were being such jerks. Still, the pile of poo was quite nasty.

Orlu took a step towards it. The Miri Bird stepped back.

"Hey!" Sasha shouted up at the hut in the palm tree. "Lady Taiwo! We're down here with your bird. Please, will you speak with us?"

No response. Sasha and Chichi went back to grumbling about how stupid this all was. They sat on the other side of one of the palm trees, as far away from the pile of bird poo as they could. Already, it drew flies.

"Maybe we're supposed to give it something," Sunny suggested. She brought a biscuit from her purse and held it out to the Miri Bird. "For you," she said. It clapped its beak and stood there looking at her. Orlu tried stepping towards it again. It stepped back.

Eventually, Orlu and Sunny joined Sasha and Chichi. They sat there for twenty minutes, munching on Sunny's biscuits, ignoring the poo pile and trying to figure out what to do. The Miri Bird slowly stepped before them and waited.

"Do you know we walked two hours to get here?" Orlu asked it. The Miri Bird blinked.

"Our instructor is Anatov and he said that coming here is our lesson for today," he said. The bird stepped closer, squawking softly as if really interested in Orlu's words. Orlu sat up straighter. They all perked up. "Could you tell us how to get up there?" Orlu asked carefully.

The Miri Bird stepped right up to Orlu and clicked its beak in his face. Sunny gasped. The thing could have taken off Orlu's nose, even his head, with one chomp if it wanted. Orlu quickly got up. "Ah, is that what you want?" he said. "You want the same thing that everybody wants, to be treated like a human being."

The bird threw its head back and squawked loudly.

"What?" Sasha said looking angry.

"Shut up," Orlu warned him. "Be nice to it. Otherwise, we will lose our ride. We should each introduce ourselves to it."

Once they did so and politely asked the bird to take them to see Taiwo, it knelt down and clicked its beak twice.

"Okay, I understand," Orlu said. "Sunny, you and I will go first."

Sunny climbed on behind Orlu. The bird's feathers were soft or scratchy, depending on the direction you rubbed them. They were also covered with a thin coat of reddish palm oil, the smell wafting from its body. Sunny didn't have time to dwell on the fact that her clothes were ruined. She held Orlu tightly around the waist.

"Are you afraid?" he asked.

"Yeah."

He laughed.

The bird took off and they both screamed. She could feel the bird's powerful muscles working as it launched itself straight up. Seconds later, they landed on the verandah of the hut. It was made of woven palm fibre and gave a little with each step. They stumbled quickly into the hut. Inside was a plump woman in jeans and a white T-shirt sitting on some pillows.

"What held you people?" she said in Igbo. She had a Yoruba accent. She switched to English when Sasha and Chichi stumbled in. "Make yourself comfortable, students."

They sat down. She looked past them. "Thank you, Nancy," she said.

The bird squawked but remained there, watching.

"Humility," Taiwo said standing up and looking down at them. "Sasha, Chichi, you both lack it. Sunny, you have it because you're new. You have yet to realise your own potential." She looked at Orlu and her face warmed. "But you, Orlu, were born with it. A rare gift these days."

Orlu smiled back at her. Sunny was both annoyed but happy for Orlu. Taiwo would obviously be his mentor, as Anatov would be Chichi's, and Kehinde would be Sasha's.

Taiwo brought a small brown sack from her pocket, poured some of its contents in her hand and blew it at them. Sunny screeched, closed her eyes and held her hands up as a great puff of white powder engulfed them.

"There," she heard Taiwo say after a moment. "All clean."

When she cracked her eyes open, she saw that Sasha was smiling. "Thanks," Sasha said. "I really liked this shirt."

Sunny looked at her clothes and was relieved to see the red palm oil from Nancy's feathers dryly falling from her clothes like ashes.

Chichi got up and held out the package Anatov had given her. Taiwo gently unwrapped the newspaper and smiled. Inside was a brown paper bag. "Since he gave this to you to give to me," she said to Chichi. "It's your job to present it to Nancy."

"Me?" Chichi said, taking the paper bag. She looked back at Nancy, who remained there waiting.

"Pour them in your hand and go to the door."

"But I don't like birds," she said. "Especially that one. It poos like an elephant! Orlu can do it, can't he?"

Nancy made a snapping sound with her beak and ruffled her feathers.

"This isn't a discussion," Taiwo said.

Chichi looked disgusted as she reached for the bag and poured some of the contents in her hand. She held one up, it looked like a large raisin.

"What are these?" she asked.

"Prunes," Taiwo said.

"Prunes?" Orlu said. "Don't people eat those to…soften their stool?"

Chichi squeezed her face with disgust. "And you want me to feed these to that bird? Are you joking?" she exclaimed. "The bird is already full of too much sh…"

"They are healthy and Nancy likes them," Taiwo snapped. "You will do as you're told."

Sunny bit her bottom lip, working hard not to laugh. She had to work even harder not to laugh as Nancy roughly pecked prunes from Chichi's hand with her enormous beak.

"All creatures have a place," Taiwo said, ignoring Chichi's sulking. "That's why all of us could die right now and life would go on. All of you must be putting the pieces together by now." She whispered something and soft jazzy music began to play. She winked at Orlu. "You think you are all too young."

She looked at Sasha and Chichi. "But the two of you super-intelligent vagabonds know, don't you?"

"Ma, are you talking about us being an *Oha* coven?" Chichi asked, perking up.

"Yes."

"It's obvious," Sasha said.

"And poor Sunny has no idea what we are talking about, isn't that right?" Taiwo said.

"Basically," Sunny said.

"The irony," Taiwo said, laughing to herself.

"What's ironic?" she asked.

"That is not for me to explain," Taiwo said. "All in due time." She paused for dramatics. Sunny wanted to roll her eyes. These scholars all seemed to like making things seem so huge and mysterious. It was beginning to get on her nerves. "The four of you will be West Africa's first pre-level *Oha* coven."

"It's true?" Orlu exclaimed.

"Hard to believe, isn't it?" she said. "None of you knows how to read the stars and none of you will be tall enough to possess the natural ability. But if you did, you would know that something is coming."

Sunny felt her heart flip. "I do," she said.

"Oh," Taiwo said, and then she nodded. "I stand corrected. Anatov told me about you and the candle. Wilderlings can show the future to those without the ability of premonition.

"We Leopard people need to be extra vigilant these days, but sometimes we need to act. Sunny, an *Oha* coven bears the responsibility of the world on its shoulders at a specific point in time. Coven members are people of action and authority but they are also people of selflessness. I trust you all have heard of Black Hat."

They all nodded. Then Chichi gasped. Sasha grabbed her shoulder and they both just stared at each other.

"That's why!" Chichi said to Sasha.

"Goddamn!" Sasha said. Then they both looked at Taiwo who was laughing.

"Both of you, are so quick," Taiwo said. She looked at Orlu and Sunny, "They have just now realised that Black Hat is a Leopard person."

Orlu nodded. "I considered it but I wasn't sure. I didn't want to say anything."

"How do you know?" Sunny asked. "Just because he's a ritual killer? All ritual killers can't be Leopard people, can they?"

"No, most ritual killers are misguided or crazy Lamb folk. But we know about Black Hat. He was a scholar. Many years before all of you were born, Otokoto Ginny passed the last level. He was thirty-four years old, a year older than I was. He shouldn't have been allowed to even take the test." She hissed in annoyance. "He passed, but he was never fit to be a scholar. His hunger for wealth and power were as strong as his hunger for *chittim*. I don't know what was wrong with him. He has to be stopped, not just for the sake of the children he is drawing from, but for the world. This is the task we are giving to the four of you."

Sunny's mouth fell open. Orlu cried out in frustration. Sasha laughed and said, "Bring it." Chichi slapped hands and snapped fingers with Sasha.

"We don't know what it is he is planning, but these killings and mutilations point towards the blackest, most secret type of juju," Taiwo said. "The kind that requires ritual sacrifices of human beings. The fact that he is targeting children means he is working with juju that draws its power from life and innocence. In three months, we will expect you to go after this man. We can easily find him but it is important to wait for the right moment to strike."

"How do you know when that is?" Orlu asked.

"We don't know, but we are sure that we will know it when we see it."

Orlu frowned. "The scholars, you mean?"

"Yes, from Leopard Knocks and other distant places. We are all working together on this. We met and decided to choose you last year. Except Sunny. We had an idea about her, but we couldn't see her clearly until you, Chichi, introduced her to your mother."

Sunny had to say something. "You expect us to capture this Black Hat who is like you, one of these people who has passed the highest of the highest level of juju ability? That's—I mean no disrespect—" She paused, the irritation that had been brewing in her for weeks suddenly flaring bright. She felt used. "That's *insane*! And—and I'm beginning to know how you people think! You'll just find some other kids to do it if we're all murdered! And why am *I* included in this?! I don't know anything!"

"This is bigger than you," Taiwo said turning very serious. "But you're part of it, too. It would be unfair for me to expect you to understand this at the moment, but you will."

Sunny exhaled loudly but looked away, working hard to shut her mouth. What else could she say that was coherent and not full of swear words, anyway?

The next morning, when she woke and stretched, something fell off her bed. It was a rolled up newspaper from Leopard Knocks, an early edition. Taped to it was a receipt that said:

Welcome, new subscriber. We appreciate your business. Please pay Chichi Nimm a sum of one small silver chittim. Have a nice day!

CONCLUSION

. . . So there you have it. All you need to know to get started. As I have repeated incessantly throughout this book, there is no direction you can turn that does not face you towards certain death. The best thing to do is be who you've been, don't move, stay where you are, drop all ambition as a Leopard person. Relax. Do not strive too high. Learn but do not use. And only learn the basics. It is best to remain in your protective shell. Ambition is not your friend. Be glad the Leopard world has been opened to you, but remain a spectator. And for the hundredth time, I repeat: KEEP YOUR SECRET LIFE FROM YOUR LAMB RELATIONS AND ACQUAINTANCES. Not only are there dire consequences for breaching secrecy, but you risk upsetting a very delicate, crucial hard-earned balance. Now go well, free agent. Be well. And again I say: Welcome.

CHAPTER TEN
FACING REALITY

Sunny spent the next month deep in all kinds of books. She was doing homework for two schools. But somehow, she was keeping up and managing enough sleep. She'd read *Fast Facts for Free Agents* cover to cover twice. She practised basic jujus and her skill of becoming invisible. She even perfected bringing forth and pulling back her spirit face.

She moved on to her two new books from Leopard Knocks. The Nsibidi one really caught her interest. Her eyes adjusted quickly to the wiggling, gesturing, animated black symbols. Soon she could actually see that they were trying to say things. For example, a symbol that looked like a stick figure of an intense man standing and punching his fists in the air meant, 'This is all mine!' The figure was placed in the front cover of the book, and next to it she neatly wrote her name.

But understanding what was 'written' in the book was coming slowly. Each symbol spoke a complex idea, and the slightest change in the symbol shifted its meaning. And the book expected her to learn the language and then read and understand what Sugar Cream had written using the language. She was only able to decipher the first third of the first page and that page mostly told her why most people wouldn't be able to read the book.

"This text won't be a bestseller," the book said. At least that's what Sunny thought it said.

She also read well into her *Advanced Juju Knife Jujus* book, though the subject was way over her head. She didn't even have a juju knife. And every charm had some crazy warning or side effect like heart failure, brain aneurysms, cancer, venereal disease, itchy rashes, terrible luck, insanity, and, most often, death.

Her mother seemed pleased with the 'fresh look' Sunny suddenly had and the happiness that radiated from her. Her father, on the other hand, avoided her. Maybe he sensed the change in her most. Her brothers actually began to talk to her. They played more soccer after dark. Several times, she even joined them in their room to watch movies on their computer.

It was a warm Monday morning. She woke up bleary-eyed but smiling. She had gone to bed very late. Something had clicked in her brain last night, and she understood the Nsibidi book's language a lot better. In those late hours, she'd read a full page.

She rubbed the crust from her eyes, sighing loudly. It was going to be a long day. She reached for the newspaper on her lap. She got one every morning now. She never heard or saw anything; it would just be there when she woke. She unrolled it and, just like that, the glowing euphoria she'd been experiencing for a month died. "Oh, no," she whispered.

The headline read: **Otokoto The Black Hat Strikes Again!** A boy of seven had been taken in the market. He was found the next day with his ears cut off, unable to properly hear even the loudest noise. Sunny threw the paper across the room. Her legs shook as she got up and retrieved the front page.

She pressed her lips together as she read the whole story. The boy had stumbled into someone's home babbling about how angels had saved him. *The poor boy*, she thought. *Why do I feel like it's my fault? It's not as if I can do anything.* But some very intelligent people believed she and the others could. She quickly got ready for school.

She had to wait until lunch break to talk to Orlu about it.

"Did you read the paper?" Orlu asked.

"Yeah."

They were quiet.

"What'd Sasha say?" she finally asked.

"I won't repeat his words. He was very angry."

"I felt more guilty than angry," she said.

"Yes."

"Have you seen Chichi?"

"I went to see her this morning," he said. "She's usually awake doing something, reading. Her mother told me she had gone for a walk after reading the paper. Maybe she went to see Anatov. Sasha sent a message to Kehinde. Taiwo's Miri Bird gave my mother a note to give me this morning. It said not to do anything."

They barely ate their lunches. Even when they both received high marks on their essays in literature and writing class, they were grim. So, when they were both leaving school and Jibaku roughly pushed Sunny aside as she passed, followed by Calculus, Periwinkle, and a few others, there was bound to be trouble.

"Hey, stop it!" Sunny screeched, running up and pushing Jibaku back. She felt the blood rush to her head. Just then, a beat-up car full of older teenage boys pulled up in front of the school. "Jibaku," the driver called.

Sunny and Jibaku turned around. The boys got out of the car and swaggered into the school yard in their baggy jeans and T-shirts. Loud hip-hop music blasted from their shabby vehicle. Sunny wanted to laugh hard. They were trying way too hard to mimic black American culture.

The driver pointed at Orlu. "You! Small boy! I know you from somewhere."

"And so what?" Orlu snapped, looking annoyed.

Jibaku and Sunny turned back to each other.

"Eh! Don't touch me with your diseased hands, you devil, *mmuo ojo!*" Jibaku said.

"Or what? Eh?" Sunny said, feeling her blood rise.

"Come o! This *oyibo* fit give una trouble!" the driver said to his friends, laughing. "Serious trouble." He laughed harder. "Jibaku, let us go."

Orlu tried to pull Sunny back. She snatched her arm away. "No!" she said. "I'm not afraid of this idiot!" Jibaku instantly whirled around and launched herself at Sunny. Sunny shoved her back and threw a punch. She had two crazy brothers; she knew how to fight. And Jibaku had it coming.

Jibaku screeched, clasping her eye. She came at Sunny again. Suddenly, they were both on the ground, rolling in the dust, kicking and punching and scratching. Sunny was a hurricane of rage, only vaguely aware of Orlu and the boys exchanging angry words. A crowd gathered. She didn't care. She rolled on top of Jibaku and slapped her face as hard as she could.

Hands locked around her arms. Calculus and Periwinkle were dragging her off. This gave Jibaku a chance to kick Sunny in the belly, knocking the air out of her. The unfairness of the situation really made her see red. She screamed and wretched her arms from Periwinkle and Calculus. She was on Jibaku again, pressing her to the ground. She revelled in the fear on Jibaku's face.

"You try and beat me again—" Sunny said breathlessly. "Remember this the next time you think about it!" Without a thought, she brought forth her spirit face. "*Raaaahhhh!*" she roared. Jibaku screamed so loudly that everyone, including the boys came running. Immediately, Sunny retracted her spirit face and stood.

Jibaku scrabbled away from Sunny into the guy's arms, her eyes wide and wild. She started crying, burying her face in the guy's chest. He pointed a finger at Orlu and Sunny. Deepening his voice for emphasis, he said, "*Bia*, if I see any of una again, I go show you pepper!"

Orlu and Sunny watched them all pile into the car and drive off.

"Come on," Orlu said. "Before the teachers come."

They walked slowly, Sunny limping a little. Her knees were scraped and she'd bruised her arm.

"So, you showed her your spirit face, didn't you?" Orlu said. "Shut up."

A blue Mercedes pulled up beside them. The window came down. "Sunny Nwazue?" the woman behind the wheel asked. She wore a green head wrap, dark sunglasses, and black lipstick.

"Who are—"

"Are you Sunny Nwazue?"

"Y-yes," she said.

"Enter. You are to be taken to the Obi Library for punishment."

"But it wasn't her fault," Orlu begged. "She is a free agent, she was just introduced some weeks ago. She didn't work any juju on anybody. She just—"

"Get in, Sunny Nwazue," the woman repeated.

Sunny looked at Orlu. "Go," he said. "God, that was very stupid, Sunny."

"What's going to happen?" she whispered.

"I don't know," he snapped. He cursed to himself and then said, "Just enter."

The woman drove in silence. From the back window, Sunny waved sadly at Orlu. He just looked at her. She slumped in her seat and took out her mobile phone. "No reason to get in trouble twice," she grumbled.

Her mother answered. "Dr. Nwazue speaking."

"Hi, Mama," she said.

"Hi, sweetie, is everything okay?"

"Um, yeah," she said, looking tentatively at the driver.

"How was school?"

"Fine," she said, lowering her voice. "I got an A for my maths exam. And I got an A for my essay in literature and writing class."

"Wonderful."

"Mama, can I have dinner with Chichi and Orlu tonight?" She held her breath. The family rarely had dinner together, but her mother liked her and her brothers to be in the house by nighttime.

There was a pause. "As long as all of you study your books," she finally said. Sunny breathed a sigh of relief. She hated lying. "Be home by seven. Anyway, it's going to be a late day for both your father and myself."

Sunny put her mobile phone in her purse. "Excuse me," she said to the woman.

She looked at Sunny in the rearview mirror.

"Will—will they throw me in jail or something?" she asked.

"I can't discuss that with you," the woman said in her flat voice.

Sunny sat back and looked out the window. The monotony of the drive and the hum of the car were soothing. Soon, she dozed off.

"Get out."

Sunny slowly opened her eyes. They were parked outside of the Obi Library. There must have been a way in wider than the tree bridge.

"Someone will meet you inside." The moment Sunny got out, the woman drove off, leaving her alone in Leopard Knocks for the first time. There were people going in and out of the library, on the street. She saw a group of kids about her age walking towards Taiwo's hut. They saw her and waved. She waved back. Then she turned to the library. A cobblestone trail led through the wildly growing grass to the main entrance. As with almost every Leopard building, there was no door, only a silky lavender cloth. She pushed it aside and stepped in.

Books and papers were stacked and piled in corners, set in bookcases as high as the ceiling, scattered on and around clusters of chairs. It was all very untidy and disorganised and the air had a stale paper odour. People read, talked, wrote, and even performed acts of juju. A man standing in a corner with a book in his hand shouted something and threw some powder in the air. *Poof!* A burst of brown moths. He coughed and cursed and threw the book on the floor.

An old woman sat beside a bookcase, surrounded by children. She snapped her fingers and all the children floated inches from the ground. They giggled, trying to make themselves go higher by pumping their legs.

In the centre of the large busy room was a round table with a silver sign hovering in midair above it. In large black letters, the sign read: **Wetin?** A young man with Yoruba tribal markings on his cheeks sat behind the desk.

"Hello," she said, nervously. "I'm—"

"Sunny Nwazue," he said. "Breaker of rule number 48. And it is such a primary rule." He called behind her. "Samya."

"Yes?" came a voice from behind a bookcase. A woman with long braids, red plastic glasses, and reddish brown skin peeked around it.

"Sunny is here," he said. "Take her upstairs."

Samya looked Sunny over and then said, "Come. This way."

They took the staircase beside the *Wetin* desk. The next floor was larger, with more bookcases and stacks of paper. The people here were older. Sunny wanted to slap herself. Her first look at the Obi Library University was basically as a criminal.

A haunted moaning came from somewhere on the other side of the floor. Thankfully, they went up another flight of stairs. The next floor had more books and classrooms, too, but she was too nervous to really pay attention. "Please. What is going to happen to me?"

"I am not allowed to speak with you about that."

It looked like they were going up another staircase. Instead, Samya led her to the first actual door Sunny had seen in Leopard Knocks. It was heavy, painted black, and decorated with a white drawing like those on the outer walls of the library. The drawing depicted a person being whipped by another person. There were squiggles, circles, and Xs around the person being whipped. She assumed they illustrated cries of pain.

Samya knocked on the door. "Stay here until they ask you to enter," she said. Then she left.

Five minutes passed. *Man, I wish the door would open*, she thought. Anything to get away from the sounds in the hallway—the moans and wheezy, hysterical laughter and whispers, like some confused ghost. A large brown bird flew by and red spiders scurried across the high ceiling. She even felt a blast of warm wet air pass. Someone was moving invisibly.

She considered sitting on the floor but more red spiders were scurrying about there. Another ten minutes passed. Frustrated, she finally tried the door. The knob turned easily. She held her breath and pushed. She peeked in. Sitting on a solid bronze chair was a dark-skinned old woman dressed in a cream-coloured *buba* and matching trousers. She was slightly hunched to the side and looked uncomfortable.

"Oh, I'm sorry," Sunny said, retreating.

"Come in. Only those who want to come in are allowed to enter."

She stood before the woman. Dozens of masquerade masks covered the walls, hanging close to one another. Some looked angry with mouths full of teeth; others were fat-cheeked and comical, sticking their tongues out.

"So I could have just turned and left?"

"Maybe," the woman said. "But you are here now." The door closed. "Sit on the floor," the woman said. "You don't deserve a chair."

Sunny looked at the floor, spotting two more red spiders a few feet away. Slowly, she sat down, drawing her legs in close. "I'm sorry for what I did," she quickly said.

"Are you?"

"Ye—" Then she caught herself. "No."

"So you would do it again if you were given a chance to redo the incident?" she asked.

She thought about it for a moment. The mere thought of Jibaku angered her. She knew her answer. She kept her mouth shut.

"You will be flogged, then," the woman said.

She gasped and shook her head.

"Or I will put you in the library basement without any lights," the woman said. "There are things roaming down there that would scare some sense into you."

"Please," she begged, tears coming to her eyes.

The woman nodded. "Yes, I will do that. Samya!"

"Please," Sunny screeched. "I'm sorry! I understand now! *Please!*"

The woman looked down her nose at Sunny, irritably flaring her nostrils. "You're a free agent," she said, her voice softening.

"Yes," Sunny said. "I just—"

"The council always knows when something like this happens, when prime rules are broken. Didn't you read that in your free agent book?"

Sunny slowly nodded, her eyes on the ground.

"Next time, I will have you brought into this office and flogged thirty times and then I will throw you into the dirtiest, dampest, oldest room in the library basement where you will stay for a week with nothing but watered *garri* to eat. You hear me?"

Sunny swallowed and said, "Yes."

"I won't tolerate stupid behaviour," the woman said angrily.

"I understand," she said.

"Do you?"

"Yes," she said. She was shaking.

"Next time fight fairly," she said. "From what I have heard, your brothers have shown you how to do that."

"Yes," she said. Her heart was slamming about in her chest.

The woman looked her over. "So how has it been?"

"Eh?" Sunny was trying not to hyperventilate.

"Since you've come into the Leopard world."

"Be—before today or after today?"

"It is not a safe world," she said. "You cannot just go around doing whatever you like. Some of us may behave like that but it is not proper. It is not what I expect of you." She sat back and shifted her position, but she still looked hunched to the side. "Anatov has told me of you," she said. "I did not think I would be meeting you this way."

Sunny cocked her head and then said, "You're Sugar Cream, aren't you?"

"Finally, you ask."

"Sorry," she said. She paused. "Yes, I *was* stupid. It's just that I wanted to put the fear of—of God into her." She paused, clenching her fists. "I can't stand her!"

"Well, that certainly is one way to do it," Sugar Cream said. "Although it is illegal."

A spider was walking towards Sunny's foot. She scooted back.

She was more afraid of Sugar Cream when there was silence, so she asked the first question on her exhausted mind, "So, ah, why do they call you 'Sugar Cream'?"

Sugar Cream smiled and Sunny relaxed a bit. "It is an old story," she said. "When I was very small, I walked out of the forest. A young man found me. I was like a little monkey, wild and feral. Some people think that actual monkeys might have even looked after me for some time. Somehow I had survived in the bush. I couldn't have been more than three years old.

"Anyway, the only way I would come to the man who found me was when he offered me his cup of tea with a lot of sugar to drink and a tube of perfumed hand cream to play with. He took me to his home and raised me as his daughter, even though he was only seventeen years old. He grew up to be a professor at the University of Lagos and I went on to the Obi Library. To this day, I drink my tea with lots of sugar and I love the smell of hand cream."

A lot of holes in that story, Sunny thought. "What of your true parents?"

"I don't know, Sunny," she said. She stood up and stretched, raising her arms over her head. Sunny stared. The woman's spine. It wasn't right. But from the front, she couldn't tell exactly what was wrong. She quickly lowered her eyes.

"I hate sitting for too long," she said. "It's uncomfortable. Even with this hard, sturdy chair. Come and walk with me."

Sunny quickly followed her out. She couldn't help staring at Sugar Cream's back. One shoulder was higher than the other, and her spine curved in a most profound S. Had she been like this as a baby? Maybe this was why her parents had abandoned her. But if they were Leopard people, they'd have jumped for joy at this deformity.

"You should know this," Sugar Cream said, turning to her. "When people stare at you from your back. You always know when they are doing it."

Sunny stepped back mortified by her own rudeness. "I—I didn't mean to."

"I have severe scoliosis. And no, I was not born this way. And I don't think I was abandoned by my parents. I think they were killed."

Despite her deformity, Sugar Cream walked briskly. She greeted the students they passed. "Good afternoon, madam," an old white man with a British accent shyly said.

"Good afternoon, Albert," she said.

When they were alone again, Sunny asked what she'd wanted to ask since Sugar Cream had stood up. "I was wondering... what ability do you have?"

"I am a shape-shifter, as you are."

"No, I'm not," Sunny said.

"Can you not turn yourself into something like warm vapour? You are a type of shape-shifter. I can become a snake," she said, making her hand move in an S motion. "My ability is a physical manifestation. Yours is spiritual. The reason you can become vapour is because you can literally step into the spirit world. I doubt you have done this yet. You would know if you had."

"How do I—"

"Only when you want to," she said. "To enter the spirit world completely, you have to die. So for you to do it, you have to die a little." She paused and looked at Sunny. "Would you like to learn?"

"I...don't know," she said uneasily. "Not really." Who would want to learn how to die?

They passed a group of students who cautiously greeted Sugar Cream. "The students you see here are the most advanced," she said. "Those who manage to get here will most likely pass *Ndibu*, the third level; most likely none of them will pass *Oku Akama*, the highest level. It has been many years since anyone has."

They passed some tall shelves and piles of books. "How does the library keep track of all the books?" Sunny asked. "A lot of them seem..." she trailed off. She wanted to say, 'thrown about.'

Sugar Cream laughed. "Don't worry, every book here is accounted for. They are marked. When they need to be found, they will be found."

"How?"

"That depends on who wants to find it," she said. They went back to her office, where she sat on the arm of her bronze chair. Sunny remained standing. "Anatov was going to send you here in two weeks. I was going to decide whether or not I would mentor you. Now that you have behaved so stupidly, my decision is harder. I will need to think about it."

Sunny's heart sank. It didn't matter that she had avoided being whipped or thrown in the library basement, Chichi, Orlu, and even Sasha—who never missed a chance to make trouble—had mentors. For them it had been so simple and obvious. Her path to anything seemed to always be difficult. And she hated how everyone was acting as if she should know the rules so well. It was ridiculous. Couldn't Sugar Cream cut her some slack?

"You chose to do what you did," Sugar Cream said. "So don't stand there being angry at me. For me to mentor you would be a great honour, an honour reserved for a mature girl or boy. You would be the only student I would mentor. Your case is complicated." She sighed. "But you most certainly should be involved in this. I have no doubt about that."

"How are you so sure?" Sunny asked. Inside she was crying. "I mean, you see how I am, what I did, and you're rethinking wanting to mentor me. How are you so sure I should even be part of this *Oha* coven group thing?"

Sugar Cream shook her head, a sad look on her face. "I was hoping you wouldn't ask me that."

Sunny waited for her to go on. "Listen. It was your grandmother, Ozoemena, who taught Otokoto everything he knows. She was his mentor. And it was Otokoto who killed your grandmother in a ritual to steal her abilities, as he stole her life. Do you want to know why he is so powerful? All you need to do is look at who your grandmother was and who Otokoto was before he became the Black Hat."

Sunny had no words.

"Yes," she said. "So you see why this is complicated."

Soon after that, Sugar Cream sent Sunny home. Sunny remembered saying goodbye and feeling even more like a criminal. She'd walked down the stairs and felt like a criminal. And she got into the council car, feeling like a criminal. She felt unworthy, childish, stupid, and worthless. On top of all this, she was the granddaughter of the scholar who taught a murderous psychopath. Her guilt tired her out so much that she slept the entire drive home.

She spent much of that evening in her room, staring off into space, thinking and thinking about all Sugar Cream told her. She still had homework to do. By 11pm, she'd fallen asleep on her books.

Sunny heard knocking. She thought she was dreaming. When it didn't stop, she swam up to wakefulness and groggily opened her eyes. Aside from her reading lamp, her room was dark. Then she saw a tiny light at the window. She froze, her brain for some reason going all the way back to when she was two and burning up from malaria. *The light watched over me.*

She blinked, fully waking up. It was the light of a firefly. She slowly opened the window. Sasha, Orlu, and Chichi stood below. "Come down," Orlu whispered loudly. "Meet us outside the gate."

She quickly dressed, then made herself invisible and swooped out of the window. When she emerged from the gate, Chichi threw her arms around her. "You are all right!" she said happily. "I heard you beat the hell out of Jibaku."

"You okay?" Sasha asked.

"Yeah," Sunny said.

"We were worried about you," Orlu said.

"You didn't sound like it when they took me away," Sunny said, annoyed.

"Why did you have to do it?" Orlu said. "You should—"

"Who cares?" she said. "And you know why, anyway. You of all people."

"I was about to fight Jibaku's boyfriend," Orlu said. "He is three years older than me and much bigger. But still I wouldn't have done what you did!"

She sighed loudly, rolling her eyes.

"I had to see the council once, too," Sasha said, putting his arm around Sunny. "Back when I set that masquerade on those guys harassing my sister." He paused. "I was caned twenty times and then ordered to be sent here."

"You were actually *caned*?" Sunny asked, looking shocked.

"I have the scars to show for it," Sasha said coldly. He met Orlu's eyes.

"Didn't know they did that in the US," Sunny said.

"Yeah, me neither," he said. "Anyway, Sunny, I never expected *you* to get in my kind of trouble."

"I just lost it, I guess."

"So what happened?" Chichi asked.

After she told them everything, including the part about her grandmother, they were all quiet. Then Chichi said, "Your grandmother would have been the one to bring you to the library, if she was alive. And she would have flogged you first."

"He must have eaten some of her flesh," Sasha said. "That's the only—"

Chichi angrily shushed him. "We don't need to talk about that now!"

Sunny felt ill. Chichi pushed Sasha away and put her arm around Sunny's shoulder.

"Sunny, try to find out more about your grandmother," Orlu said. "If they know about your grandmother's abilities, then we will know more about Black Hat."

"Yeah," she said quietly.

"Sugar Cream is very tough," Orlu said.

"I know," she said.

"If she refuses you, Anatov will find you another mentor," Chichi said.

This was not a consolation. She wanted Sugar Cream.

But she did feel better. Her grandmother was no criminal. She'd only been the teacher of a student gone bad. Still, by the time she was back in her room, she wanted to cry again. She couldn't get Black Hat out of her head. As she went to turn off the light, she saw the red ghost hopper standing on the post of her bed.

"You just have to sit yourself there, don't you," she said. It just looked at her with its huge compound green-blue eyes. She turned off the light. As she closed her eyes, she heard a soft, wavery singing, like a tiny dove who was using its voice to more than coo. It was lovely.

"You could do a lot worse than a ghost hopper. Some people would love to have those," Orlu had said. Now Sunny understood why. She settled down and let it sing her to sleep.

CHAPTER ELEVEN
LESSONS

"You're lucky your back isn't stinging," Anatov said. "Sugar Cream has the flogging done by a very muscular lad." He stood up and strolled around them with his hands behind his back. "This changes things some. If it weren't for Sunny's recklessness, I'd have sent y'all to meet Sugar Cream and get a tour of the Obi Library—not including the fourth floor, of course."

Sunny was relieved when no one seemed angry.

"Today will be short," he said. "I'll lecture on some important jujus. Then you can try a few of the advanced ones." He sat down and flicked his long beard over his shoulder. "Healing juju is tricky. Do it wrong and you worsen the ailment. First you find the cause. Let's say that a man has a boil on his *nyash*."

Orlu, Chichi, and Sunny snickered. Sasha only frowned.

"You don't know what *nyash* means, do you?" Anatov asked Sasha. "Come now. Of all words."

"It's 'ass,' in Pidgin English," Sunny said, still laughing.

Sasha humphed and looked away.

"Work harder on your Pidgin English and your Igbo," Anatov told Sasha. "You don't even know any general curse words yet? Pathetic. How will you be able to move on to Yoruba?!"

"I'm working as hard as I can," Sasha replied in perfect Igbo. He even managed to hide his American accent. Sunny had to admit, she was impressed.

"Work harder," Anatov replied in English. "So, back to the *nyash*. I am a man with a boil on my *nyash*. I want it gone before my wife sees it. What do I do?"

"Squeeze it," Sasha said. They all burst out laughing.

"That would leave a sore that could get infected," Anatov said, remaining serious. "Such a simple problem and not one of you can tell me how to quickly cure it?"

"You'll have to make a strong medicine," Chichi said.

"Yes, but a strong medicine can take all night," Anatov said. After a moment, he said, "Open your books to page one hundred and eighteen."

The chapter was titled *Reknitting: Fast Healing By Hand*. Anatov read the second paragraph aloud:

"'There is only one way to swiftly heal the body. You must undo and then reknit the cells. Those who excel at this must have fast hands and superb spatial skills. Males possess this skill in greater quantities than females. With young people, simply look to their ability to play video games for your answer.'"

Anatov looked up from his book. "I want you all to look at yourselves and locate an ailment. Could be a cut, a scratch, bruise, or pimple."

Sunny still had plenty of bruises and scratches from her fight with Jibaku.

Anatov held up a small vial containing a light blue substance. "You're to go to Leopard Knocks on your own time and buy some of this," he said. "It's called Healing Hands Powder. Come and take a pinch. You should have this with you at all times—just in case."

The powder was hot between Sunny's fingers, but not unpleasantly so.

"If you hold it long enough, the part of your skin that is touching it will develop a cancer," Anatov said.

They all froze. "What!" cried Sasha.

"Patience," Anatov firmly said. "I know this might be hard, knowing what you know, but you need to stand still enough to hear your heart beat. If you don't, it won't work." He waited.

"Close your eyes," he said. "The blood your heart pumps nourishes every part of you, including the part you wish to heal. Imagine sailing through your veins to that ailing place. You see it? Now imagine that you're bringing that part of you forward. It detaches and now floats before you. See it rotate so you can look at it from all angles."

Sunny imagined the dark purple black bruise on her bicep where Jibaku had punched her, the bruise she wished would go away before her mother saw it. She imagined the flesh under her skin, full of burst blood vessels.

"Keep your eyes closed," Anatov said. "Now, quickly, blow the powder at what you see!"

She held her fingers to her lips and blew. Immediately her bicep felt as if it had caught fire. She screeched, grabbing her arm.

"Looks like we have a result," Anatov said, smiling wide.

Sunny's arm gradually began to feel better. She looked at it and laughed. "It's gone!"

"Yours worked?" Chichi asked, surprised. "Nothing happened to the rash on my ankle."

"Nothing happened to my scratch, either," Sasha said.

Sunny smirked, feeling even more satisfied with herself.

"You didn't visualise well enough," Anatov said.. "Orlu? What of you?"

"The wound I had on my leg is gone," he said. "But I didn't feel any pain, like Sunny did."

"You have more control," Anatov said, placing a hand on Orlu's head. Then he placed a hand on Sunny's. "You, Sunny, have more power. Sasha, Chichi, you need more practice. I'm not surprised you couldn't get it to work at all. All of you, go scrub your hands of every trace of the powder."

The next two hours were tough. Sunny could barely keep up, even when he discussed things from the juju knife book. And because she had no juju knife, she was forced to shadow everyone else's motions, which felt silly. She soon went from feeling powerful to pathetic. It was more than clear that Orlu, Chichi, and Sasha had years on her, had *upbringing* on her. They were so natural as Leopard folk, whereas she was stumbling around in the dark.

When they were finished, Anatov made an announcement. "Next Saturday, we go to Abuja. We go for two reasons. First, Sunny will pick out her juju knife."

"We are going to see Junk Man!" Chichi exclaimed.

"Second, I'm taking you all to the Zuma Festival to see your first Zuma National Wrestling Match finals. I need to be at an important meeting of scholars, so this trip will kill multiple birds with one stone."

Sasha looked delighted and, for once, Orlu's reaction matched his. "I've always wanted to see the finals," Orlu said. "I hope no one's killed, though."

"Yes, it's often a fight to the death," Anatov said with a mysterious smile.

How was Sunny supposed to pull this one off? An entire day and night? And Abuja was hours away by car. She had to lie. It was the only way.

Chichi was in on the plan. Two days later, Sunny invited her to dinner. Chichi made sure to dress up. She wore black trousers and a top made from Ankara cloth with rose designs and a green background. Her short Afro was brushed out. She even wore silver hoop earrings.

Sunny's father was still at his office working on a case, but that was fine. It was her mother they had to really convince. Why did her brothers have to be around, though?

"Good evening," Chukwu said as she showed Chichi in. He looked her up and down. Sunny almost wished Chichi had come in her usual shabby clothes. Chukwu held out a hand. "I'm Sunny's oldest brother, Chukwu."

"A pleasure to meet you," Chichi said, shaking his hand. She looked him in the eye as she did so. Sunny didn't like that either.

"My sister has told me so much about you," he said.

Sunny rolled her eyes. She hadn't told him a thing. Ugonna stood behind him, apparently unable to speak.

"Mhm?" Chichi smirked flirtatiously. "There is plenty of me to talk about."

Chukwu's eyes were flashing with interest as he sidled closer, a lazy smile on his face. Sunny wanted to gag.

"You know," he said, "I'm captain of the football team at my school—and the best player."

"Oh," Chichi said. "Is that because Sunny can't play in the sun?"

Ugonna and Sunny snickered.

"Come on now," Chukwu said in his buttery voice, trying to hide the fact that Chichi had thrown him off. "Football is a man's game."

That was enough. Sunny groaned and took her friend's arms. "Back off," she said, pushing Chukwu aside. She took Chichi to the kitchen to meet her mother.

"Your brothers are pretty," Chichi said as she pushed her along.

"Yeah, pretty stupid, maybe." But Sunny was more nervous about what was coming next. "Okay, now don't say anything weird or anything, all right?"

Chichi rolled her eyes.

"Hi, Mama," Sunny said. Her heart was beating so fast. "This is Chichi."

"Hello," her mother said, putting down her wooden spoon. "So finally I get to see this girl that my daughter spends so much time with."

"Good evening, ma. It is nice to meet you," Chichi said. Sunny had never heard Chichi sound so respectful, which was a good thing. If Chichi stepped out of line once, Sunny knew there was no way they could get her mother to agree to a sleepover.

"How is your mother?" Sunny's mother asked, looking Chichi over and sitting before them at the table.

"Oh, she's fine," Chichi said.

"Your mother and I went to the same secondary school."

"Oh, I didn't know that," Chichi said, frowning.

"Mhm," her mother said. "Asuquo was my senior by a year but we all knew her. She was good in literature and writing, like Sunny here."

"My mother doesn't talk very much about her school days," Chichi said sounding annoyed. "At least, not the ones here. She says school is—"

Sunny stepped on Chichi's foot.

Chichi smiled. "Oh, never mind."

Her mother's smile wavered. "What does your mother do now?"

Sunny pressed her foot harder on Chichi's foot.

"She—she teaches," Chichi said. "She teaches writing."

"Oh? Where?"

"There's a—small school in Aba," she said. "She teaches there."

"Well, that's very nice," her mother said. "Is this the school you attend?"

"Mama, her father's that famous musician Nyanga Tolotolo," Sunny blurted out.

"What?" her mother said, surprised. "Really?" Chichi nodded. "Sunny's father absolutely loves his music. I didn't know that!" Her mother looked more closely at Chichi, probably remembering the hut that Chichi lived in.

"Yes," Chichi said. "We are not in close contact with him, though. The most I have seen of him has been on his DVD, or in music videos and magazines."

"Oh, I'm sorry to hear that," her mother said. There was an awkward pause. "Well, there's some jollof rice and plantain. Take as much as you want." She got up. "It was good to finally meet you, Chichi. Greet your mother for me."

As she was leaving, Chichi said, "Excuse me, Mrs. Nwazue?"

She turned around. "Mhm?"

"Can Sunny stay at my house over the weekend?"

Her mother stood there for a moment.

"We will behave ourselves," Chichi added, with a winning smile. "I know how Sunny was late getting home the other day. It will not happen again."

Her mother looked shrewdly at Chichi. Then she said, "Make me a promise, then. Promise that—promise that you'll both behave and be responsible."

Sunny almost shivered at her mother's intensity. "We will, Mama," she said.

"Of course, ma," Chichi said.

Her mother stood there looking from Chichi to Sunny. She seemed to think for a moment, as if she was making a big decision. Then she nodded. "Make sure you return by Sunday, by dinner." The girls stood in silence as her mother filled a plate and left the room.

"What was that about?" Chichi asked. "She sounded like she was sending you to your death." Sunny just shook her head.

Chichi grabbed Sunny's shoulders. "You are going! This is going to be great!"

Sunny smiled, but still felt ill at ease.

"Whoo!" Chichi said, sitting down. "That felt like a job interview."

"Yeah," she said.

"Well, it's over. Cheer up, eh? Come on, let's eat! I'm so hungry." Chichi took a few mouthfuls. "Your mother cooks so well!" She paused. "Have you ever been to Abuja?"

"Shhh, lower your voice."

"Sorry," Chichi whispered, giggling.

"Twice. My aunt, my father's oldest sister lives there."

"I love Abuja," Chichi said. "The air is so dry and the National Mosque is lovely."

"And the roads aren't so bumpy."

Chichi laughed. "Yes o."

"So is there anything I'll have to do?" Sunny asked. "You know, like when I was initiated?" She shuddered, remembering the mud, dirt, and rushing river water.

"No," Chichi said. "But don't go and become lazy. You know what we have to do about Black Hat."

Sunny shuddered again. "Just—just tell me about this juju knife stuff."

"We go to this man called Junk Man and you buy one from him. It's simple." She smiled. "You'll see, don't worry."

Sunny hoped so.

CHAPTER TWELVE
ABUJA

It was Saturday morning and the sun was just getting into gear. The friends were part of a crowd waiting on the busy street in front of the path to Leopard Knocks. Sunny couldn't stop smiling. Since she was with Leopard people, there was no reason for her to pretend she needed her black umbrella. She was standing in the sunshine, just like everyone else. She'd considered asking Anatov why she was no longer light-sensitive, but really she didn't want to know.

"How long is this man going to keep us waiting?" a woman standing in the shade of a tree mumbled. She hissed with annoyance.

"*Kai*, no sense of time," a man in a suit muttered. The armpits of his jacket were already dark with sweat.

In the distance, Sunny spotted an ominous red cloud—the funky train, approaching at a ridiculous speed. "Wish you'd brought a box of tissues?" Sasha asked Sunny.

"Not funny," she said. She didn't tell him she actually had. This was going to be a snot fest.

The funky train was covered with sayings embellished with colourful loops and swirls. **Jesus Is Mine**; **No One But Christ!**;

The Blood Of God!; Nothing Bad!; Slow But Sure!; Life Is Short!; Jesus Save Us!" In the centre was a crude painting of a very white-faced blond-haired Jesus flashing the peace sign.

"Is this for Leopard people?" she whispered to Chichi. "Or Christian fanatics?"

Chichi only laughed. "It will change to different things about Allah when we enter Hausaland. And the Jesus painting will become a crescent moon and star. You know the saying—'When in Rome do as the Romans do.'"

The vehicle stopped abruptly in front of the crowd causing the car behind it to screech to a stop. Loud profanity-laced hip-hop blasted over the vehicle's sound system. The driver was a man who called himself Jesus' General. But Sunny suspected that there was little holy about him. She wondered if he changed his named to 'Allah's Captain' when they crossed into Hausaland. She laughed to herself.

"*Oya!* How many una dey?" Jesus' General shouted, getting out of the vehicle.

"Sir," said a stately woman, "does this nonsense piece of rubbish run on fuel?"

"Dis kin bus sef!" A man groaned a few steps away. He spat something in what Sunny thought was Yoruba and then threw his dusty backpack on the ground.

"Ah beg, no vex," Jesus' General protested humbly. "Na mix-mix bus be dis one. E de use small fuel, plenty juju, and plenty plenty of de power of God's will. Come, I no go disappoint una. Just enter bus, I go give una better price to reach de festival."

"Please! We will probably die from the fumes," a woman said. "Me, I'll wait for the next one."

Jesus' General waved an annoyed hand at the angry people and turned to Anatov.

"Anatov," Jesus' General said, shaking, slapping and snapping hands with him. "Am happy to see you, my man! No be small thing o."

"I swear!" Anatov said, putting an arm around the driver's shoulder. Anatov looked at them and said, "Get on," then turned back to Jesus' General. "*Oya*, talk now." They moved a few steps away, obviously to discuss prices. It took a while to find a seat because the long vehicle was mostly full. Sunny's backpack was slung over her shoulder and as they made their way to the back, it smacked a boy in the head. "Oh! I'm so sorry," she cried, patting his head. She snatched her hand away when she realised what she was doing. "Sorry," she said again.

Rubbing his head, the boy nodded. Her face grew hot. He was gorgeous. Of all people she could have bashed in the head, it had to be him. He gave her a reassuring smile. "No problem," he said. "I never faint, *abi*?"

She laughed and quickly moved on.

There were exactly five seats at the very back of the funky train. The chair in the centre was large, clean and throne-like with much more legroom than the others. It was obviously for Anatov. Chichi plopped down beside Sunny, Orlu, and Sasha on the other side of Anatov's seat. Not surprisingly, Sasha took the window seat.

"Young men wey strong *kakaraka!*" Jesus' General shouted from the front of the bus, "*Abeg* make una help us push de bus small."

Sunny almost laughed. Clearly, even a vehicle powered by juju needed a push so the driver could pop the clutch. Several men got up and went outside, including Anatov. Jesus' General got behind the wheel.

They pushed and pushed and the funky train began to roll. Finally, the engine popped, banged, and chugged. At the same time, she heard another noise that sounded more like wind blowing through the top of a dry palm tree. Blue lights running along the vehicle's walls and on the floor lit up. The air began to smell of flowers. Sunny sneezed and groaned.

They were officially on their way to the Zuma festival.

Anatov said they'd be staying at the Hilton, the biggest and most lavish hotel in the city. Even one of America's presidents had stayed there. Sunny was only able to relax when Anatov said that Leopard Knocks was paying for the room. She barely had enough money to afford two meals, and she doubted they'd take *chittim*.

It was going to be a very busy day. First they would get her juju knife. Then they'd attend the wrestling finals. After that, Anatov would attend a meeting of scholars from all over Africa. They'd have the rest of the day and evening all to themselves. "There's an 'arts and crafts' fair all day and a student social tonight," Anatov said. He looked at Orlu and Sasha and smiled. "And, as always, there's the Zuma Football Cup match around five o'clock."

Sunny frowned. Why didn't he look at her when he said this? She liked soccer, too. And she was good at it.

Their rooms were on the tenth floor of the Hilton. And they weren't just rooms—they had a suite! Orlu and Sasha had one room and Chichi and Sunny had another. The rooms were joined by a door. Anatov's room was farther down the hall. "We leave in an hour," he said. As soon as he was gone, they looked at each other and then howled with excited laughter.

"I can't believe I'm here!" Sunny screeched, throwing herself onto her bed.

"This hotel is toxic," Chichi said, chidingly as she looked out the window. Sunny joined her and for a moment, they both stared out at Abuja. Sunny could see the National Mosque perfectly. It looked like something out of a dream. Abuja as a whole looked like something out of a dream with its smooth roads, lush greenery and new-looking buildings. So different from home. Chichi sat on the bed and unwrapped one of the chocolates that had been placed on their pillow. She popped it in her mouth and said, "I think that is why Anatov is making us stay here."

"I thought you'd like it," Sunny said.

Chichi frowned at her. "Why?"

"Imagine the books they'll be selling at the festival," Orlu said, coming into their room and sitting on the cabinet beside the TV. Sasha went to look out their window.

"Bet there'll be a lot of hot girls there, too," Sasha said.

"There will be even more fine boys," Chichi said, giving him a look. "There are always more boys."

"Hey, don't go off with anyone," Orlu said. "We're not at home."

"I should say the same to you," Chichi said.

"I'm a man," Orlu said in total seriousness. "You're a girl. It's not the same."

Chichi scoffed.

"It's not," Sasha said with a shrug. "Anyway, Chichi, come here. Look at this."

"So what do you think of things so far?" Orlu asked Sunny. Behind them, Chichi and Sasha had started whispering to each other and snickering as they looked at Sasha's book.

"Ask me in a few days," Sunny said.

"I hate this hotel and everything it stands for," Orlu said. "This kind of over-extravagance when people are living so badly just outside the hotel; it's terrible."

"It's not all bad."

Orlu shook his head. Chichi and Sasha quickly shut Sasha's book. Sasha shoved it back into his bag.

"What are you guys up to?" Sunny asked.

Chichi wouldn't meet Sunny's eyes. "Sasha's just helping me out with—something. Nothing you and Orlu would be interested in."

"Sunny, you going to get in that soccer game with me?" Sasha asked. "Or football, I mean. Whatever you guys call it here."

"I still call it soccer, too," she said, laughing. "Part of my Americanness, I guess. You think I can play in the game?"

"Definitely. I've seen you handle the ball, man," he said. "Orlu, you in?"

"No, I'll watch with Chichi."

"So, they let girls play?" Sunny asked, tentatively.

"Doesn't matter," Sasha said. "You're playing."

They split up to bathe and change. Everyone wore their best. Sasha had on baggy jeans and a short-sleeved blue dress shirt. He paused to look at Chichi, who wore a bright green wrapper and matching top. "You look nice," he said. "You should dress up more often."

"It's ok, I only dress like this when there is a reason," Chichi said, but she looked pleased.

Sunny fidgeted. She knew she looked good in her navy blue dress trousers and blue top with orange and yellow designs, but it didn't really matter to her. "I hate dressing up," she said.

"It's ok I don't mind it," Orlu said. He wore a long light blue caftan and matching trousers. "But there are more important things."

The same funky train that dropped them off picked them up. It was a tenth of the size they'd left it in, even smaller than a van, and it was empty. There was a white throne for Anatov in the second row.

"Hey," Sasha asked, sitting behind Jesus' General. "What music you got?"

"I get de type of gam-gbam dim-dim music wey go shake the air." Jesus' General said. He and Sasha slapped hands. Sasha flipped through Jesus' General's CD collection.

Anatov sat in his seat, opened up the day's paper, and began to read. Chichi sat beside him and did the same. Orlu and Sunny went to the back. As they drove off, Sasha got the music going. He and the general bobbed their heads to the beat.

"Sunny," Orlu said. "Remember I told the two of you to be careful. Chichi knows her way around, but you are new, so you have to be extra careful."

"Sure," Sunny said, rolling her eyes. "So, did you and Chichi come to this together last year?"

"Yes," Orlu said.

"Your parents and Chichi's mother are friends?"

Orlu frowned and cocked his head. "Yes, well...in a way." He lowered his voice. "Chichi is not normal. She gets that strangeness from her mother. Her mother is really, really brilliant. She's an assistant to Sugar Cream and she's a Nimm priestess."

"What's—"

"Women who become Nimm priestesses are chosen when they are born. Their intelligence is tested before their mother is even allowed to hold them. If they pass, they are 'sold' to Nimm, a female spirit who lives in the wilderness."

"Like *Osu* people?" she asked, horrified. These were Igbo people sold as slaves to an Igbo deity.

"In a way. Nimm women aren't outcasts like the *Osu*," he said. "Nimm women all have 'Nimm' as a last name, and they are never allowed to marry. And they reject wealth."

"Is that why Chichi's father left?"

Orlu laughed bitterly. "No. I overheard my mother telling my auntie that he was one of the most selfish men she had ever met. He doesn't know that Chichi's mother is Leopard person, though." He paused. "I'm sure if he knew that he was not allowed to marry her mother, he would have fought to marry her."

"Oh," she said, realising something. "So Chichi's not pure Leopard?"

Orlu shrugged, "No one is 'pure.' We all have Lambs in our spiritline somewhere. Anyway, Nimm women are...somehow strange. My parents are friendly with her, but not friends."

There was a silence. Music drifted back from the front of the funky train.

"Orlu," Sunny finally said, glancing at Chichi who was reading her newspaper, "what do I...*do*?"

"What do you mean?"

"Am I supposed to keep all this stuff from my family for the rest of my life? Who can live like that? It's already weird. What do free agents do?"

"Well, for one, the pact we made prevents you from telling anyone about it," Orlu said. The trust knot, the symbols on the book, and the juju knife—it seemed like years ago, not just a few months. "I don't know, Sunny. But you know what?"

"What?"

"You really need to find out about your grandmother," he said. "Especially from your mother. You didn't inherit the spiritline from her, but maybe your mother knows more than you think."

Wuse Market was about ten minutes from the Hilton. Sunny hadn't expected them to go to a Lamb market, especially not this one. It was the first African market she had visited, a few months after her family had returned to Nigeria when they'd stayed with her aunt. Talk about culture shock!

American supermarkets were neat, the prices rigid, and everything was so sterile. At first, to her American eyes, Wuse Market seemed ripe, unpredictable, and loud. She'd been overwhelmed by what the market sold, and how the vendors sold it. Now that she knew better, she realised it was one of the nicest markets in Nigeria. It was clean, had brick stalls instead of wooden tables, open gutters that were relatively free of debris, and nice wide spaces between the shops.

After Anatov paid Jesus' General, they all went straight to a shaded part of the market. A crude roof of wooden planks was built over all the booths here.

"One man's junk is another man's money!" a man announced in a gruff voice. Junk Man. He had a look that practically screamed that he was far more than what he seemed. He was short and fat, his head shaven so close that it shone like a black bowling ball. In contrast, he had a bushy grey moustache and a long equally bushy grey-black beard. He wore a bronze ring on every finger. His cushioned chair creaked whenever he moved.

His booth was the same size as everyone else's, about twelve feet by twelve feet. Wooden dividers separated his shop from a utensil shop to his right and a basket shop to his left. But his place was packed! A narrow path led through his wares. He raised his fat hands and shouted, "Hey! Anatov!"

"Junk Man," Anatov said, as they vigorously shook hands. Junk Man's rings clicked loudly.

"That one?" Junk Man said, pointing at Sunny. Anatov nodded. "Ah, na albino now," he said. He smiled, and a dimple appeared on his left cheek. "*Oya*, make you come look. Make you no shame. But no any one of dem be for free o. Look am well-well before you buy. But make you no touch de things wey you know say you no suppose touch, especially those parrot him feathers. Those ones dey make people talk plenty-plenty. Dem go reach house, na so so talk dem go dey talk, and dem no fit answer why, na so-so nonsense talk dem go like to talk."

Sasha, Orlu, and Chichi were already looking around. Sunny had no idea what not to touch. There were so many items—most on tables, some on the ground or hanging from nails on the wooden dividers.

There were baskets; ebony and bronze statues; rings, necklaces, and anklets of various metals; piles of colourful stones and crystals; ancient looking coins; cowry shells the size of her pinky and larger than her head; scary and smiling ceremonial masks; a jar of gold powder; a pile of jewels and rusted daggers; bags of coloured feathers. An eight foot tall ebony statue of a stern-looking goddess watched from the far corner.

"Hey, you see this?" Sasha asked Chichi. The two huddled close around something. That snickering again.

Sunny stopped to look at a mask emitting a very foul odour.

"Sunny," Orlu said, "the knives are here."

They were piled in a beat-up cardboard box. Some had jewelled handles; others were made of metal, copper, bronze, or what looked like gold. Another looked like it was made of wood. Another was plastic.

"How do I—"

"Come, you be Americana?" Junk Man asked. Suddenly, he was right next to her.

She jumped. "Um—yeah, sort of. I was born there and lived there for nine years before we came back."

"You and him, na who senior who? Him?" he asked, pointing at Orlu.

Sunny shrugged. "Only by a few months."

"Dem born your parents for here?" he asked.

"Yeah," she said.

"Then you be from here and also from there. Two place, you *sabi*?"

She laughed. "If you say so."

"Na so."

"So what's that make me, then?" she asked.

"Dat one no concern anybody." he said. "Na juju knife you want, *abi*?"

She nodded, grinning. She liked Junk Man very much.

"*Oya*, close your eyes, put your hand inside there, collect one knife."

She shut her eyes. As she rummaged around, one of the knives cut her. "Ah!" She snatched her hand away and opened her eyes.

Junk Man immediately reached into the box. "E don land!" he said. The knife he brought out had a small smear of her blood on the blade. "Na wetin be this?" he quietly said, frowning.

She stared at it. "What is that?"

"Oh. Look at it," Orlu said.

"Is that the one that chose you?" Chichi asked, coming over.

"Oh, that's— uh, that's different," Sasha said.

Its handle was an unremarkable smooth silver, but the blade was paper-thin, made of a clear green material, like glass.

"Na one man from the north dash me dis after I buy many other knife from him," Junk Man said. "I no even see de man face becos he wear one thick veil wey cover him. But him eye fine like woman own and him voice sound very kind. Na voice dem dey take know as man nature go be. And na woman eye dem dey take know as her nature be. Dat one na true talk, *sha*. Anyway, see your knife o. Na de knife pick you, correct-correct. Na thirteen coppers last price."

They all gasped.

"That's crazy!" Chichi said.

Sunny frowned, annoyed. She had expected to pay three. "Do you want—"

"I *sabi* wetin you want and I *sabi* de thing wey want you," Junk Man said. "When na juju knife matter, I no dey talk price at all. This knife, na him choose you, so no other knife go choose you until this one destroy or spoil. If I like I for charge you one thousand *chittim,* and you no go fit do but to pay me."

Thankfully, Sunny had brought twenty copper *chittim*. She dug out thirteen while Junk Man polished the knife with a white cloth.

"Let me see," Anatov said to Junk Man when he'd finished with it. Anatov held it before him, pointing it straight ahead. He peered down the blade. "Nice."

"Lucky girl—maybe," Junk Man said. He looked at Sunny. "Come, put de *chittim* inside dat basket under de table." She dropped the *chittim* into the half full basket. "*Oya*, take am."

Slowly, she took the juju knife. She yelped and almost dropped it. Junk Man grinned. "Ah, na only that look for your face remain wey I need to see."

"Is—is this normal?" she asked, staring at her hand and the knife. It felt as if her hand and the knife had merged. She'd read about it in the juju knife book, but experiencing it was very different from reading about it.

"Yep," Anatov said. "It's a sensation best understood by experience."

She touched the tip of the knife. It was amazing—she felt it right through the knife. She tapped it lightly against the table. It was like tapping her finger.

"Now make you try something," Junk Man said.

"But I'm not that good at—"

"Call music," Chichi said. "That one isn't too hard."

Sunny did remember how to do it, but she was still nervous. "Tell me again."

"Cut down, twist your wrist, and then catch the invisible pouch," Chichi said. "Then speak the activation words into it: 'Bring music.'"

"All right," she whispered. She carefully cut the air and flicked her wrist as if tying the invisible pouch in a knot. The wet, cool juju pouch dropped into her hand. She smiled. "Bring music," she said into the pouch in English.

It wasn't classical music that came. It was fast, high-pitched guitar. Highlife music. Her father's favourite song by Nyanga Tolotolo. She laughed and grinned. She glanced at Chichi and was relieved to see her grinning, too. Two copper *chittim* fell to her feet.

"Ha! You see? It done dey pay for itself!" Junk Man shouted.

The loud music startled people, most of whom were Lambs and probably assumed it was coming from a boom box somewhere in Junk Man's booth. A woman passing by shimmied her shoulders a bit, and a man did a few dance steps. Seconds later, the music faded away.

"Well done," Anatov said.

"Your first juju charm by knife," Sasha said, patting her on the back. "You're a new woman."

"It's just the beginning," Chichi said.

"Come, take dis one also," Junk Man said handing her a small blue bean. A sound was coming from it. She held it to her ear. The thing was giggling! "Na *jara*. I dey always give my customers small-small gifts," he said.

"Thanks," she said, looking at the bean. "What is it?"

"Take am go home, put am for under your bed. Wait for some days."

"How much is this?" Sasha asked, holding up a polished brown conch shell the size of his hand.

"Hmm. Do you know what that does?" Anatov asked.

"Sure do," Sasha said. Anatov and Sasha exchanged a look.

"One copper, one silver," Junk Man said.

"How about one copper," Sasha said.

"*Oya*, bring money."

CHAPTER THIRTEEN
ZUMA ROCK

The funky train had miles to go, but already Sunny could see Zuma Rock. It was about two hundred feet high, the size of a football field, and dark as a humongous piece of charcoal. At its centre was what looked like a crude, gigantic white face.

Sunny's mother had brought her to see it during their visit three years ago. The man who gave them a tour said it was believed that Zuma Rock possessed mystical powers. He said anyone who climbed or went too close to it would never be seen again.

Zuma Ajasco, the Abuja Leopard headquarters, was set right at the foot of Zuma Rock, hidden from Lambs by powerful old juju. This was where the festival took place, too. Now the Zuma Rock myth made sense to Sunny.

About a mile from the rock, they turned onto a narrow road. People walking on it had to scramble aside to avoid getting run over. Most of them were dressed in different kinds of traditional attire but some wore jeans, trousers, and dresses, too.

When the festival came into sight, Sunny wasn't sure if she was more in awe of its sheer hugeness or of Zuma Rock itself. The festival grounds were the size of seven football fields, partially in the rock's shadow on the other side of the highway. Because of the rock, passersby wouldn't have seen the festival even if there wasn't strong juju hiding it.

"How come Zuma Ajasco isn't the central West African headquarters instead of Leopard Knocks?" The moment the words were out, Sunny wanted to take them back. Anything to avoid the look Anatov gave her.

"In 1992, they made Abuja the capital of Nigeria instead of Lagos. Now the scholars of Zuma Ajasco think that that Abuja should also become the Leopard central headquarters of West Africa instead of Leopard Knocks," Anatov said. "Bullsh— nonsense. Leopard Knocks has been Leopard Knocks for over a millennium. To move it would dislocate all that they hold dear."

He paused. When he continued, he sounded less angry. "I want you to know this now, before you all officially enter the extravagance of Zuma Ajasco. The idea of what is appropriate and respectable differs amongst scholars. The people are like people anywhere, but the scholars are the leaders. If they are rotten, things can go very wrong.

"Zuma Ajasco has only two scholars. You'll know Madame Koto when you see her. I'll introduce you if the chance arises. You can't miss her; she's a descendent of the ancient line of Tall Men. She's also quite...wide. People say she eats five-course meals four times a day. It's believed she secretly owns one of the world's biggest oil companies; no one knows which one. When you see her, she'll be surrounded by very attractive men, none of whom she is married to. She refuses to marry on principle.

"Then there's Ibrahim Ahmed. He might be a hundred and twelve, but he looks as if he's lived for over three hundred years.

He has fifteen wives, owns a hundred-and-fifty-room mansion that changes shape and location every five months, and is rumoured to be working with some Iraqis to break the physical plane between Earth and Jupiter. It's also rumoured that he's dined in the White House many times with various American presidents. He makes his money in oil. You see the problem?"

Sunny did. These didn't sound like Leopard scholars, who were supposed to live by the philosophy of modesty and only be interested in *chittim* and the welfare of the people.

"These fools passed the fourth level?" Sasha looked sceptical.

"Oh, those two aren't fools," Anatov said. "No, no, no. And yes, they've passed the fourth level. They're capable of great things, but potential doesn't equal success."

Jesus' General pulled the funky train up to the festival entrance, which was marked by a red wooden arch, and they got off.

The arch was huge, and carved to look like braided plants—but as the breeze blew, the wooden plants swayed with it. Lurking at the arch's peak was a life-size wooden leopard. It inspected all who entered. Sometimes it sat up, stretched, and even growled. Mainly it crouched and watched.

"It watches for Lambs," Anatov said. "That great piece of juju was brought here for the festival by one of the scholars from Cameroon."

Sunny felt sick. What did it do when it spotted a Lamb? It may have been wooden, but it looked alive. And hungry. She wasn't a pure Leopard person. Would it sniff the Lamb-ness on her skin? She walked as close to Anatov as she could. Her legs felt like boiled cassava. They passed under the arch. All the while the leopard stared intensely, specifically at her.

"It's watching me," she whispered to Chichi.

Chichi laughed. "Maybe it thinks you look tasty."

Sunny held its stare as they passed. The leopard growled deep in its throat. It turned around to watch her once they were through. Minutes passed before she stopped expecting it to come bounding through the crowd to tear her apart.

The festival grounds were paved with cobblestone, and there was highlife, hip-hop, and jazz playing from three different stages. There were booths selling food and souvenirs, and there were tons and tons of people. She must have heard over fifty different languages. She saw a group of children crowded around a man claiming to have gone to the moon; a large tent with a cross in the front that said, **The Leopard Society of the Lord**; another where she heard hundreds reading from the Koran.

People used juju to light their cigarettes, push baby carriages, and block out cigarette smoke (she needed to learn that one). She even saw some kids batting a *tungwa* around. As it floated inches from the ground, they dared each other to kick it. The brown skin ball finally exploded on an unlucky boy and all the others laughed and pointed.

"Let's get something to eat," Anatov said. The wrestling match wasn't for another forty-five minutes.

The food was the usual, and Sunny was grateful. She ordered a large bowl of okra soup and *eba* and a bottle of Fanta. It was hot, spicy, and good. But, as she sat at the table with the others, that feeling of being completely out of her element crept back in. Suddenly, she felt claustrophobic, drowning in the unfamiliar and unpredictable. "Where do you think the bathroom is?" she asked, wiping her hands with a napkin.

"On the other side of that booth," Chichi said, pointing.

She got up before Chichi could say anything about coming with her. She needed a moment alone. There was a long line. She tried to hold back tears. Still, a few harmless tears were better than picking a fight or destroying things. She walked past the bathroom and came to an open field of dry grass. After making sure no one was around, she broke down sobbing.

"Excuse me, are you all right?" someone asked in strangely-accented English.

When she looked to the side, she started. Then she wanted to cry some more. More strangeness. The man wasn't just tall; he was like a human tree. He had to be over seven feet. He wore a long yellow caftan with a heavily-embroidered neckline and yellow pants. He was dark, black-skinned like some of the yam farmers back home who worked in the sun all day.

She just stared at him. Instead of getting annoyed, he smiled. It was the brightest, warmest smile she'd ever seen, and she couldn't help smiling back. He handed her a yellow handkerchief.

"Thanks," she said, looking at it. "Are you sure, I—"

He gave her the beautiful smile again and said, "My gift to you."

She blew her nose into it and looked up at him. She figured she owed him some sort of explanation, but all she could say was, "I— I'm a free agent." She felt so stupid.

"Oh, I see," he said, understandingly. He put his arms behind his back and looked at the field. She followed his eyes, straightening up and putting her hands behind her back, too. He just had this aura about him that said, "Whatever I do is good."

"I found out only months ago," she said. "My teacher brought me here with my other, um, classmates."

"Who's your teacher?" he asked.

"Anatov," she said. "The Defender of Frogs and All Things Natural."

"He still uses that title?" He laughed. "Brother Anatov earned it years ago when he first came to Nigeria from America. The man used to shout and shout about being a vegetarian and how frogs were the thermometers of the Earth. I know him well. Good man," he said. "You are from Leopard Knocks, then."

She nodded.

"Well, let me tell you this," he said. "You're neck-deep in Leopard society right now. The good thing is that it doesn't get any deeper than this. Sometimes it's best to just jump in. Then, after that first shock, you can handle anything."

"Yeah," she said, wiping her eyes again. "I—I got my juju knife today, too."

"That's wonderful," he said. He looked down at her. "Use it well and true. There are more valuable things in life than safety and comfort. Learn. You owe it to yourself. All this"—he motioned around them—"you will get used to in time."

He patted her on the head, and walked away. She held the handkerchief to her chest. Only when she turned around did she realise a crowd had gathered to watch them.

They had really good seats for the match.

Within the hour, the open field was filled with rows and rows of folding chairs. There was a large area in the centre for the match. Within minutes, the chairs were all taken. It looked like everyone at the festival was here.

They sat in a special section in the left front specifically for the scholars and their chosen students. On the way to their seats, Anatov introduced them to Madame Koto. He had described her perfectly. In height, she easily rivalled the man that she'd spoken with. But where he was stick-thin, Madame Koto was very, very fat. She was surrounded by three very attractive men, each wearing an expensive designer suit and a smug smile. They treated Madame Koto like their queen.

Madame Koto looked down at the four of them and haughtily said, "It's good to meet you." Then she made for her seat with her three men in tow. Two boys and two girls, presumably her students, also followed. They looked at Sunny, Chichi, Sasha, and Orlu with great interest but Madame Koto didn't introduce them.

Sugar Cream was there, too, sitting with a group of very old men near the back of the special section. They were having an animated discussion, and didn't seem interested in the wrestling match at all. They stopped talking when Anatov brought Sunny, Chichi, Sasha, and Orlu to say, "Hi." The old men didn't return the greeting, instead staring at the four of them like they had sprouted wings.

Today Sugar Cream wore a long, silky, European style cream-coloured dress and several cream-coloured bangles that clacked whenever she moved her arms. "Chichi, Sasha, Orlu. It's wonderful to finally meet you." She only gave Sunny a stern look before moving on. Sunny felt like a dirty dishrag.

The old men finally broke out of their staring trance and introduced themselves. Sugar Cream had to translate. They were from the Ivory Coast and Liberia.

"How many languages does Sugar Cream speak?" Sasha asked Anatov as they sat down.

"At least ten," Anatov said. "Probably more."

"What about you?"

"Who knows?" Anatov said. "Who's counting?"

"Where are Taiwo and Kehinde?" Orlu asked.

"Home, of course," Anatov said. "Someone had to hold down the fort."

There were several other students with their teachers, some Sunny's age, most older. One boy, the student of a scholar from Ghana, knew Chichi and Orlu.

"Long time," he said.

"Not long enough," Chichi said.

"You, I will make sure I flog you tonight," the boy said pointing at her.

"You can try. But you know you are just talking," Chichi said playfully, but Sunny detected a real threat behind her words. "Oh, by the way, these are my new classmates, Sunny and Sasha. You know Orlu. Sunny, Sasha—this, unfortunately, is Yao."

Yao and Sasha looked each other up and down. *Instant tension there*, Sunny thought. "Isn't Sasha a woman's name?" Yao asked with a smirk.

"Do I know you?" Sasha asked. "Because you obviously don't know me."

"Ah, American," Yao said.

"Can't you tell, jackass?" Sasha said.

"All right, enough of that," Anatov said, pushing Yao towards his teacher. "Save that for the social tonight."

"Who the hell is that?" Sasha asked Chichi, still shocked at Yao's nerve.

"He's the one I was telling you about," Chichi said. "You know, what we discussed."

"Oh, I see," Sasha said. "A'ight, we'll handle that later then." Chichi nodded.

"What did you discuss? 'Handle' what?" Orlu asked. Chichi and Sasha just laughed. "Ah, this is going to get crazy. I can feel it."

A regal woman briskly walked onto the field. She brought out her juju knife and Sunny nearly screamed with horror as she dragged it across her throat. Then she remembered where she was. There was no blood, not even a cut.

"My name is Mballa and I will be your commentator this fine day," the woman said in a highly amplified voice. "Welcome to the two hundred and forty-sixth annual Zuma International Wrestling Finals. Make sure to notice our sponsors who have worked sponsorship jujus on your seats. Remember their names when you go to our vendors to ease that mysterious craving. Special thanks, of course, to Abuja's own Madame Koto and Ibrahim Ahmed for making all this happen.

"Now we all know that this year's finalists have come a long way to get here. Fifty undefeated victories each and both have passed the seven Obi Library tasks to get here. These are two truly gifted men o!"

The entire audience recited the next thing she said. "This is the final test of brains and brawn, so let them show and prove!" Everyone burst into applause, howls, and cheers. People stamped their feet and pumped their fists in the air. Then the drumming began. Sunny looked around. She didn't see anyone with drums.

"These two warriors are the greatest West Africa has to offer," Mballa said dramatically. "Kind, generous, loving, loyal, both of these men would give their lives for Africa without a thought. Both of these men know when one must stand up and fight. They are what Western society fears most.

"On this side, from the country of Burkina Faso, comes *Saaaaayé!*"

The crowd burst into noise as Sayé, a brawny brown-skinned man of about forty, jogged and bounced around the arena. Orlu leaned towards Sunny's ear and said, "You see that leather sleeve he's wearing?"

She nodded.

"When he was young, he was hit by a car and they had to amputate his arm."

"So his arm is fake?" she asked.

"It's more complicated than that," Orlu said. "He was born with this...ability that was only discovered when the accident happened."

"On this side," the commentator continued, "from the country of Mali, comes *Miiikniiikstiiic!*"

The crowd shouted again as a very, very tall black man ran in. Sunny recognised him—he was the man she'd talked to an hour ago. No wonder a crowd had been gathering!

"Miknikstic can see into the near future," Orlu said into her ear. "About five seconds. So he will know all of Sayé's moves before he makes them! They're as evenly matched as I've ever seen."

"But if these two guys are so great, why are they fighting each other?" she asked. Orlu just shushed her. "It's an old West African Leopard tradition," was all he said. She sat back. At least she knew who she was rooting for.

The opponents stepped up to each other and warmly shook hands.

"Rules," Mballa said. She spoke more to the audience than the competitors. "One. Stay in the arena at all times. The arena ends six metres above the ground. Two. You can only use your natural abilities—no powders, dusts, juju knives, et cetera. Three. This is hand-to-hand. Whatever your ability, the fight must remain so. No mental or spiritual manipulation is to be used against your opponent. The powers who watch over you will decide what the winner wins. Good luck and may Allah help you." She threw down what looked like a flat black stone and quickly left the arena. She took a seat in the front, two rows away from them.

The two men circled each other, Miknikstic crouching low and Sayé moving sideways. The drums beat a steady rhythm. The men ran at each other. When their bodies collided, the crowd shouted, "Wah!"

They grasped each other's shoulders, their muscles flexing as they tried to throw each other down. But, as Orlu had said, they were evenly matched. They grabbed each other, let go, and grabbed again. Sayé's leather sleeve bulged more and more as the fight intensified. Mik.nikstic pushed Sayé back. Sayé paused then grabbed the zipper of his sleeve. He pulled.

"Now they start!" Mballa announced. "Mik.nikstic crouches low as Sayé prepares to give him the worst."

The zipper caught a little on Sayé's sleeve and he looked down, but even before this, Mik.nikstic was in motion, quickly moving to the side and lunging at Sayé. Sayé had barely ripped the sleeve off when Mik.nikstic threw a hard punch at his head.

"Wah!" the audience shouted.

"Look at that!" Sasha screamed, standing up.

Sunny wanted to close her eyes. But she didn't. She knew that no matter what she did, the fight would continue.

Sayé staggered several steps and fell. Everyone in the crowd stood up and started shouting.

"Ah! Get up o!"

"Brilliant!"

"*Chineke!*"

"Why did I bet on that man?"

"Allah will protect you! But only if you get up!"

"Use your ghost arm, you idiot!"

Mik.nikstic didn't prance about talking trash as Muhammad Ali did in old TV footage. Nor did he spit on Sayé, gesticulate, taunt, beat his chest, or laugh, as they did in pro wrestling. Instead, Mik.nikstic stood over Sayé, looking down at him, waiting for him to get up or call it a match.

Sayé slowly got up. Miknikstic was ready. He must have seen what was coming next because he did everything he could to block it.

"Oh my goodness!" Sunny shouted when she saw Sayé's right arm. It seemed to be made of a blue substance somewhere between water and mist. At first it was shaped like an arm, but as Sayé rushed at Miknikstic, it shifted and morphed.

Miknikstic held his arms up to block it, but it kept changing shape. It split in two. Miknikstic threw himself to the side. Sayé's arm missed Miknikstic's head by a fraction of an inch. Miknikstic tumbled and then quickly got up.

"I think I'm going to be sick," Sunny muttered. She'd just spoken to Miknikstic, and now he was out there fighting for his life. He'd been so kind to her.

Sayé landed a punch, sending Miknikstic flying and the crowd to its feet again. Sunny pressed her hands to the sides of her face. "No, no, no!"

"That was a heavy blow. Is he dead?" the commentator asked.

"No. He still moves. Miknikstic is getting up. He spits out a tooth. Brushes himself off."

Sunny shut her eyes and jammed her index fingers into her ears to block out the commentator's gleeful descriptions. She sat like this for minutes, listening to herself breathe and the muffled sound of the crowd.

"Okay," she finally said to herself. Her voice was loud with her ears plugged. "We'll be going home after this, so—take it in. Even if it hurts. Miknikstic would be proud."

Slowly, she opened her eyes. When she saw the two opponents, her vision blurred with tears. They were bleeding profusely, and neither would give up. She looked around at everyone. It was as if they'd become actual leopards, leopards who smelled blood. They were shouting and laughing and encouraging—nostrils, mouths, and eyes wide, trying to take it all in in as many ways as possible.

The only people who seemed calm were the scholars, who sat stiffly and clapped once in a while. Anatov had stopped getting up whenever Sayé or Miknikstic fell. His face was unsmiling and stern. Sunny, Sasha, Orlu, and Chichi were the only students who had stopped enjoying the spectacle. Chichi was frowning. Orlu had a stunned, blank look on his face. Sasha looked angry and glared at the commentator whenever one of the competitors fell, as if waiting for her to put a stop to it.

Miknikstic was wrestling with Sayé's ghost arm, which kept escaping his grasp. A part of it extended away from Miknikstic. It threw a punch at Miknikstic's chest. Miknikstic doubled over but didn't fall. He wiped the blood from his face. Sayé took the moment to spit out a tooth.

Suddenly, Miknikstic's face undulated.

"What the hell?" was all Sunny could say.

His face had become a wooden square mask. It looked like a robot—if a robot were made of wood. The crowd gasped in shock.

"Oh, Jesus," Chichi said, looking away.

Sayé brought forth his spirit face, too—a grey stone face of a lion.

"And now they are down to it," Mballa said. "The blood is flowing and the true selves emerge. Don't turn away, people. These are two truly noble and selfless men."

They went at each other again. This time, their spirit selves took the lead. Miknikstic lumbered forward, and Sayé leaped. Miknikstic dodged Sayé, rolled around him, and grabbed his arm. He yanked. There was a loud *crack*, and Sayé's good arm was dislocated from its socket. Sayé gave a mighty roar, rolled over Miknikstic, and drove his ghost hand right through Miknikstic's chest.

A silence fell over the crowd. Sunny clapped her hand over her mouth.

Miknikstic fell to his knees, gushing blood. Sunny whimpered, tears rushing into her eyes. She wiped them away.

He whispered something to Sayé, and then fell to the ground. He was dead.

It started raining *chittim* on the field. As they fell, Sayé straightened out Miknikstic's body. Not one *chittim* hit either of them. Sunny would never forget the metallic clacking. When the *chittim* stopped, Mballa the commentator found her voice. It cracked as she said, "Bow down to this Year's Zuma International Wrestling Cha—"

Miknikstic suddenly got up. He gazed up at the sky as brown feathered wings unfurled from his back. He crouched down and then leaped, shooting into the sky like a rocket.

"Oh, praise Allah! What a fight this was tonight!" Mballa shouted. "We have witnessed yet another fallen wrestling competitor become a guardian angel! People give our new champion, Sayé, and Saint Miknikstic a hand! Oh, this is just amazing! Amazing! Ah-ah!" She started clapping. The whole crowd could hear her soft sobs because she'd forgotten her voice was still amplified.

"I want to go home!" Sunny shouted, getting up. Anatov reached over his chair and grabbed her by the collar. "Let go! I hate this, I hate all of this! You people are crazy!"

Chichi stared at her feet. Sasha was furious. Orlu took Sunny's hand. Anatov let go. Orlu pulled Sunny to him into a tight hug, and she sobbed into his chest.

"Keep her there," Anatov said. "I have to go with the other scholars."

Still holding on to Orlu, Sunny watched as Anatov joined the scholars walking into the arena. A woman ran in screaming. Another tall woman with long dreadlocks slowly followed.

"Ladies and gentlemen, meet Sankara, wife of Sayé and architect of the Leopard Town of Zerbo—and meet Kadiatou, wife of Saint Miknikstic and warrior of the Women of the Cliffs," Mballa said. "Please give them a round of applause."

The crowd thundered with applause as Sankara threw her arms around Sayé, wiping his bloody face with her garments. Kadiatou, Miknikstic's wife, just stood there in the middle of the arena looking up at the sky.

"Now the scholars will help heal Sayé, so please don't worry about our champion. He will be fine. The match is over," Mballa said out of breath. "I hope you enjoyed the show." She ran her juju knife across her throat again and then just sat there.

They watched as people left, talking excitedly about the match. In the arena, the scholars had surrounded Sayé, who now lay on the ground. Sunny couldn't see what they were doing, exactly. Miknikstic's wife stood in the middle of the arena, gazing at the sky. No one comforted or congratulated her.

Sunny pulled away from Orlu and, without a word, pushed some chairs aside. "What are you doing?" he asked.

She jumped into the arena and ran as fast as she could. She passed the group of scholars surrounding Sayé. They were humming and something was swooping about. She focused on Miknikstic's wife. She was a lot taller up close. She wore a long dress made of the same yellow material as Miknikstic's outfit, her long dreadlocks tied with a matching cloth. Sunny stepped up to her. She could smell the woman's scented oil, like jasmine flowers. "Excuse me, Mrs.—"

"I am not 'Mrs.' anymore," she said, her back to Sunny.

"I'm sorry."

"It's what he'd always known he would become. He's dreamed about it since he was a baby. But he didn't know it would be so soon."

Sunny began to feel as if she was imposing on the woman's grief.

"I—I met your husband just before the match," she ventured. "I'm a free agent and I just found out a few months ago and here I am now. I was upset because I was overwhelmed." She paused. "He saw me and he...he talked to me and made me feel better. He gave me this." She held up the yellow handkerchief. Miknikstic's wife still didn't turn around. "I just wanted to tell you how grateful I am to him."

Silence. Sunny turned to leave.

"Wait," Kadiatou said, turning to Sunny. She had a wide nose, round eyes, and two dark squiggles tattooed on each cheek. She wore a thick metal bracelet around each wrist. "Thank you," she said. "My husband was a good person, but he picked and chose who he spoke to." She clicked her bracelets together and they produced a large blue spark. "You have my blessing, too, child." She tilted her head back to the sky.

Sunny put the handkerchief back in her pocket and hurried over to Orlu, who stood a few feet away.

"So you met him?" he asked.

"Yeah, when I went to the bathroom."

They walked past where Sayé still lay. He was groaning and his wife was sobbing, "It will be okay, it will be okay, my love! Be still."

"He'll be fine," Anatov said, walking over to them.

"Now I know why my parents never brought me to watch," Orlu said.

"This one was especially...eventful."

"Why didn't they stop it?" Sasha asked.

"Because life doesn't work that way," Anatov said. "When things get bad, they don't stop until you stop the badness—or die." He paused. "That's an important lesson for all of you. This is why I brought you all here. This is why you're staying in that hotel. Look around, listen and learn. This is *not* a holiday. In a month, you all will be facing something as ugly as what these two men faced this afternoon."

O

CHAPTER FOURTEEN
THE FOOTBALL CUP

Anatov left for his meeting and they were free until 11pm. There were things to buy, the possibility of a football match, and a social for the students. But they had just witnessed death. And then something beyond death. They returned to the same booth where they'd bought lunch and ordered glasses of very weak sweet palm wine. It was the only type the vendors would sell to anyone underage. The four of them sat in brooding silence and sipped their drinks.

"Let's cheer up," Chichi said, suddenly. "We are in Abuja without our parents and it's not even two o'clock!" She pinched Sunny's thigh and, after a moment, Sunny smiled. "Okay, okay," she said, pushing Chichi's hand away.

"Man, this place is wild," Sasha said looking around. Someone stood on a box, belting out a song in Arabic. A man walked by on shiny red metal stilts trying to make children laugh. A group of old women and men was at a table arguing as they threw down cards. "I'll bet there's a lot we could get into if we just look around. Where's that art fair?"

"Somewhere that way," Orlu said, pointing towards the man on stilts. "And we are not going to 'get into' anything while we are here."

"Yo, you need to relax," Sasha said, annoyed.

A boy of about nine walked up to their table. "Do either of you want to join the football match?" He spoke only to Orlu and Sasha.

"Yeah," Sasha said. "Put me on the list. Name's Sasha." He pointed to Sunny. "Put her on, too."

The boy frowned. "I don't think—"

"You don't think *what*?" Sasha asked, leaning menacingly towards the boy.

The boy looked adequately scared. "Well...she's a girl."

"So?"

"What about him?" the boy said, pointing at Orlu. "He can play instead."

"Nah, man," Sasha said. "Put her name down. If they ask you, just say she's a dude. My name's girly, and I'm a guy. So same with 'Sunny,' got it? We'll deal with the consequences when the time comes, not you."

"O-okay," the boy said, writing her name on the list.

"When's the game?" Sasha asked.

"In one hour," he said. He reached into his satchel. "Here are your uniforms. Both of you will be on the green team."

"Woohoo!" Sunny yelped when the boy had left. "I can't wait!"

They both ran to the public restrooms to change. She was glad to get out of her dressy clothes and take off her earrings. Thankfully, she'd worn sandals; if she'd worn dress shoes, she'd have had to play barefoot. She ran out to Orlu and Chichi, and kicked her leg up as if she were scoring the biggest goal ever. "Gooooooooooal!" she shouted. "I hope they let me play."

"Sasha will scare them into it," Chichi said confidently.

"Maybe not," Orlu said. "The boys you will be playing will be older. I have seen the football match. They are unplanned, but brutal."

"What do you mean, brutal?" Sunny asked, frowning.

"They are not like the wrestling match," Orlu quickly said. "Brutal like a good football match."

She relaxed some and shrugged. "I'm playing. I don't care."

"You sure are," Sasha said, throwing his rolled-up clothes on the bench and sitting down.

"Well, I can't wait," Chichi said. "I've never seen you play."

"I've never really played," she said, smiling. "I mean, I've played with my brothers, but only after dusk. I've been itching to play for years. I don't care if it's against boys or if they stick me in defence. I want to be out there."

"Oh, you're not gonna be our defence," Sasha said. "We've kicked the ball around some. You've got killer footwork and aim. *You're* playing centre forward."

"Centre forward?" she exclaimed. She laughed. "Please. They'll never—"

"Let me handle it," Sasha said. "You just prove me right."

Sunny and Sasha decided to go for a warm-up jog and see if they could meet up with the other players.

"We're going to check out some of the shops," Chichi said. "We'll see you on the field."

Orlu slapped and grasped Sunny's hand, then did the same to Sasha. "Be cool," he said.

The game was in the same field as the wrestling match. Sunny didn't like the idea of playing soccer where someone had just died. Still, when they got there, everything from the match was already cleared away; it looked as if nothing had happened. A boy was walking around the goals inspecting the bright, crisp white lines.

"The lines," she said, looking over the field. "They look so perfect."

"They have a little machine to help," Sasha said. "Let's jog."

After the first lap, she realised the field was really uneven. There were rocks sticking out and small holes probably made by snakes or rodents. This was going to be a challenge for everyone, not just her.

"Who's your favourite soccer player?" Sasha asked as they jogged.

"Pelé," she said. "You know, during the Biafran War—that's the Nigerian civil war back in the sixties—the Nigerian and Biafran sides stopped fighting for two days to watch him play."

"Really?"

"Yep. As one man, he stopped all the killing. He was *that* good."

"So you like playing forward, like he did?"

"Well, as far as I know," she said. "I haven't had much real experience."

"I wish we had a ball to kick around," he said.

"You know, I think I saw a *tungwa* floating around over there," she said. They both laughed so hard they had to slow down.

More boys joined them as they ran. Nobody spoke, but those in white uniforms congregated at one side of the field, those wearing green at the other. An audience slowly gathered, too. Most of them were teenagers.

"Green team over here!" a tall guy said. He looked about seventeen, and wore a green uniform and nice football shoes, one of which he rested on a beat-up ball.

"Hey," she said to Sasha as they walked over. "He was on our funky train."

Sasha raised his eyebrows.

"I hit him in the head by accident with my bag when we were getting on. He's Igbo." *And gorgeous*, she added to herself.

He had a clipboard. The boy who had taken their names stood behind him. He made eye contact with Sunny and quickly looked away.

"My name is Godwin," the older boy said in English. "I'm captain of the team this year." He paused. "Do you all understand me? Who understands English?"

Everyone raised a hand except for three boys.

"No English?" Godwin asked them.

"*Français,*" one of the boys said.

The boy next to him nodded and said, "*Oui, je parle français, aussi.*"

"*Moi aussi,*" the third boy said.

She wondered where they were from. They didn't seem to know each other, so most likely they were from three different French-speaking African countries.

"I speak French," a stocky boy of about fifteen spoke up.

"Good," Godwin said. "What's your name?"

"Tony."

Godwin nodded. "Translate. I'm going to call names, tell me where you're from and your age." As Tony translated, Godwin looked at his clipboard. "Mossa?"

One of the French speakers stepped forward.

"My name is Mossa and I'm from Mali," Tony translated. "I'm twelve years old."

Godwin looked the boy over. He kicked the ball to Mossa.

"Dribble it and then kick it into the goal as hard as you can. Aim it into the left side," Godwin said.

Tony translated. Mossa jumped into action. When he dribbled the ball, he almost tripped over it. He kicked it with all his might and it flew over the right side of the goal, along with his shoe.

Sunny pinched Sasha's arm as they both tried not to laugh. A few of the taller boys held nothing back and bellowed with laughter. Mossa looked embarrassed and quickly ran to get the ball and his shoe.

"Kouty?" Godwin said.

"I am from Nigeria," he said. "I am fourteen years old," he said.

"Good to see you again." Godwin looked him over. "I know how you play. What do you want to play this year?"

"Goalkeeper."

Godwin laughed and shook his head. "That position is filled. What else?"

"Centre-back."

Godwin nodded. "That's what I had in mind." He looked at his clipboard. "Sasha?"

Sasha pushed through his teammates and stood before Godwin with a smirk on his face. "I'm from the United States of America. I'm fourteen."

Godwin looked him over. "What are you doing in Nigeria?"

"Parents sent me to live with family friends—to keep me out of trouble."

"This one is going make sure we are slapped with penalties," Godwin said to the rest of the team.

Everyone laughed, including Sasha. "Do what I asked Mossa to do."

Sasha took the ball, dribbled, and then kicked it as hard as he could into the goal. It went in, but through the centre instead of the left side.

"That's not bad," Godwin said writing something down. "Agaja."

The tallest and brawniest of them all stepped forward. Sunny imagined the ground shaking with his every move. He had a shiny bald head and the most muscular legs she had ever seen. "I'm from Benin," Agaja said in a deep voice. One of his front teeth was chipped. "I'm eighteen."

"Dribble and kick it into the goal, right side," Godwin said.

Agaja's feet were lightning fast, whirling and juggling the ball, making it obey his every whim and then POW!—he blasted it dead into the right side of the goal. They all clapped.

"That's encouraging," Godwin said with a grin. He looked at his clipboard and paused. "Sunny?"

She moved past the staring boys. She felt like she was in slow motion.

"Uh-uh," Godwin said, shaking his head. "No girls."

"Do you want to win?" Sasha cut in. "Because I've been watching that other team. Most of them are over sixteen. Look at them."

They all did. Those in white were all not only older, but a lot bigger. Whoever had gone around searching for players had taken it more seriously than the boy from the green team.

"*Kai!*" Godwin said. "I should not have allowed my brother to do it." He gave the boy a dirty look. Godwin hissed and said, "That's even less reason to allow a girl on the team."

"Why not?" she demanded.

"Because you're a girl," Agaja said in his monster voice. "It's simple." Several of the others agreed.

"So?"

"Give her the test," Sasha said. "It's stupid to judge without knowing what you're judging."

Godwin threw the soccer ball hard at Sunny. She caught it and glared at him. Then she turned and glared at all of them. *Idiots*, she thought. "What do you want me to do?" she asked Godwin.

"Agaja," Godwin said, "go and stand in front of the goal. No, better yet, I will." He handed his clipboard to his brother. "Agaja, you play defender."

She watched Godwin walk to the goal and Agaja position himself in front of him. Her palms were sweaty. Godwin bent into a ready position. "Okay, Sunny," he said. "Get the ball past us."

She dropped the ball, placed her foot on it, and glanced at Sasha. He looked nervous, but nodded his head in encouragement. She began dribbling. The motion warmed and soothed her body. It felt so good to kick a soccer ball out in the open, under the sun. She dribbled, weaving left and right as she worked to avoid Agaja and move the ball towards Godwin—her feet flew faster, forward, back a half-step, forward, diagonally, in a circle around the ball, faking to the right. She got the ball past Agaja and he grunted in frustration. She danced with the ball the way she danced over the tree bridge to Leopard Knocks. She felt her spirit face stir just behind physical her face. But she had her in control and kept her there.

She brought her foot back and fired the kick. The ball flew to the far right. Godwin jumped, his eyes wide, his mouth open. It was almost in. Almost. Then Godwin managed to tip it away just in time. He fell onto his side.

She slowed down, putting her hands on her hips. She looked down, ashamed that she hadn't made the goal.

"*Na wa o!*" she heard one of the team members say, impressed. She looked up.

"Man!" another cried. "*Ah-ah*, did you see that?"

One of the French speakers excitedly said something in French. Agaja patted her on the shoulder, "Not bad."

Godwin rose. He walked up to Sunny and just stared.

"See?" Sasha said, grinning.

"Yes o," he said, taking the clipboard from his brother. "Okay."

Sunny was all smiles. "I'm almost thirteen," she said. "And I'm—I was born in America but both my parents are Nigerian and I've lived in Nigeria since I was nine..."

"So you're Nigerian?" Godwin said, frowning, unsure what to write down.

"No," Sasha said. "American."

"Whatever you want to put," she said. She was just glad to play.

There were eleven of them in all. Godwin was goalkeeper. Sasha was assigned centre half. Sunny was centre forward. Her accomplices, the left and right wings, were the two other best and oldest and biggest boys on the team, Ousman and Agaja. As they stretched, she looked up and was surprised at the size of the audience that had gathered. It was huge—more than half the size of the one for the wrestling match.

"Hey, Godwin. Are you ready?" the other team captain asked.

"Yes," he said. "Give us two minutes."

They huddled. "Is everyone here?" Godwin asked.

They all said, "Yes."

"The other team looks like they are all seventeen- and eighteen-year-olds who ate steroids with their *fufu*," Godwin said. Those of them who could understand laughed. Tony translated for the French speakers and then they laughed, too.

"Doesn't matter," Godwin said. "Just looking at our centre will completely distract them. Don't be offended, Sunny."

"None taken," she said. A thought crossed her mind. *Are they going to use juju in the match? And if not, what of natural abilities?* Her natural abilities would be useless. How could she kick a soccer ball while invisible?

"They're going to play dirty," Godwin said. "So if you have to, do the same. We'll use an attack formation, so three-three-four. Sasha, you're going to be in front with Sunny, Agaja, and Ousman when you need to be." He paused. "For those of you who are new to this, you can't use juju in the Zuma Football

Cup. If you do, we will all be disqualified. And you cannot use your natural mystical abilities. This is football, Lamb style."

A few team members groaned, the French speakers groaning seconds after Tony translated. Sunny had never been so relieved.

"Stop complaining!" Godwin snapped. "Buck up. This is real."

"We're ready," Agaja said. He hadn't groaned at all.

"I'm definitely ready," Sasha said.

Sunny slapped hands with Ousman. Godwin held a hand out and they all took it.

"For the Zuma Football Cup!" he shouted.

"For the Zuma Football Cup!" they shouted back.

The referee stood in the middle of the field with a pad of paper and stick of chalk. He was drawing a series of loopy symbols that apparently meant: *I will not use juju or my Leopard abilities.* Both teams faced each other.

"Do you all know the rules?" the referee asked loudly.

"Yes," they chorused.

"Each of you step up and seal it."

Everyone crowded in and the referee watched closely to make sure that each player pressed a thumb to the centre of the symbol.

"You won't like the result if you break this pact," he told everyone. "So don't even try."

All the players ran to their positions for the kick-off. The white team had won the coin toss, so Sunny stepped into the centre circle as the green team stepped back.

"The players are getting in position," an amplified young female voice said. Sunny saw the commentator in the front of the audience. "It seems that the green team will play the ball forward first. Not since fifteen years ago when Onyeka Nwankwo played for the green team has a girl participated in the Zuma Cup. But this albino girl is certainly the first ever to play centre forward! What excitement we are having on this warm Zuma Festival Day!"

"What is this?" the centre forward for the white team asked his teammates in English. He pointed at her and turned to his teammates. "You see this?"

One of the other boys in white laughed and said something in a language she didn't understand. Two other boys in white laughed hard, too. There was a rise in the chatter from the audience. She was used to ridicule, but this hurt more than usual. This wasn't just about her being albino, this was about her being a girl— an ugly girl. *Stupid boys. Stupid, blockhead, idiot boys*, she thought.

"Hey, Godwin, since when are they allowing ghosts to play?" the boy in front of Sunny loudly asked.

Godwin only shook his head, hunkering down into position. The white team's centre was about to say something else when he suddenly fell backward. Behind her, Sasha laughed hard. "Asshole," Sasha said, putting a pouch of juju powder back into his pocket. Sunny grinned.

"Hey, no more of that," the ref said, pointing at Sasha.

Sasha held his arms out, "The game hasn't started yet."

"Well, it has started now." The ref took out a pocket watch, put a whistle to his lips and blew, handing the ball to Sunny.

She placed it on the centre spot and took a deep breath. The moment she brought her foot back, five copper *chittim* fell next to Sunny, but she was too busy to care. She kicked the ball diagonally to Ousman and ran.

"And they're off," the commentator said. "Ousman kicks it back to Sunny. Sunny takes the ball around Ibou, the centre forward from Senegal! Look at those feet!"

She remembered what Godwin said about the other team being distracted by her, and she took full advantage of the element of surprise. She dribbled the ball with speed, zigzagging around the other team and checking her peripheral vision for flashes of green. She spotted Agaja to her left. When she got close enough to the goal post, she passed the ball to him. He took the shot. It flew in like a bullet. The crowd jumped up and shouted.

"GOOOOOOOOOAL! The green team scores!" the commentator shouted.

"Ha-ha!" she shouted, running over to Agaja and hugging him. She heard someone shout her name and saw Orlu and Chichi standing up and jumping in the front seats. She blew a kiss at them and they cheered louder, "Sunny, o! Sunny, o!!!"

The other team barely knew what hit them. As he stepped into the centre circle, Ibou the white team's centre looked angry as hell. His nostrils flared like an infuriated bull's. Sunny glared right back at him. Adrenaline was blasting through her veins. *Have to move really quick now,* she thought. *He's going to try to hurt me.*

But she wasn't afraid. She was playing soccer in the sun with other players and she was good. She knew the minute that ball had dropped. She wasn't just good at kicking a ball around, she was good at playing with a team. "I've had your *chittim* given to your friends over there for safekeeping," the ref told her.

She nodded, stepping away from the centre circle and keeping her eye on Ibou. The ref blew his whistle as Ibou placed the ball on the centre spot. He kicked it to his teammate who dribbled it.

"Pass it back here," Ibou roared. "Let me show this girl." Sunny ran at Ibou as soon as he got the ball and they scrambled for it. Ibou tried to elbow her in the ribs, but she dodged him and took the ball with her.

"And Sunny makes a fool of Ibou, again," the commentator said.

She ran with it, looking around for the others.

"Sasha!" she shouted, passing to him. It was intercepted. They all turned and ran to the other side. The boy who took it was fast. Before she knew it, the ball was dribbled through the defensive line. Ibou elbowed Mossa as he passed and Mossa fell to the ground clutching his chest. The ref blew the whistle as Ibou passed the ball to his teammate. The boy kicked it hard towards the goal. Godwin leapt and knocked the ball out of the way. Then he ran to Mossa. "You okay?" he asked, helping the boy up.

"Sorry o," Ibou said. Then he shook his head, laughing.

By the second half, Sunny could barely think straight, she was in such ecstasy. The white team was made up of brutes, but when they weren't hurting people, they were really good. Somehow Sunny's team managed to hang on, down only two to three.

Godwin had them go from an attacking arrangement to a defensive one when he realised that the boys on defence were terrified of the white team. It was Godwin, Sasha, Ousman, Agaja, and Sunny who really held them together.

"Kouty, kick it out of bounds!" she shouted as she pushed past the white team player trying to block her. Kouty was surrounded by four opponents like a trapped rabbit. He kicked wildly towards Sasha. Ibou swooped in, stole the ball, and soon after the white team scored.

"Oh, no!" she said stamping her foot. She tried to give Kouty an encouraging smile. "Nice try," she said, and went back to the centre.

"One minute left in the game," the commentator said. "Can the green team make two goals by then? It's doubtful, but they don't seem to be ready to give up."

"I'm certainly not," Sunny said, as she faced Ibou.

"You people never had a chance," Ibou said. "Girls belong on the sidelines."

"Do you know what century it is?" she asked.

"What do you know about time, you ghost girl?" he said.

"Trash-talking Muhammad Ali-style on the field, I see," the commentator remarked. "One of the richest traditions of the Zuma Cup. It seems we are witnessing the creation of a new rivalry between the white and green!"

"Ey!" Sasha said to Ibou. "Why don't you shut your mouth before I make your lips fatter?"

Ibou pointed angrily at Sasha and ran his finger across his neck.

Sasha just laughed and said, "Bring it." He'd already fouled Ibou six times. It didn't compare to the number of times the white team had fouled the green defensive line, all of whom were younger, smaller, and more afraid. Ibou had fouled Sunny three times and she had the bruises on her shins and cuts on her knees to prove it.

The ref blew his whistle as Sunny put the ball down. She passed it to Agaja who passed it to Sasha who passed it back to Sunny. Ibou immediately came at her and the two fought for the ball. Ibou grabbed it with his foot; she put her foot on his foot and snatched it away. He swerved around her and took it. She shot out her foot and got it back. They went on like this for several more seconds, Ibou cursing as he fought with her. Sunny was laughing. Two members of the green team came running over to triple-team Sunny.

"Stay back!" Ibou shouted, out of breath.

"A foot battle," the commentator said. "The albino girl against the superstar boy."

Sunny didn't know she could be so fast and quick. Eventually, he got it away from her and he laughed, victorious. She was so tickled with herself that she forgot to be angry.

"Sasha, stay there!" she shouted as she pursued Ibou. He was zigzagging, trying to shake her off. But she anticipated his every move. She saw her chance and snatched it from right between his legs. She took off, passing back and forth with Sasha. Most of the white team's offence was overconfident, so they'd left the other half of the field open. Sasha passed the ball to Agaja, who dribbled past the two remaining white defenders and then squared the ball to Sunny. She played in a perfect cross to Sasha, who slammed it in just as the ref called time.

"GOOOOOOOOAL!" the commentator shouted. Everyone cheered.

In the end, they lost three to four, but it was hard to tell. Godwin went running from his goal post and the whole team smashed together in one big group hug. "Ah! That was amazing!" Godwin exclaimed.

"Did you see her?" Kouty exclaimed.

"Like Pelé!" Sasha shouted.

The French speakers were shouting in French.

The white team looked half as happy. They gathered and calmly slapped hands, turning to look at the green team celebrating its loss.

"And this year's Zuma Cup goes to the white team, captained by Ibou Diop. We hope you enjoy your gift certificates to Fadio's Furiously Fascinating Book Shop located in Abuja. Congratulations to you and your scholar teachers."

CHAPTER FIFTEEN
HOLD YOUR BREATH

"How am I supposed to go back home after a day like this?" Sunny asked. "Regular life is going to seem so boring."

She and Chichi were in the bathroom. Since there were no places to bathe at the festival, she'd done the best she could with a wet washcloth, then sprayed herself with perfume she'd bought with some of the *chittim* she'd earned at the soccer game kick-off. She looked at her new braids in the mirror. Chichi had taken her to a hair stall right after the game where the stylist had used skill and juju to speed-wash then braid Sunny's hair. The tiny, neat braids framed her face and fell just above her shoulders.

Chichi laughed. "Don't worry, the night is still young."

"What's this social thing anyway? Is there any way we can skip it? I'm exhausted."

"No, anyway, we have to wait for Anatov to get out of that meeting."

Outside was early evening and a nice cool breeze was blowing. Sasha and Orlu sat waiting on a nearby bench.

"Man, what were you all doing in there?" Sasha asked.

"None of your business," Chichi said.

"Orlu, do you know who we give these uniforms back to?" she asked.

"Keep it. You are on the green team if you want to play next year."

"Excellent," Sasha said. "I'm in."

"Me, too," she said.

The social had already begun by the time they got there. It was in a tent beside the field. Inside, bass-heavy dance music blasted. Two older students stood at the entrance.

"Welcome," the female one said. She looked them up and down. "Who's your teacher?"

"Anatov," the male student said. He pointed at Sasha and Sunnny. "At least those two. They're the football players from the green team."

"Oh!" she said, recognising Sunny. "You were great! I always wanted to play, but I didn't know I could. At least the girls who come after you will know now."

Sunny was delighted. She hadn't even thought of that.

The boy chuckled. "They'll have to play as well as her, or they shouldn't bother." Sunny frowned. Why should girls be held to higher standards to play?

"Anatov is our teacher, also," Chichi said, looking a little annoyed.

"All right," he said.

"Go on in and enjoy the food. No teachers are allowed, so you can relax." He handed them each a small white towel. "You will need these."

The air inside the tent was humid, and smelled like rich soil, headily scented flowers, and leaves. Vines with tiny purple glowing round flowers hung from the ceiling. There were small bushes and trees lining the walls, and a large one in the middle.

Sunny watched, open-mouthed, as the central tree lifted up on its roots and slowly rotated to the loud music. Beneath the tree, students danced. On the far side of the tent was a buffet. It started raining and thundering, and all the people on the dance floor raised their hands and shouted, "Heeeeey!"

"Oh, this is wild," Sasha said, wiping his face.

"Let's get some food," Orlu said, making for the buffet. "I'm so hungry."

The rain soon stopped, but the air was so humid that their clothes were soaked.

Several people recognised Sasha and Sunny and told them that they'd played a great game. Godwin, who was surrounded by girls, waved hello as they passed. Sasha slapped and grasped his hand. He greeted the girls and they all twittered and grinned. *Ugh, sometimes I'm embarrassed to be a female*, Sunny thought.

"Girls always chase the athletes," Chichi said as Sasha blabbed with Godwin. Sunny only gave Godwin a brief smile on their way to the buffet.

There was *egusi* soup and *eba*, fried plantain, pepper soup, stew and rice, roasted goat meat, and a bunch of dishes Sunny didn't recognise. Not a bad selection at all. Sasha rejoined them as they were sitting down. "If they really want to represent, they should add some cornbread, fried chicken, and collard greens,"

Sasha said. "But, oh, I forgot, this is the West African festival, as if African Americans ain't West African."

"Maybe some KFC?" Sunny suggested, laughing.

"Better yet—Popeye's," Sasha said. "Or Harold's."

"What's this yellow rice thing?" Orlu asked. "Isn't it Ethiopian or something? It's delicious!"

"Nice game." They all looked up. The boy who'd spoken was carrying a plate heavy with fufu and a large bowl of soup. Three of his friends stood behind him.

"Thanks," Sunny said. It was Yao, the one who'd mocked Sasha's name. Sasha hissed and looked away.

"Chichi," Yao said, "you look nice tonight. Too bad it won't help you."

"You just don't know when to hide," Chichi said.

"You think I would hide from *you*?" Yao said, trying to sound condescending. He only succeeded in looking stupid. It was painfully obvious that he liked Chichi.

"You want me to embarrass you again? You must be one of those boys who enjoy humiliation."

"Whenever you are ready," Yao said, gritting his teeth.

"Why don't you sit down and fill your stomach first," Chichi said loftily. "Maybe have a dance or two. Enjoy it while you have time. Then we will see."

Yao narrowed his eyes. "Boys, let's go." They walked away.

"What's the deal with you two?" Sunny asked Chichi.

"*Wahala*," Orlu said.

"Yao and I hate each other," Chichi declared. Sunny scoffed. How stupid did Chichi think she was? "But I'm more intelligent,"

Chichi continued. "I showed him pepper last year but he won't listen, so I have to show him again."

What is it with Leopard people and competition? But Sunny wasn't one to talk. Only two hours ago, she'd been high on adrenaline herself.

"I see that look in your eye, Chichi," Orlu said. "I hope you're not planning anything dangerous."

"I wish I was back at the hotel sleeping," Sunny said. She shovelled jollof rice into her mouth.

After they finished, they sat back sipping Malt and patting their full stomachs. The music was louder and more people were dancing.

"Ah-ah, what is this?" Orlu grumbled as Yao approached again.

"Didn't I tell you—" Chichi started to say.

"Do you want to dance?" Yao asked, holding out a hand.

"No," Sasha said, looking very annoyed. "She doesn't."

Yao glared at him. "Did I ask you?" He looked at Chichi, waiting for an answer.

"All right," Chichi said, getting up. "Let's go."

Sasha scowled as Chichi walked hand and hand with Yao to the rotating tree. Then he turned and waved at Agaja and Ousman, who were standing with a group of older boys and girls. They waved back, motioning him to come over.

"I'll see you guys later," Sasha said, getting up.

Sunny took a gulp of her malt and looked at Orlu. "Wanna dance?" The words were out before she'd really thought about them. She felt her face grow hot.

Orlu half-smiled and looked at the dance floor. "That tree looks dangerous."

"I know," she said laughing louder than she meant to.

There was a long pause. "All right," he finally said, putting down his can. "Come on."

As they walked towards the dancing, jumping, laughing, wiggling students, Sunny remembered how tired she was. She'd always liked dancing, making it a point to hit the floor at all the parties her parents took her to, but right now her legs were sore. She was worn out. And it was so hot and humid.

The moment they got near the tree, the music grew louder and she jumped. Then she smiled. She could feel her spirit face just behind her face rejoicing. After that, she was in the zone, shaking her hips, throwing her arms in the air, shuffling her feet and sweating like everyone else. Orlu wasn't bad, either. Chichi saw them and dragged Yao over. For that hour and a half, they were all joyous.

As it grew late, the tree switched to slower music; not couples music, but cool-down music. The social was almost over. People started leaving. There was a notebook at the entrance for people to write their contact information so everyone could keep in touch. Chichi had scoffed and said this was a useless practice. In most African countries, it was hard to keep in touch with people from far away, even with email. In the Leopard community, it apparently wasn't much different. "Only the scholars know how to communicate easily across large expanses of space," Orlu said as they returned to their table.

"Scholars, and people who are born with the ability," Chichi added.

"Are you finished with Yao?" Orlu quickly asked.

"Where's Sasha?" Sunny asked.

They looked around.

"Look at him," Chichi said, narrowing her eyes. He was surrounded by at least five girls. "I thought you said he was with your teammates," Chichi said.

"He was," Sunny said.

Chichi stormed over to him. Orlu and Sunny laughed. Sasha and Chichi were always so dramatic.

As Chichi was going towards Sasha, Yao met up with Ibou, the soccer player. They spoke for a moment. Then they started towards Chichi. Orlu's smile dropped away. "Oh no. Trouble. Come," Orlu said, taking Sunny's hand.

Chichi called Sasha's name. The girls stepped aside as she approached. Yao called Chichi. She turned around. Sasha pushed past a particularly eager girl trying to press herself against him.

"So, what do you have?" Yao was saying to Chichi by the time Sunny and Orlu got to them all. Ibou stood quietly beside Yao.

"What do *you* have?" Chichi asked.

Yao took out his juju knife. It looked like it was made of pure, smooth gold. The tip was curved. He cut the air in a complex series of motions and caught something. He blew it at Chichi. A heavy wind pushed her back several steps. When it stopped, everyone gasped. Chichi's bright green wrapper and top was now metallic gold. Then the dress started growing much tighter around the chest, pushing up her bosom.

Ibou's eyebrows rose and then he laughed loudly. "*Ah-ah!* That was a good one," he said, slapping Yao's hand. "You should have made it even tighter in the backside." Yao and Ibou laughed even harder.

The girls who'd been hovering around Sasha all went, "Oooh," and then clapped. "How pretty," one girl said in Igbo, feeling the material of Chichi's sleeve. Chichi snatched her arm away.

"*Abeg!*" she said. "Petty juju. You are the only one who is impressed."

Several of the girls hissed, one of them grumbling, "Look at this girl. She might as well be a man if she can't appreciate that material."

Chichi brought out her knife. By this time, Sasha had stepped forward. He put his arm around Chichi's shoulder and looked with amused eyes at Yao and Ibou. "Yao, you're an idiot," he said dismissively. "And Ibou, first you're bested on the soccer field by one of my classmates and now your best friend's gonna be bested by another of my classmates. You're inferior."

"Have you forgotten," Ibou said "your team lost."

"Only because you chose the oldest players," Godwin said from the gathering crowd. "The game is supposed to be about brains and brawn, not just brawn."

Yao, who had been looking at Chichi the entire time, said, "You won't beat me this year."

"Careful," Orlu whispered to Chichi.

Chichi slashed in a square and then spoke something in Efik.

When nothing happened, Yao grinned and said, "I guess it didn't work. You're losing your touch."

"Maybe her dress is too tight," Ibou said. Several people laughed. Chichi frowned, close to tears. She looked down.

"I guess you are right," Chichi said, quietly. She looked up. And slowly held her hand up and whispered, "You win."

"Obviously," Yao said, looking more triumphant than ever. He brought his hand up to shake hers. A third of the way there, it hit something. He gasped, his eyes growing wide. He banged on the invisible barrier with his fists.

"See!" Chichi said, laughing hard. "You can't even touch me!"

Yao cursed and banged on the barrier. Then he turned to the side and found that there was a barrier there, too. She'd literally boxed him in.

"Take it off!" Yao said, in a panic. "Take it off!"

Ibou tentatively knocked at it and then reached around to make sure he wasn't enclosed either. This made Chichi grin wider.

"Nice," Sasha said.

"I know," she said. She lazily raised her knife and made another square. This time, she did it in the opposite direction and the words she spoke were different. Yao's hand instantly went through the air, the barrier gone.

"How did you—"

"*Abeg*, as if I'd tell you."

"That's third level juju," Ibou said. "We're not allowed—"

"Obviously I have full control of it," she said. "Na easy thing for me. But you, you no go fit understand." She lifted her chin, looking at the people behind Ibou and Yao. "Anybody else?" Chichi said loudly. No one stepped up.

"I'm not finished," Yao angrily said.

"Yes, you are. You don't have anything stronger than what I just did."

"How do you know?"

She paused, cocking her head. "Ok, what of this," she slowly said, "I will call up a masquerade and you will never challenge me again."

"Chichi, enough!" Orlu said. "You always go too far! Why are you taking it there?"

"Orlu, relax," Chichi said. "I have wanted to try this for some time." She turned to Yao. "Did you hear how I said 'try'? You are no match for me, so I might as well challenge myself. Why not kill two birds with one stone? Finish with you once and for all and also do something I have never done."

Yao and Ibou looked worried. In a low but shaky voice, Yao said, "You don't even know how—"

"We do," Sasha said.

"Oh! What is wrong with the two of you?" Orlu said, throwing his hands up. "You think I don't know where you got the juju? That book was trouble from the minute you saw it, Sasha."

"I've done it already," Sasha said.

A loud murmur flew through the room.

"Do it, then," someone said.

"Yes, I want to see," someone else added.

"I hear that you could die if you fail."

"Do it!"

"What do you mean, you have already done it?" Orlu asked. Then something seemed to dawn on him.

Sasha smiled. "Yeah, it was that day at your house."

Orlu was silent.

Yao and Ibou whispered to each other and when they stopped, they didn't look so terrified. "Okay, I accept," Yao said. "Do it. But you have to be the one to do it, not him."

"And who do you think taught him how?" Chichi said mysteriously. "And if you didn't know, my mother is a Third Leveller. I come from thick spiritual blood."

Yao and Ibou's smiles faltered. Sunny glanced at Orlu, wondering if she should grab his hand and get them both out of there. Even she knew a masquerade was bad news. And there was no stopping Sasha and Chichi combined.

"What of your father?" a girl behind her said. "I hear he's Lamb. Your spirit blood cannot be that thick."

Chichi glared at the girl. "Don't worry about my father," Chichi said. "I certainly don't."

"Chichi, don't do this," Orlu said.

"Masquerades are hard to control even when they're successfully called. They can force their freedom."

But Chichi had already sat down. "I have it all in my head," she softly said. She started drawing in the dirt with her knife.

"Oo! For God's sake," Orlu angrily whispered to Sunny. "I want to just kick her! Do you know how bad this is?"

Even before becoming a Leopard person, Sunny knew about masquerades. They were supposedly spirits of the dead, or just spirits in general who for various reasons came to the physical world. During weddings, birth celebrations, funerals, and festivals people dressed as and pretended to be them. That was the key word, *pretend*. But in the Leopard world, they were real.

"Chichi," she said. "Maybe you should—"

"Leave me," Chichi said, still drawing. "I know what I'm doing."

"Of course you do," Orlu said. "Until you get us all killed."

"Didn't you hear? We've done it before," Sasha said. "Chill."

The entire tent was quiet as everyone watched. For the first time that night, Sunny wished some figures of authority were allowed to keep an eye on things. "Are you sure you won't get sent to the Abuja Leopard Council?" Sunny asked loudly.

"Do you see any nonsense Lambs around?" Chichi snapped. The design she was drawing looked like a giant circle with lines radiating out and into it. She quickly made a cross in the centre and then sat back, looking at her work.

She stood up and began chanting something in Efik as she cut the air with her knife.

"Look," Sunny said to Orlu. People started to whisper to each other. Many either stepped back or ran out of the tent, especially when the dirt in the centre of the drawing began to churn up into a small mound.

A minute passed. The mound grew taller and taller. It looked like the beginning of a termite mound, the places through which masquerades were believed to enter the physical world. It reached about six feet before it stopped. Termites emerged from tiny holes throughout the hill. The winged ones immediately took to the air. Sunny swatted at one that landed on her arm.

"This juju charm," Chichi said dramatically, "is straight from *Udide's Book of Shadows.*"

Several of the remaining people gasped. More turned and ran out of the tent.

"*Udide's Book of Shadows?*" Yao almost shouted. Now he looked highly alarmed. Ibou must have fled because Sunny didn't see him anywhere. "*Haba!* Are you crazy! Do you know what you've just invited?"

"Udide respects the intelligent, the creative, and the brave," Chichi said, turning back to the termite mound.

Only friendship kept Sunny from running—especially after the wailing started. It was a high-pitched wavery sort of ghostly noise, like the ululations of women from the Middle East. Then the trademark *tock tock tock* started, the sound of tiny drums. A playful flute wove in and out of the wailing and drumming. Then there came the tooth-vibrating *DOOOM DOOOM* of a deep-barrelled talking drum.

"Sunny, if you value your life, do not run," Orlu warned.

The mound was caving in at the centre. They all stepped back as a wooden knob rose from it. It was attached to the top of a large tuft of thick raffia. Then the termite mound expanded. They backed away some more. The creature's body was large and bulbous, covered with beautiful blue shiny cloth. Cowry shells and blue and white beads hung from pieces of blue yarn. They clicked and clacked as the masquerade grew.

When it reached over fifteen feet high, it stopped. The drumbeat and the flute reached a crescendo. The large tuft of raffia at the top fell away, revealing a four-faced head.

Students called for Allah, Legba, Chukwu, Jesus, Mawu, God, Chineke, Oya, Ani, Asaase Yaa, Allat, and many other deities to protect them. Sunny moaned and pressed close to Orlu, who was cursing under his breath. Chichi seemed to be in a trance, Sasha watching wordlessly behind her.

The masquerade faces looked around at them, the expressions animated. The smiling face grinned. The angry face scowled. The surprised face looked more and more shocked. And the curious face looked very, very inquisitive. The knob at the top grazed the tent's ceiling.

Then the wooden mask fell away. Orlu and Sunny dodged the falling pieces. On the other side, a student beside Yao shouted in pain as one hit her on the shoulder.

"Oh my God!" Sunny screeched. Orlu grabbed her arm.

Underneath the mask was a huge undulating mass of red termites, wasps, bees, mosquitoes, flies, and ants! It wasn't raffia and palm fronds that stuffed the masquerade's blue cloth-covered body—it was stinging insects. People started screaming and the masquerade began to dance, a cloud of insects rising around it.

"Everyone! Get down!" Orlu shouted. "Right now! Right now!"

But people were too panicked. They were running amok. Orlu shoved Sunny to the ground. Something stung her arm. "Stay down!" he said. Then he shouted, "Chichi, Sasha, down! It's going to happen any minute!"

The masquerade danced, whirling and whirling faster and faster. It whipped thousands of insects to the rhythm and speed of the drums and flute, laughing its shrill womanly laugh and buzzing its insectile buzz.

Orlu dropped down beside Sunny and said, "Hold your breath."

As soon as she did so, the buzzing grew a thousand times louder. Insects blasted in all directions. The blue cloth collapsed, empty. Sunny was buried in thousands of ants, and bees and wasps smacked into and flew around her head. She screamed and cried along with everyone else.

Death by stinging. It could happen. A boy in her town was killed by a swarm of angry wasps when he tried to knock down a hive behind his house. *We're all going to die here*, she thought, curling herself tighter. She felt two more stings on her legs and wondered what her parents and brothers would think when she was returned home all swollen and red and dead. *I should have stayed home*, she thought. *This is what I get for lying.*

She felt Orlu start to get up. "What are you *doing*?" she screamed, pulling him back down. Something stung her arm.

He pulled away and got up again. She shielded her eyes and looked at him. Orlu seemed far from himself, calm and unafraid. He was holding out his hands and bringing them in, holding out his hands and bringing them in. Each time he did this, more insects piled themselves under the masquerade's cloth.

"Go home," he coaxed in Igbo. She could hear his voice through the screaming and buzzing. "You have seen, you have stung, you have terrified—now, go home."

Soon Orlu had made the masquerade gather itself completely and there it stood. It pointed at Chichi, who was looking up from her crouched position. It spoke something in what Sunny assumed to be Efik. Then it slowly descended back into its termite mound and the mound descended back into the earth.

"Is everyone all right?" Orlu asked.

They walked briskly to the festival entrance. It was a quarter past eleven. They were late. "Don't," Orlu said, walking fast. "I hate false apologies."

"I am not apologising," Chichi said, almost running to keep up with him. "I'm just thanking you!"

"Shut up," Orlu snapped.

"Don't be such a tight-ass," Sasha said, rubbing one of his many stings.

Orlu stopped so abruptly that Sunny ran into his back. She didn't want to talk about any of it. She just wanted to find Anatov, go back to the hotel, check her skin for stingers she'd missed, rub her entire body with calamine lotion, and go to sleep.

"Do you have any idea what could have happened?" Orlu shouted. "Everyone knows how brilliant you are! So you needed to show how stupid you are, too, eh?"

"No one was really hurt," Chichi said defensively.

"Not because of you!"

"*Ah-ah*, I knew you were there, now," she said. "You think I didn't consider that?"

"You always make a mess and assume I'll clean it up," Orlu said. "Why don't you try to learn some undoing jujus for yourself?"

"Because you were born with it," Chichi snapped. "You can always save the day."

Orlu looked disgusted. "Don't make this about me. People could have died because of you. You called up *Mmuo Aku!* If it had decided to start really stinging—ah! Don't you research things before calling on them?" He took a deep breath. "And what did it say to you?"

Chichi opened her mouth but then just stubbornly looked away. "It's my business," she mumbled.

"Let me guess," Orlu said sarcastically. "The thing said 'thank you' before it went back."

"Sorry," Chichi said quietly.

"I said I don't want your apologies!" Orlu shouted, walking off.

Anatov looked angry, but very tired when they got to the entrance. About fifty other people were also waiting for the funky train.

"You're lucky it's late," he said. "Otherwise, I'd have left it to y'all to find your way to the hotel." They apologised. He yawned and waved a hand at them. "So I hear you four have made a name for yourselves this year."

They all looked at their feet.

"How many *chittim* fell when it was over?"

"Seven coppers," Orlu mumbled. "We could have gotten people killed and we got paid for it."

"As a group you made a mistake and you learned you could also right it," Anatov said. "Get on the bus. Sasha, you're an idiot."

Sasha looked surprised and then looked at his hands.

Disgusted, Anatov continued, "Orlu's mother told me right away about all the noise that night and how the house felt as if it were underwater. Obviously, you called *Mmuo Miri*, and she is not like that small one you called back in the States. *Mmuo Miri* is a masquerade that only an experienced Third Leveller has any business calling. You could have all drowned in that house. Do you have some sort of death wish?"

He didn't wait for an answer. "Orlu's mother and I agreed that you'd survived an episode of stupidity and probably wouldn't make the mistake again. You proved us both wrong tonight, Sasha." Anatov leaned towards Sasha. "I will have you caned by the strongest man in Nigeria if you pull something like this again. Understood?"

Sasha nodded.

"I will let you keep that book, but I expect you to act like you have some brains." He turned to Chichi. "And you are to report to the council with me first thing when we get home."

The trip home was nothing like the trip there. Chichi barely spoke a word, nor did Orlu. Sasha and Sunny chatted briefly with Godwin before he took his seat. "I couldn't sleep last night," Godwin said.

"Me neither," Sunny said.

"I slept well," Sasha said, smiling brightly. Sunny could tell he was lying. There were bags under Sasha's eyes.

"The four of you—everyone is talking about you," Godwin said. "No one has seen juju like that performed and then stopped by students so young. And of course people are still talking about your fast feet, Sunny, and your fast mouth, Sasha."

"Do people hate us?" she asked.

Godwin laughed and shook his head. "Ah, no! They will be talking about this festival for years, man."

CHAPTER SIXTEEN
TROUBLE AT HOME

The funky train stopped right in front of Orlu's house. Chichi had only looked away when Sunny, Orlu, and Sasha tried to say goodbye. She was going straight to Leopard Knocks with Anatov.

"I'll see you all in two weeks," Anatov said. "That's Thursday in the p.m." He too had been quiet through the trip. "Sunny," he said, taking her hand before she got off, "did you have a good time?"

"Best time of my life!" she surprised herself by saying.

"Good," he said.

"You sure say you no wan make I drop you in front of your house?" Jesus' General asked.

"Oh, here is fine," she said, quickly hopping off.

They watched the funky train drive away. "What'll they do to her?" she asked.

"I think she'll get caned," Orlu said. "That masquerade was bad, but the fact that she called it in a public place like that..." He shook his head.

"This is what I hated back in America," Sasha said.

"What? That people get punished when they deserve to be?" Orlu said. "You should be going with her."

"I should," he said, looking at his feet. Then he hissed loudly and kicked some dirt. "No one is willing to push the envelope. So what if she called up a damn *Mmuo Aku* and it went wild! She still did it! She still performed the most sophisticated juju any of them had ever seen."

"True, but you're wrong," Orlu said. "We can't live in chaos. The ages are set for each level for a reason. You can be able to do something and not be mature enough to deal with the consequences. It is just like—like a girl who develops breasts too fast. It doesn't mean she's mature."

"Ooooook!" Sunny suddenly said. "I'm going home. I'll see you when I see you."

"Peace," Sasha said, hugging her.

"See you in class," Orlu said. After a moment's hesitation, he kissed her on the cheek. She touched her cheek and looked at Orlu with wide eyes. Sasha chuckled. She didn't dare look his way. As she walked slowly down the street, she heard them start arguing again.

Sunny returned home to music playing and her father's laughter. His friend Ola was visiting and they were mildly drunk on Gulder, as usual. "Ah, Sunny, is that you?" Ola said when he saw her trying to slip unnoticed to her room.

"Good afternoon," she said, trying to shake the dislocated feeling she was experiencing. It was like two realities fighting for dominance. "Hi, Dad." She froze. The ghost hopper was sitting on his head.

"How was your weekend?" he asked with a lopsided smile.

"Um, it was good," she said, working hard not to look at the ghost hopper. "Dad, there's a—a leaf on your head."

When he brushed his head, the ghost hopper leaped onto the arm of the couch. She slipped away before he could say any more. She heard her mother laughing in the kitchen and speaking in rapid English. She had to be talking to her sister, Chinwe, who lived with her African American husband in Atlanta.

"Ah, you know you miss it," her mother was saying. "You can't even find half the ingredients there for a decent *egusi* soup." Pause. "I know. Mhm. I plan to, but only when she's"— she noticed Sunny come in and smiled—"ready. You want to talk to her? She just walked in. Hold on. Sunny, come and talk to your auntie."

Auntie Chinwe was one of Sunny's favourites. Her mother said that she was the free spirit of the family, and that Sunny's grandfather considered her a disappointment. In addition to marrying an 'akata,' as her grandfather called her African American husband, Auntie had also decided not to become a doctor. Instead, she'd studied dance.

Now she was a professional dancer with a group called the Women of the Bush and she also taught dance at Columbia University. The DVD of one of her shows was one of Sunny's most valuable possessions.

"You must have had fun," her mother said, kissing her cheek and giving her the phone. "Every time I called to speak with you, you two were out doing something or another."

Though Chichi's mother didn't keep a phone, her mother had Orlu's parents' phone number. "It was great, Mama," she said. "Thanks for letting me go."

She patted Sunny on the head.

"Hello?" Sunny said, holding the phone to her ear. Her mother left the room to give them a little privacy.

"Sunny," Auntie said. "How are you?"

"I'm fine."

"I hear you were out with your friends yesterday."

"Yeah. It was great. It was nice to be out of the house and all."

With her peripheral vision, she could see two ghost hoppers sitting on a bunch of plantains on the floor. One of them was munching on the stem. So there *was* more than one.

"Well, I'm glad that you've made some good friends, and that my sister has finally loosened the leash. You're a responsible girl and you should be treated that way."

Sunny felt a little guilty.

"Auntie?" She stepped over to look into the hall to make sure her mother wasn't hiding behind the door, as she knew she often did.

"Mhm?"

She lowered her voice. "Tell me about Grandma—just a little bit. Something. Every time I ask Mama, she refuses to tell me." There was a pause, a long pause. "Auntie? Are you there? Hello?"

"Yes, I'm here," Auntie said. "Where's your mother?"

"She'll be back in a minute."

"Why do you want to know? Was someone teasing you?"

"No," she said. "No—nothing like that."

"You sure?"

"Yes," she said. She heard footsteps. "Mama's coming! Can you tell me—"

"No," Auntie Chinwe said. "I can't tell you much of anything. Our mother—your grandmother—wasn't crazy, but she was full of secrets that she took to her grave. She never let any of us really know her."

"But how do you know there were secrets?"

Her mother walked in.

"Because I have eyes and I have ears," Auntie said.

"Okay, Sunny," her mother said.

"Let me finish talking to my sister before her phone card runs out."

"Look in your mother's side of their bedroom," Auntie said quickly. "She keeps some things in a box, I think."

"Okay," she quickly said. "Love you."

"Love you, too, sweetie," Auntie said as her mother took the phone.

"Sister? So how are little James and Gozie?"

Sunny took a small package of biscuits and went to her room. She closed and locked the door and sunk to the floor. Never in her life had she had so much swimming in her head. Never, ever, ever. She would have curled up and gone to sleep right there if she hadn't seen a ghost hopper sitting on her bed.

She dragged herself up. Carefully, she picked up the ghost hopper. She was surprised when it didn't struggle. She'd seen one move lightning-fast when it wanted to, and she was sure its legs were very powerful. It weighed about a pound, and she had to use both hands. Its body felt substantial, despite its ghostly appearance. She set it on her dresser.

She lay on her bed and brought out her new juju knife. It truly was magnificent. What was the blade made of? She held it and at once felt that odd sensation of it being part of her.

She yelped when she felt something moving in her pocket. She was about to tear off her jeans, thinking it was a remaining wasp or ant from the masquerade, then she remembered. It felt like so long ago since Junk Man had given her the small blue bean. She held it up as it softly giggled and shook between her fingers. She placed it under her bed as he had instructed. Then she picked up her newspaper.

When she unrolled it, a smaller circular newspaper fell out. *Special Leopard Report*, it read. There was a soft drum beat that reminded her of the terrifying masquerade.

CORRUPTION IN THE OBI LIBRARY

Otokoto The Black Hat Steals Top Secret
Book From The Fourth Floor

"My God!" Sunny flung the newspaper across the room. "No more!" Not a second passed before she heard a loud crackling sound. The bean. "Thought he said to wait a few days," she said, frowning. She hung over the bed and watched a small blue wasp emerge. She shuddered, but then she relaxed. This wasp didn't seem full of stinging, deadly mischief.

It moved groggily around the empty casing. Then it picked up half, flew to her dresser, and dropped it. It retrieved the other half and did the same. Then it rested for a moment. A minute later, it began to loudly eat the casings, making loud crunching and cracking sounds.

"I hope you're not poisonous," she muttered, putting the opened package of biscuits next to the wasp. Before she knew it, she was asleep.

Something woke her around midnight. NEPA had taken the light, and because it was a cool night, the generator had not been turned on. A clicking sound came from her dresser. She grabbed her torch and turned it on. The biscuit package was empty, and beside it was a castle the size of her hand made of what looked like crumbs. The blue wasp stood on top of the castle as if waiting for applause.

"Oh my goodness," she said, smiling at the nonsense of it all. "That's—wow!" She softly clapped and the wasp buzzed with pleasure. She spent the next two hours doing homework before finally going back to bed.

CHAPTER SEVENTEEN
BASIC JUJU

The next two weeks passed quickly. Sunny spent most of it studying and reading and practising and reading some more. She was living two lives. In Lamb school, she did well in her classes and kept away from Jibaku, who seemed to believe that what she'd seen during their fight was just Sunny's extremely ugly face. In Leopard school, she did as well as she could.

The next time they met after Abuja, they didn't do much. Chichi was still recovering from her caning. Sunny winced when she saw Chichi's back. The skin wasn't broken, but it was very bruised and tender. The council people didn't make empty threats; if you broke the big rules, you paid a big price. Chichi refused to talk about it and got angry at the slightest mention of Sugar Cream.

After that, to Orlu's great dissatisfaction, Sasha and Chichi grew more obsessed with *Udide's Book of Shadows*. Thankfully, they only read and discussed the book.

They also grew obsessed with something else. Days after Chichi's caning, Sunny and Orlu had gone to Chichi's hut after school, only to find Sasha and Chichi standing in the doorway locking lips.

"What the—!" Sunny exclaimed. Sasha and Chichi jumped apart, straightening their clothes. Sasha grinned and shrugged. Chichi only laughed. Orlu rolled his eyes and Sunny just stood there, shocked. Totally unexpected. She glanced at Orlu and looked away.

"It's nothing," Chichi said, going into the hut.

"Yeah," Sasha said.

But Sunny saw how he watched Chichi go inside. This was not 'nothing.' And it wasn't the last time she saw them kissing, either. On top of this, Orlu was careful around her. He was the same Orlu she'd always known, except that he made it more of a point to open doors for her, things like that. Once, he even bought her some chocolates. They were delicious. Chichi and Sunny never discussed her and Orlu, or Chichi and Sasha. It was an unspoken agreement between the four of them.

By the second week, Sunny knew several basic knife jujus, like how to amplify her voice, move small things, and keep mosquitoes away. But nothing that would harm a monster like Black Hat Otokoto.

"It's so weird," she said one day as they sat outside Chichi's hut. "It builds something new every day. I leave my window open so it can go out and find new materials and hide from my mother."

"It's a wasp artist," Orlu said. "They live for their art. If you want it to live for a long time, make sure you let it out like you've been doing, and show it that you appreciate its work."

"I'd smash the thing," Sasha said. "My sister had one when she was small, and when she forgot to give it praise once, it got pissed and stung her. Its sting paralyses you for ten minutes so you can do nothing but watch it build its 'final masterpiece' and then keep watching as it dramatically dies. The damn things are psychotic."

"Not if you treat them well," Orlu said.

"You shouldn't be *forced* to treat anything well," Sasha said, giving Orlu an annoyed look. "It should be your choice."

"Not all things are a choice," Orlu said. "Some things should come naturally."

"For me, it—"

"*Abeg*, both of you, just shut up!" Chichi snapped.

Sunny laughed. Things were back to normal.

CHAPTER EIGHTEEN
SEVEN RAINY DAYS

Even though it was the middle of harmattan, it had been raining for seven days. The markets were muddy. The streets were flooded. The schools had closed two days ago. The rain was so unexpected that, though it was perfect mosquito weather, there were no more mosquitoes out than usual. It was as if someone had flipped a switch marked **rain**.

The morning of the seventh rainy day in a row started like almost any other.

The first thing Sunny did when she woke up was look at her cabinet. Her wasp artist, whom she'd decided to name Della (after the famous sculptor she'd read about on the Internet named Luca Della Robbia), had built a mud sculpture of Mami Wata. As always, the wasp stood on top of its creation waiting for her response.

"That's really beautiful, Della," she said, meaning it.

It buzzed its wings with glee, circled its creation, and then flew out the window. Sunny unrolled her *Leopard Knocks Daily*. Tomorrow they were to meet with Anatov and probably find out what they were expected to do about Black Hat. She braced herself for news of his latest act of debauchery.

Instead, the headline read: **Rain, Rain, Please Go Away!**

She laughed, relieved. Everything was rained out. Even the criminals seemed to have taken cover. Maybe Black Hat's hat wasn't broad enough to protect him from the rain, either.

She went to get some breakfast and froze. Her heart threatened to leap from her chest. There at the kitchen table sat her mother and she was handing a cup of hot tea to…Anatov.

"Good—good morning?" Sunny squeaked.

"Sunny," her mother said, looking uncharacteristically rattled. "Sit."

Sunny had to really force herself to move.

"This is—this is the son of a friend of your grandmother's—my mother." Her mother's hands shook as she picked up her cup of tea. She laughed to herself. She sounded on the verge of tears.

"Yes," Anatov said. He poured a large amount of evaporated milk into his tea, stirred it and took a sip. "I was in town and decided to…drop by."

Sunny could only nod.

Suddenly, her mother whirled around and faced her. She obviously wanted to say something. Instead she kissed Sunny's cheek and nearly ran out of the room.

Anatov took a calm sip of tea. Sunny waited. "We're going to Leopard Knocks," he said.

"What? But it's—isn't that tomorrow?"

"Bring your knife, your powders, and one of your umbrellas."

"Won't my mom—"

"She won't stop you," he said. "Go fetch your things. There's little time."

One of the official Obi Library cars waited outside. Behind the wheel was a short, unsmiling Hausa man. A lit cigarette hung from his lips.

"Put it out, Aradu," Anatov snapped.

"Sorry, sir," Aradu said, quickly flicking the cigarette out the window.

Sunny looked back at her mother, who stood like a statue in the front doorway. Sunny waved. Her mother didn't wave back. She just stood there as they drove away.

Maybe she knew she would never see her daughter again.

The driver manoeuvred the car easily, first on the muddy road and then on the slick street. It was an oddly smooth ride. When they accelerated, there was no sound at all. Clearly, like the funky train, the car ran on some kind of juju. Sunny wondered why the Leopard people didn't share this technology with the rest of the world. It would solve some serious environmental problems.

They passed Orlu and Chichi's houses. "Aren't we picking up—"

"They'll meet us there," Anatov said. "Your home situation is not so easy, so I had to come get you."

"What's happening?" she asked.

"When we get there," Anatov said. She nodded and looked out the window. "You've made good progress, Sunny."

"Thanks."

"What I'd like you to think about, though, is *who* you are. Because within that knowledge is the key to how much you can learn."

She frowned, thinking about what had just happened with her mother. "*Oga*," she whispered, "these days I don't really think

I know who I am." Anatov was silent. "What do you know of my grandmother? Who was she?"

"Only her oldest daughter, your mother, can tell you that."

"Why won't you tell me?" she asked desperately.

"It's not my place," Anatov said.

"Was she bad?"

He didn't respond.

"Why was she Black Hat's teacher? Of all people?" she asked.

When Anatov remained silent, she pounded her fist against her leg. For a while, the windshield wipers going back and forth was the only sound.

Anatov patted her shoulder. "We have a half-hour drive," he said. "Take the time to relax while you can." He leaned forward and tapped the driver on the shoulder. "Put on some Lagbaja."

Sunny closed her eyes and listened to the afrobeat music.

The car stopping woke her up. They were outside of the Obi library. Sasha and Orlu were already there. "Wait here," Anatov said, and went inside.

They were too nervous to talk. Instead, they just stood together, shoulder to shoulder. Five minutes later, Chichi arrived with her mother, walking under a large green umbrella. Even with the umbrella, both of their cheeks were wet. Chichi looked shaken. Her mother sniffled and wiped her eyes. Chichi gave her a tight hug and watched her mother walk down the street towards the Leopard Knocks markets.

Sunny hugged Chichi. Sasha and Chichi exchanged more than hugs. Sunny and Orlu just avoided each other's eyes. Standing out there in the rain, it was as if they were waiting to be sent into battle, to their deaths.

"Okay," Sasha said standing up straighter. "Everyone lighten up. God."

Orlu sighed. Chichi put her arm around Sasha's waist and said, "Children are dying and being maimed, right?"

"Right," Sasha said. "We're lucky, really. We're going to have a chance to prove what we're made of. Some people never get that, man. Not in their whole life. But what's up with this rain?"

"That's what bothers me," Orlu said.

Sunny was about to say something when Sugar Cream came up behind them. She held a white umbrella and wore white trousers and a long fringed top. She smelled like flowers, even in the rain.

"They're ready for you," she said. "Let's go."

The library felt different. People weren't smiling and no one spoke, even when they reached the university on the second floor. Students walked close with their heads together, whispering. And when they saw the four of them, they stared, some occasionally giving them fake reassuring smiles.

To Sunny's surprise, there were buckets and towels all over the floors and on the stairs, catching drips. She'd have thought that the library, of all places, would be protected from something as simple as heavy rain. She hoped the books were okay.

They followed Sugar Cream to a large door on the third floor. "Behave yourselves," she sternly told them. "Don't ask any questions until you are told that you may."

She opened the door. Another indoor jungle. Sunny had to work not to groan. She was reminded of the tent at the Zuma Festival, and that brought back memories of the terrible masquerade.

But this jungle was more controlled—the foliage grew only around the edges of the room. A toucan sat in a tree near a window. The bird looked at them suspiciously. In the centre was a large oval table. Around it sat seven people, all of them ancient except for Taiwo, Kehinde, and Anatov. Sugar Cream motioned them to sit in the four empty chairs.

A bent woman with black skin and milky blind eyes laughed loudly and said something Sunny couldn't understand. The language she spoke was full of click sounds, most likely Xhosa. The man beside her wheezed with laughter, slapping the table with a rough hand. Sugar Cream sat down in a chair beside the blind woman and said something. Sunny only understood the last word: "English." Two of the scholars on the far side of the table, both women, hissed loudly.

The blind woman said something else in her click language and the old man beside her added his two cents, pointing accusingly at Sasha. Sugar Cream responded soothingly. The two old women on the other side of the table joined the conversation. One of them switched languages and started speaking something that sounded like French. Kehinde, Taiwo, and Anatov remained silent.

As the heated conversation ensued, the toucan whistled and flew a circle over the table. It landed in an empty seat next to the two women on the end. Sunny gasped as the bird slowly grew into a large-nosed old Middle Eastern looking-man with green eyes. He wore a white turban and a white caftan. He slapped his hands on the table and scowled at Sasha.

Sugar Cream politely said in English, "It must be this way. Sasha's American. And this one here is American, too, though she's Igbo also and speaks the language."

The toucan man scoffed. "They don't teach them to understand others, they teach them to expect others to understand them," he said in English. He humphed and said, "Americans."

"Hey," Sasha, said growing annoyed. "I'm not deaf! Don't insult my country."

"Yes," the toucan man said. "You *are* deaf. Dumb and blind, too! Now shut up!"

Sasha jumped up, angry.

"Sasha, sit," Anatov said firmly.

"Now!" Kehinde said, pointing a long finger.

Sasha sat down, looking pissed. There were even tears in his eyes.

"Let me open your ears, mind, and eyes a little," the toucan man said, leaning forward. "Your beloved country, Sasha and Sunny, the United States of America, has made Black Hat economically wealthy enough to push his plan forward."

"Let's not get ahead of ourselves, Ali," Sugar Cream said.

"Actually, we are far behind," Ali said, looking away and thumbing his long nose.

Sugar Cream got up and stood behind them. "These are the four of the *Oha* coven brought together to handle Black Hat," she said. She touched them each on the head. "Sasha Jackson.

Sunny Nwazue. Chijioke of Nimm. And Orlu Ezulike. If you object, speak up."

The room was silent but Sunny could feel the deep scrutiny. The two women on the left had closed their eyes. The blind woman had turned an ear to them. The old man next to her was staring. And Ali, the toucan man, hummed to himself. A small breeze flew through the room, rustling the leaves of the palm trees in the corners.

"That one carries rage," Ali said, gesturing at Sasha. "At small, small things like his country and his awareness of the politics."

"They fight plenty," said the blind woman.

"They make up just as much," one of the women on the left said. "There's love, too."

"And lust," Ali added, laughing slyly. "That's good."

"Mhm," one of the women on the end said, nodding. "You're right, Ntombi and Ali—love and lust. They have checks and balances."

"Otherwise, they'll be dead moments after they meet Black Hat," Ntombi said.

"So this is Ozoemena's granddaughter, eh?" the blind woman said, nodding at Sunny. "Looks nothing like her."

How can she tell? Sunny thought, irritated.

"I was born blind but I see better than everyone in this room," the blind woman snapped. Sunny felt her face turn red and she looked down.

"What does it matter that she doesn't look like her?" Ali said. "I hear she's an athlete like Ozo."

"That one," the man next to the blind woman said, pointing at Chichi. "Fast, fast, fast, and sharp like a Ginen-made sword." He clapped his hands together. "Oh, I'm impressed. But royal blood will mean extra danger for her."

"Royal blood means royal responsibility," Anatov said, speaking for the first time since they'd walked in.

"The free agent," the blind woman said. Her voice was shaking. "She's—she's seen it." They went silent. "Haven't you?" the blind woman asked.

"Seen what?" she asked, feeling her throat constrict.

"You know what I speak of," she said. "It's why you all are here today. It's why Black Hat has been kidnapping, killing, and maiming children. He is only one leg of the centipede, and the centipede's head is yet to emerge."

"It's going to happen? For sure?" Sunny said.

"It will," the blind woman simply said.

"You've really seen it?" Ali asked, his voice softening for the first time. Sunny nodded. "I'm so sorry. No one so young should witness the end of the world."

"The beginning," the blind woman corrected.

"Can someone speak straight?" Sasha said. "We've been told we have to fight Black Hat. We four, not you all. Sunny is the youngest, Chichi is the oldest"—he looked at Chichi but she said nothing—"or maybe she's the youngest and I'm the oldest. I'm fourteen. Why us? What can we possibly do? Who is Black Hat?"

"He's right," Orlu said, standing up. He placed his hand on Sasha's shoulder, a sign for Sasha to keep his mouth shut. "We need information." He addressed the two women on the left and the toucan man, "Great Madam Ntombi, Madam Bomfomtabellilaba, *Oga* Ali." He turned and addressed the blind woman and the man beside her. "And Great Great Madam Abok and *Oga* Yakobo, you are all very, very old and wise beyond imagination. You've travelled a long way. But what seems clear to you is confusing to us.

"Please, tell us how Black Hat is only one leg of the centipede, as you said, Madam Abok. Why do we have to do this and not a group of older, wiser people? Tell us what to do!" Orlu sat down and the room was silent.

"Checks and balances, you see?" said the woman Orlu had called Bomfomtabellilaba.

Abok, the blind woman spoke. "There will be a nuclear holocaust, but there will be something else, too. It will bring green and everything will change. Many laws of physics will shift and become something else. This place will become a new place. Sunny isn't the only one who's seen it. Several old ones have seen it, too.

"Whether Sunny knew it or not, she has always been a Leopard person. Just as her grandmother was. All free agents are what they always were—Leopard. And she is a child of the physical and spirit world. Sunny, you have friends and enemies in the spirit world, for before you were born you were a person of importance there. What kind of person were you? Well, that is something you'll have to figure out. A friend or enemy of yours showed you that vision in the candle. It changed you, no?"

Sunny nodded. It had been the first sign of what she was.

"Now, as I said, many know of what's to come. Some see that they can take advantage of it. Imagine chaos, and then in the middle of it all, someone comes with a logical blueprint for a new order. What would you do? You would follow that person, no? The closer the change comes, the more Black Hat types we will see. I say he is a leg of the centipede because I believe he is one of several, a minion. Above him is the true leader.

"Black Hat's real name is Otokoto Ginny. As you know, he passed his fourth levels which means he is an expert; he is a master; he is powerful. But something went wrong, and now he is corrupt, too.

"Otokoto was a Nigerian oil dealer who did big business with the Americans. But he had greater aspirations than financial wealth, just as he sought more than just *chittim*. He wanted power. That remains his greatest hunger, and his hunger has opened him up to terrible powers of the earth. There is a forbidden juju, a black juju. It is old and secret. He had only part of the juju and needed the book he stole from the library for the rest. The juju is to bring the head of the centipede through—Ekwensu."

Chichi and Orlu gasped so loudly that Sunny jumped.

"Why would anyone do that?" Orlu asked in a strained voice. Chichi looked like she was about to cry.

"The hunger for power will lead a person to dark, dead places," Abok said. "He's lost control of himself. He is lost. He will attempt it. Especially now that he has that book. If he brings Ekwensu through, Ekwensu will build an empire. She did it once before, thousands of years ago, and it was only by coincidence that Ekwensu was sent back." Abok paused. "People say it was a combination of lightning, an angry willful girl, a rotten mango, and perfect timing."

"What's expected of you four is simple," Abok said. "Two children have been taken. It happened two hours ago. Your job is to bring them back safely to their parents.

"This rain is not a coincidence. It is sent by Ekwensu. The thunder and the lightning and the water cleanse the atmosphere in preparation for Ekwensu's arrival. It's like rolling out the red carpet for a great queen. Do you see all these leaks? No natural rain could penetrate library walls.

"In about six hours, Black Hat will perform a ceremony on these two children. He will have them drink Fanta laced with calabash chalk, a substance that will enhance the spirit life within the children. Then he'll kill them. And when he completes this ceremony, he'll have gathered enough force to bring Ekwensu through."

"Will..." Sunny hesitated. But she had to know. "Will he recognise me?"

Sasha, Orlu, and Chichi all looked at her, baffled.

"He might," Abok said. "Though you don't look like your grandmother, there are other ways to know a spirit line when it runs strong."

She clenched her fists. "How do we find him?" she asked.

"He owns a fuel station near Aba," Taiwo said. "Start there, follow his tracks. Use the element of surprise. He is arrogant and has no respect for young people. He will not be expecting you and when he sees you, he will think you harmless."

"Why didn't people do this for—for all of the other children?" she asked.

"Timing is everything," Abok said. "It wasn't time."

"We had people try but they all came to a bad end," Ali added quickly.

"Timing," Abok said again. "This time, it will be right."

"We hope," Ali said.

She frowned. "You mean you've sent other groups like ours? And—"

"We have and will continue to until Black Hat is taken down," Yakobo said. "More is at stake than your lives."

"Black Hat is a shrewd sorcerer," Abok said. "He has protection, but we have watched for loopholes. The children that returned maimed but alive were all rescued by *Oha* Covens."

"Did the rescuers escape, too?" she asked.

None of the scholars replied. That was answer enough.

Sunny held the phone closer to her ear and turned away from the others. They were on a funky train, speeding down the road in the rain. The line remained quiet but she knew someone was there. "Mama, hello? I can hear you breathing."

"What do you want?" her brother Chukwu said. "What did you do?" There was the sound of a struggle. "I want to know!" her brother demanded.

"Let me talk to her," she heard her other brother Ugonna say.

"Give me the phone," she heard her mother snap. "Sunny?" Her voice sounded thick and she sniffed loudly. "Is that you?"

"Yes, Mama," Silence. "Hello? Mama?"

"Yes?"

Silence.

"Is—is it raining there?" her mother finally asked.

"Yeah."

"Of course it is," she said quietly.

"Mama, do you…" Sunny tried to speak, but it felt like something was softly squeezing her throat. It was the pact she'd made with Orlu and Chichi.

Silence.

"J-just come home," her mother whispered. "Make sure you come back home." Silence. "Be brave. I love you."

Sunny closed her phone, wiped her tears, and put all her questions out of her head. She had to focus. She turned to her friends. "Tell me about Ekwensu."

"She is like what Satan is to Christians," Chichi said. "She's one of the most powerful masquerades in the wilderness. If she comes through, if Black Hat succeeds—then think of what you saw in that candle. Now see that vision controlled by a demented monster that no one and nothing can stop."

They had twenty minutes before they reached the fuel station. Sunny held her head in her hands.

CHAPTER NINETEEN
UNDER THE HAT

It wasn't hard to find, even in the rain. Trouble is never hard
to find.

All they had to do was follow the line of cars. It started where
the funky train dropped them off, and led them to the shiny,
spotless fuel station. They huddled under Sunny's large black
umbrella as they walked—the umbrella she once used to protect
herself from the sun.

"What's the point?" Sasha asked. "These people will probably
get stuck in the mud on the way home. These are all Lambs."

"I think the fuel station is selling really cheap," Chichi said.

"So?" Sasha said, frowning. "Is it really worth it?"

"Fuel is already hard to find," Chichi said. "Cheap fuel is like
gold." She paused. "I wonder if having all these people around
helps with whatever Black Hat is planning."

"Probably," Orlu said. They were almost there. "Stop. Wait."
Orlu paused. "Cross the road. Hurry up."

They waited for two cars and a truck to zoom by, which
splashed them with water. Quickly, they scrambled across the
street and stood in a muddy parking lot.

"Rude drivers," Chichi said, slicking muddy water from her arms. "Rubbish."

"Doesn't matter now," Sunny said. "We're already soaked."

"What is it, Orlu?" Sasha asked.

"I don't know," Orlu said. "As we were getting closer, I kept feeling…you know, when I undo things, it's not always voluntary."

"Something there?" Chichi said. "Protecting the place from Leopard people?"

"I think so," Orlu said. "You didn't feel anything?"

"But you can undo it, right?" Sasha asked.

"I'm afraid," he said simply. Sunny felt sick. Orlu was a proud person. For him to admit this was serious. He let out a deep breath. "If I do this—everything will start. I know it."

"Then do it," Sasha said. "That's what we're here for."

"What about the element of surprise?" Sunny asked. She was thinking about how surprise had helped her team score its first goal.

"You can't always have things the way you want them," Chichi said.

"We'll be like cowboys walking into a bar full of criminals," Sasha said, laughing almost hysterically. He had a crazy look in his eye. "Forget surprise. Let's just go in there. We've all got big guns." He took out his juju knife. Sunny, Chichi, and Orlu did the same.

Like the team they were, they clicked their knives together. As the knives touched, they seemed to become one thing—one being made of four people. They all jumped back and looked at each other.

"Let's go then," Orlu said quickly.

Sunny closed her umbrella, dug its point into the mud, and left it behind. They held their juju knives ready.

People watched from the dry comfort of their cars. Several frowned, blinked, and wiped their eyes, probably unsure of what they were seeing. One woman was pointing at them and shouting something to the man in the passenger seat. The car's windows were closed and thus Sunny couldn't hear exactly what she said. But Sunny could imagine what she saw: four kids, one who seemed to glow because of her albino skin. One moment, the kids' faces looked like ceremonial masks and their motions utterly changed, the next they were just kids again.

More than a few people who'd seen Sunny and her friends or sensed something bad was about to happen got scared and drove off. Some, not wanting to lose their places in line, moved their cars up to take the spots, killed the engines, and fled. Others sank down in their seats, but not so much that they couldn't see what was about to go down.

When the four of them got within a few yards of the fuel station, Orlu stopped, a nauseated look on his face. Suddenly, he started moving—grasping, slicing, chopping, punching at the air with both his free hand and his juju knife. He was fighting with something. Gradually, he fell to his knees, still fighting.

"Can we help?" Sasha shouted.

Orlu didn't answer. Sunny had never seen him move his hand and knife so fast. He was like Bruce Lee, except Orlu didn't look so confident.

Then she felt it—a very slight shift in space, as if they were all moved forward by about a foot. "Ah! Did you see that?" someone exclaimed from behind them.

"What?" someone else shouted.

"No o, I'm getting out of here!"

More cars started. Several screeched away. In front of them, people still pumped gas. A gang of men came running out of the station, and there was a loud sucking sound. Orlu fell flat on the soaked concrete.

"Orlu!" Sunny shouted.

He'd rolled on to his back, breathing heavily. "Help me stand," he wheezed.

Sasha and Sunny pulled him up. He felt very warm, steam rising from his wet clothes. He leaned on them, rubbing his eyes. Otherwise, he seemed okay. He looked to the side of the fuel station, pointed, and said, "You see it? There."

Before, there was only an empty lot full of trash and weeds. Now, in the middle of the trash and weeds, was a patch of tall wild grass and an *obi*. It wasn't a normal *obi*. It had the usual thatch roof, but it was held up by steel pillars; there were drawings burned into the metal. Inside, they could just make out a large man and two small shapes on the floor. Lightning flashed across the sky, followed a second later by a bone-shaking crash of thunder. Sunny jumped, clutching Orlu tightly. Now he held *her* up.

"The storm's right above us," he said. "This is where it is."

A green-yellow blur streamed out of the obi and came rushing right at them, chirping and squawking. Sunny wiped her face to make sure she was really seeing a flock of angry-looking parakeets.

"Bush souls!" Sasha shouted.

"I see them," Chichi said quickly, holding up her knife. The flock undulated and rolled around the trees, spiraling at them. "There are five."

"Hey! All of you!" someone shouted. "Where you dey go?" It was one of the thugs from the fuel station's store.

Orlu broke into a sprint, and Chichi, Sasha, and Sunny did the same.

"We're going inside," Orlu shouted to her.

"We'll cover you," Sasha said.

Sunny saw Sasha whirl around and slash at something, a gash appearing on his arm, just as he disappeared in the hail of green-yellow birds. Chichi threw some sort of juju at another black shadow and then was covered by flying parakeets, too. Before Sunny could figure out how to defend herself, something cold hit her in the head. Everything became redness and pain. Then Orlu was shaking her and dragging her on. She fought through the lingering pain.

They ran for the *obi*. She could see the shapes now. They were children. Toddlers. Lying on the floor. One in a dress, and one in shorts with no shirt. So small and innocent and, perhaps, dead.

They stepped into the *obi*.

Her eyes met those of the man who had murdered her grandmother

Black Hat Otokoto had dark, smooth, shiny skin; arm muscles so thick they pushed at his clothes; and a barrel of a pot belly.

His chubby-cheeked face was unsmiling and his eyes were set deep between folds of fat. He sneered at her and she nearly dropped her juju knife.

"This is the last effort?" he laughed, turning away as if they were nothing. He began drawing something with chalk around the children. Behind them, Sunny could hear Sasha and Chichi making their way over as they fought the bush souls, fled the birds, and worked jujus to hold back Black Hat's thugs.

"If you come any closer, you will ruin what is already in motion. Then I will have to slaughter the two of you instead of just these children. Get out," Black Hat said. Then he seemed to be speaking to someone else. "All of you can also leave. These children are harmless. Go and watch for real threats," he said. All the commotion and squawking behind Sunny instantly stopped as the bush souls obeyed. Even his thugs went back to the fuel station. Sasha and Chichi came running in.

"What have you done?" Chichi shouted the minute she saw the children. "You evil bastard!"

Sasha took one look at the children, pulled something out of his pocket, and blew into it. It was the conch shell he'd bought from Junk Man. Its deep guttural sound made Sunny's head vibrate. "Come now!" Sasha shouted. "Take Otokoto's blood!"

Every insect in the area obeyed as if they knew the world depended on it. The air grew black with them, all trying to bite, sting, or defecate on Black Hat. Taken by surprise, Black Hat screamed and staggered back. Orlu and Sunny each grabbed a child. Sunny got the boy. He was limp in her hands, his skin cold. He was dead.

Black Hat shouted something in a language she didn't understand and all the insects fell to the ground, dead. He raised a hand and Sasha's shell dissolved dust. He glared at Chichi and Sasha. "You're as pathetic as suicide bombers," Black Hat said. "You will die for nothing."

Sasha brought his juju knife up and Black Hat laughed, doing the same. Orlu and Sunny took off with the children. When they reached some bushes a few yards away, they put them down. "They're not alive!" Sunny said, frantically wiping rainwater from her face. "They're dead! We're too late! They're dead! We—Sasha—"

"Quiet!" Orlu hissed. "Just go. Go help the others."

She moaned when she looked towards the *obi* where Sasha and Black Hat were having some sort of juju battle. Sasha was slowly sinking to the ground as a white cloud hovered around him. But he still held his knife. She couldn't see Chichi.

"They're dead!" she shouted. "We're all going to die! Why'd we come here?"

Orlu knelt in the mud beside the children. He put his knife down and clapped his wet hands loudly. He pushed his sleeves back, shook out his hands, and wiped his face. Lightning flashed, immediately followed by the bellow of thunder and heavier rain.

"Orlu, what are we going to—Orlu?"

He had a faraway look on his face, the same one he'd had at the Zuma Festival when he handled the masquerade. He began rocking back and forth, drawing symbols in the mud with his finger; they melted back into the mud seconds later. "Go," Orlu said calmly, not looking at her. "These children are dead. I don't know what I'm doing, but I have to do it alone."

She turned, about to flee.

"Wait," he said. "Cut off one of your braids."

She used her juju knife to cut it. She was in such emotional shock, she barely noticed she could feel her knife make the cut. "The hair of one who walks between," he said, taking it. "Now go."

She had no plan. The rain was now a deluge. The children were dead. Black Hat was killing Sasha. Where was Chichi? Sunny stepped into the *obi* just in time to see a bolt of red lightning shoot from Black Hat's juju knife and slam into Sasha's chest. He went flying out of the *obi* into the rain, skidding backward in the mud. Then he was still.

Sasha! she screamed in her head. She grasped her juju knife. She had no intention of using it to work juju. She was going to bury it in Black Hat's back.

"*I am a Princess of Nimm!*" Chichi screamed, standing at the front entrance. She slashed her knife from left to right and shouted some words in Efik. She stabbed her knife hard on the concrete floor of the obi. Sparks flew, but it did not break. "This charm is from Sunny's grandmother Ozoemena, to my mother, to you, Black Hat Otokoto."

Black Hat stared at Chichi as if seeing her for the first time. Chichi nodded, a wild look on her face. Then the colours came. Red, yellow, green, blue, purple. They blasted Sunny with heat as they flew past and went right for Black Hat. As they whirled around him, he shrieked.

"Past sins will always come back to haunt you," Chichi said.

Black Hat shrieked and shrieked, smoke rising from his skin, his clothes catching fire as the colours harassed him. One of his ears fell to the ground. Chichi scrambled to the side as he ran out of the *obi* into the rain. The drops of water hissed and vaporised as they made contact with his skin. But then, his screams changed to laughter. It was an awful, awful sound. "You can kill me," he said, his voice gurgling. He coughed wetly and laughed again. "But I am just a vessel! You're too late!" He threw his head back and shouted, "*EkwensUUUU!*" He grinned at Chichi, his mouth all teeth now.

"No!" Sunny shouted as Black Hat brought his knife to his neck and slit his own throat.

"Just needed one more death," he said in his gurgling voice. He fell over, gouts of blood and life pouring out of him.

Silence. Sunny met Chichi's eyes and even in the rain she could tell Chichi was crying.

Suddenly, the ground shivered with the most terrifying beat she had ever heard. THOOM! THOOM! THOOM!

"Sunny!" Chichi shouted. "Help me!" She'd run to Sasha and was trying to drag him back into the obi.

"It's too late!" Sunny shouted over the deep beat. It came from within everything around them. She grabbed under Sasha's armpits. Chichi took his legs. They hauled him in. Then Chichi knelt beside him and checked his pulse. "He's alive," she said, her eyes wide and twitching.

Outside, with each beat, the mud rose into a higher and higher mound.

"Oh God, she's coming," Sunny moaned.

"Stand your ground," Chichi said, looking angry. "Where's Orlu?"

"Out there," she said. "With the children. On the other side, near the bushes."

She couldn't tear her eyes from what was happening. The heavy downpour was causing the ground to flood. The thunder and the lightning had become one. But nothing drowned out the steady drum beat of the masquerade. The mound was now three feet high, pushing aside Black Hat's body as it rose.

Chichi cursed, patting Sasha's wet cheek. "Sasha, wake up!" She pushed his eyes open. Only the whites showed.

The termite mound was six feet high now. Termites buzzed from it but the rain beat them into the mud. Something enormous was coming through. It looked like the leaves of a dead, dry crackling palm tree tightly packed together. They crackled more when the rain hit them. Chichi held Sasha's hand and then took Sunny's. "He has done it," she said. "We have failed."

Sunny was speechless, frozen with terror. A monstrosity was growing before her eyes. The *Aku* masquerade was nothing compared to Ekwensu. She was of such deep evil that her name was rarely spoken, even in the Lamb world. As her monstrous form grew, she gave off a smell—an oily, greasy smell, like car exhaust.

Ekwensu was over seventy feet high and thirty feet wide. She was all tightly packed dried palm fronds.

"Pull him back," Chichi suddenly said. "Get back!"

"What are we gonna do?" Sunny asked as they dragged Sasha to the middle of the *obi*.

"Pray," Chichi said. "There is no use in running."

For over a minute, the horrifying thing that was Ekwensu just stood there. Then there was a heavy gust of wind and Ekwensu slowly began to fall. When she hit the ground, water and mud spurted in all directions.

The two girls huddled over Sasha. Chichi wiped the mud from his face so that he wouldn't suffocate.

The drumbeats stopped. So did the thunder. Sunny wiped mud from her arms, legs, and face and slowly stood up. "Is it dead?" she whispered. She hoped. Maybe Black Hat hadn't performed the juju properly or maybe he'd done things prematurely.

But then the flute began to play.

It was a haunting tune that made her want to tear off in the other direction screaming. It was the tune of nightmares. It was fast and melodious and full of warning, like the song of a sweet-throated bird happily leading the devil into the room.

Slowly at first, Ekwensu started rotating. Pulling up mud and soggy plants Ekwensu groaned, a deep thick sound that seemed to come from another place. She rotated faster. And faster, and faster.

Soon the air was red with flying mud. Ekwensu's wind rushed through the *obi*. She was spinning so fast that she was lifting back up. There she stood, whirling like a giant car-wash brush. The flute music urged her into dance and the drumbeats started up again. Around the open area in front of the *obi,* yards from the fuel station, she danced, spraying mud and water and uprooted plants and hunks of grass.

Ekwensu let out a high pitched scream, as if to tell the Earth she was back. And then everything shook so heavily with the deepness of the drumbeats that the obi, even with its steel foundation, began to crumble. Sunny felt it deep inside her, just below her heart—a vibration, then a tug. She clutched her chest.

She stood up.

Her body felt light. She felt strong. She realised that, above all things, she didn't want to die huddling away, afraid, helpless. She was going to go out there and face Ekwensu, damn the consequences.

She'd often wondered how she'd react if she were in mortal danger. If held at gunpoint of the dark road during a carjacking, would she be able to look the thief in the eye and negotiate for her life? Or if she saw a child drowning in a raging river, would she jump in to save it? Now she had her answer. She gathered together everything she had learned over the past few months and walked out of the obi.

One step at a time, she approached Ekwensu, who was so happy to be back in the physical world that she didn't notice Sunny until she was standing before her.

On instinct, Sunny let her spirit face move forward. In that moment, her fear of everything left her—her fear of Ekwensu's evil, of being flayed alive by the monster's fronds, of her family learning of her death, of the world's end. It all evaporated. Sunny smiled. She knew how the world would end. She knew that someday she would die. She knew her family would live on if she died right now. And she realised that she knew Ekwensu.

And Sunny hated her.

Ekwensu stopped dancing. She had no visible eyes, but she was looking down at Sunny. Relaxing her shoulders and mind, Sunny let Anyanwu, her spirit, her chi, the name of her other self, guide her.

She grasped her juju knife. Her motions were smooth. The world shifted. Suddenly, all things were—more. They were in the tall grass in the rain but they were in another place, too, where colours zoomed about, where there was green, so much green.

Ekwensu howled and began to spin again, faster than before. Sunny knew she had only one word to speak. She spoke it in a language she didn't even know existed.

"Return," she said.

Ekwensu shrieked and lashed out several fronds and smacked her to the side. She flew back, hitting a tree. Ekwensu whirled faster. But no matter how fast Ekwensu spun, she was sinking. Sunny struggled to her feet. As she watched Ekwensu sink, she was reminded of the Wicked Witch of the West's death in The Wizard of Oz. Ekwensu wasn't melting, but she looked like she was as she sunk into the wet, red mud.

Gone.

"Good," Sunny whispered.

CHAPTER TWENTY
I SEE YOU

Everything settled. Mud and plants and small trees dropped from the sky, the noise stopped—except for the *chittim* falling at her feet. The heavy pressure of fear lifted. In its place came a pain in her lower back and a general ache all over her body.

"Chichi!"

"In here," Chichi called.

Sunny slipped and fell in the mud twice before she got to the *obi*.

"I think he's waking up," Chichi said. "Go find Orlu!"

Sunny stumbled out the back of the *obi*. Orlu was still there with the two children, but everything had changed.

They were alive.

They looked at her with terrified suspicion as they clutched Orlu's chest and leg. Orlu was on his back, his eyes closed.

"*Orlu!*" His dark brown skin was covered with mud, his body was so still.

"Leave him!" one of the toddlers screeched in Igbo, clinging more tightly to Orlu as Sunny approached. The child kissed him on the cheek, muddying her lips, and looking fearfully at Sunny. "Don't hurt our angel. Please!"

"I won't," she softly said. "He's my friend. His name is Orlu."

"Oh-loo," the other child said, also kissing Orlu. He spit the mud from his lips, wiped Orlu's face, and kissed him again.

Slowly, Sunny knelt beside the children and felt Orlu's face. It was still warm. She touched his chest and felt a strong heartbeat. "Thank God, thank God," she sobbed. She whispered his name into his ear and softly shook him. When nothing happened, she kissed his ear and whispered his name again and again. When he still didn't respond, she shook him hard, starting to panic.

"What?" he finally said. His eyes opened and he looked at her. He turned to the toddlers. "What happ—it worked?"

Sunny nodded, tears in her eyes.

He raised his hand and wiped some of the mud from her cheek. She leaned forward and hugged him for a very long time.

"Can you stand up?" she finally asked.

"Yes," he said. She nearly had to drag him to his feet. "They were dead," he said, as he straightened up. "I reversed...Now they are alive." He laughed and pointed to a huge pile of *chittim*. "I passed out as it was falling," he said.

They walked to the *obi*, the toddlers following close behind.

"Black Hat brought Ekwensu through," Sunny said. "He took his own life to do it." She felt a little sick. "I...something happened where I...I don't know, but I sent her back."

Orlu stared at her for a moment. "The old ones sent us for a reason."

Sasha was sitting up and rubbing his chest when they entered. Next to him was a pool of vomit. When he and Chichi saw Orlu and the toddlers, they smiled.

"Sasha, you okay?" Sunny asked.

He nodded, looked at his vomit, and shrugged. "She used Healing Hands powder on my head. I guess she finally learned how to make it work...too well."

Chichi laughed. "Well, you're alive, at least."

"Let's gather our *chittim*. A council vehicle will probably be here soon," Orlu said.

"How are we going to carry all of that?" Sunny asked, noticing another pile on the wide path to the fuel station, earned by Chichi and Sasha, and another in the *obi*, earned by Chichi when she used whatever juju she'd used on Black Hat.

The library council van arrived half an hour later. Sunny laughed. She'd expected at least ten council cars to come running, carrying all the scholars in West Africa. Silly her.

"Sorry we're so muddy," Orlu said apologetically to the driver. The toddlers clung to his legs.

"No problem," the man said. "Been rainin'." From his accent, she could tell the man was from the Caribbean. "Get in," the driver said. "No worries, Star. Mud ain't paint, ya know."

In the van, the toddlers refused to leave Orlu. They snuggled against him in the backseat and were soon fast asleep.

"So your mother told you that charm?" Sunny asked Chichi.

"My mother knew your grandmother," Chichi said. "But not very well. Your grandmother visited my mother last night in a vision and gave her the juju that she gave me. My mother called it a 'bring back.' Only powerful scholars can make one. After they die, they bring it back to someone living and whoever the juju is worked on will have his worst sins brought back to him, if it is the will of the Earth."

"Classic," Sasha said. "Black Hat's sins really did catch up with him."

"I wonder how the other *Oha* covens saved those few children," Chichi said.

"Black Hat probably killed those coven members instead, using their lives to further open the way. But their lives probably weren't as effective as the children's."

"He may have forced them to drink ten times more calabash chalk before he killed them," Orlu said.

The driver stopped at the Aba police station and got out.

"You," the driver said to Orlu. "Help me bring 'em in. Let me do de talkin'."

Orlu nodded, as the driver carefully took the boy. Orlu carried the girl. They were in the station for half an hour.

"We were questioned a little bit," Orlu said, as they drove away. "We just told them we found them wandering near the fuel station. I didn't even bother trying to explain why they were covered in mud. Driver, will they be ok?"

"Right as the right kinda rain," the driver said. "Pickney dem resilient likle tings."

Orlu had developed an attachment to the children, as they had to him. It made sense; he had returned their lives. Sunny patted him on the shoulder, "It was for the best. They have to go home to their families."

"Hope they don't blab about what they saw," Sasha said.

"Even if they wanted to, they don't really have the words to describe it," Chichi said. "And who is going to believe what a small child says?"

"Hey, is this going to take us to Leopard Knocks?" Sunny asked. They'd turned onto a narrow bumpy road, flanked by forest on both sides. She could have sworn she saw a blue monkey swing by on a branch.

"Tis," the driver said blandly. "Only official dem can enter this way."

She looked attentively out the window. Minutes later, they approached a wide concrete bridge that ran over the river. Everyone closed their eyes, the driver included. He even let go of the wheel. Sunny kept her eyes open. She considered asking what was going on. *Nah, let me just watch*, she thought. The moment the car moved onto the bridge, she felt her spirit face pushed forward. It was involuntary. She looked around. Everyone else had changed, too!

Orlu's face was square and bright green. It was decorated with thousands of wiggling Nsibidi symbols too small for her to read. Sasha had the wooden head of a fierce-looking parrot, his thick beak a bright yellow and the rest of his head a bright red. She'd already seen Chichi's long, marble-like spirit face. She couldn't see the driver's because he was in front. Then they were over the bridge. She quickly shut her eyes and pretended to open them with everyone else. She looked out of the window, embarrassed and a little guilty. What she'd viewed was very, very private. But she was glad she'd looked.

When they reached the Obi Library, the sun was just coming out.

"Your *chittim* be taken to your homes," the driver said flatly.

"What about mine?" Sunny said. "My family won't know what it is."

"It's taken care of," he said. He drove off without saying goodbye. None of them really cared. When they stepped into the library this time, the change was obvious. Though several buckets still collected drops of water, people were walking about quickly and talking excitedly, some looked agitated and some happy. News travelled fast.

Samya jumped up from behind the *Wetin* desk when she saw them. "You're here!" she shouted. People stared. Samya ran over to them. "Come!"

Again they were led to the third floor, to Sugar Cream's office. Sugar Cream stood up and hurried over.

"Samya," she said, "get them fresh clothes."

"Yes, ma," she said, leaving.

"What happened?" Sugar Cream said. "Tell it all to me."

It took them half an hour. Samya came with a stack of clothes, setting them on the floor next to Sugar Cream's chair.

"The four of you did an excellent job," Sugar Cream said when they finished. She smiled at Chichi. "And you, Sunny, you put the deepest fear into Ekwensu. But because of what Black Hat has done, it will be easier for her to return now, and she'll start gathering in the spirit world. So we here in the physical world must also prepare. I've known this time would come." She paused. "I will tell your teacher and each of your mentors about all you did." She stood up and hugged each of them and took Sunny aside.

For several moments, Sunny and Sugar Cream looked into each other's eyes. Sunny held her breath but didn't look away. Then Sugar Cream pursed her lips and said, "You've proven yourself today in more ways than one," she said. She crossed her arms over her chest and nodded. "Okay."

Sunny grinned. She finally had a mentor.

CHAPTER TWENTY-ONE
TIMING

By the time Sunny got home, the sun was setting again.

She'd been gone for over twenty-four hours. The air was heavy
with mist as the rain water evaporated in the heat. Her brothers
were outside, kicking a soccer ball around. She wore a clean
green wrapper and white T-shirt. Her sandals, the ones she'd
left home in, were encrusted with mud, as was her hair. She ran
over and stole the soccer ball from her brothers with her feet.
Even in her wrapper, she was quicker than them.

"Where have you been?" Chukwu asked. He looked angry.
"You look terrible." She kicked the ball to Ugonna.

"Trying to save the world," she said.

Ugonna kicked the ball to Chukwu who kicked it to her.

"Daddy is going to flog the hell out of you," Chukwu said,
looking her up and down. "Mama defended you and said she
gave you permission to go, but Daddy..." He looked at his watch.
"You better get ready for it."

She brought her foot back and sent the ball flying across the
street into the neighbours' wall. Chukwu cursed at her as he
ran after it. Ugonna punched her in the shoulder as he followed
Chukwu. She went inside.

The smell of pepper soup filled her nostrils as soon as she opened the door. Highlife music came from her parents' room. It was half past six. She didn't care what time it was. She had reason to be late. And her father's issues weren't hers. She went to the kitchen where her mother stood bent over a huge pot of pepper soup.

"Hi, Mama," she said.

Her mother whirled around, her eyes inspecting every part of Sunny for injury. She grinned and tears came to her eyes. Then the grin fell from her face. Sunny turned around to face her father.

Neither of her parents had been to work in a day and half because of the rain. It was rare for them to enjoy free time. Her father wore his favourite home outfit, a yellow and blue wrapper and a T-shirt. But there was not a trace of relaxation on his face.

"Where have you been all day?"

"Dad," she said. Her voice shook. "I was up to nothing unholy or shameful or dirty. I was with my friends and—" She skipped back as her father's hand flew at her face. He missed. She held up a shaky hand. "Wait, let me explain!" He came at her again and again. She dodged him each time. He pushed aside the dinner table.

"Emeka!" her mother yelled at him. "*Ah-ah*, stop it now, *biko*, please!" She pulled Sunny behind her.

"This is why she runs wild," her father bellowed, breathing heavily, more irrational. Sunny's anger at him flared as he kept shouting, "It's all you! You protect her and she thinks she can do whatever she wants. She's got your genes, your damn mother's genes! She'll come to no good like your mother! Aren't you concerned about that? Eh?"

Her mother was quiet.

"You don't speak because you know I'm right," he said. "Your mother started disappearing at night around this age, no? Didn't you tell me that? Then one day she came home carrying you in her belly! She's lucky your father married her." He turned back to Sunny, disgusted. "A beating won't save you. Look at you, you're lost!" He turned and stormed out of the kitchen.

Sunny sat down at the table and just stared off into space, tears running down her face. It was sad, so sad. She put her head on the table. Through all her thoughts of Ekwensu, her friends, her parents, the fights in school, her grandmother, one question burned bright and hot: "Who am I, Mama?"

Sunny didn't see what her mother was doing because she had her head on the table. Her mother must have stood by the stove looking at her as she stirred the pepper soup because minutes later, she set a bowl of it in front of Sunny. She could feel the heat from the bowl against her arm. She could smell the pepper.

Her mother pulled up a chair and sat down with another bowl. Sunny could hear the click of the spoon as her mother ate. Slowly, she sat up. Her mother handed her several tissues and watched her wipe her red eyes and blow her nose. Then Sunny picked up her spoon and began to eat. The soup was hot and there were large chunks of chicken and tripe in it. It was good.

"Your father never wanted a daughter," her mother said.

Sunny spooned more soup into her mouth. Delicious.

"You see your brothers, they are just like your father," she said. "When they are sons, to him they're safe." She smiled sadly. "He doesn't understand that with them he was just lucky. It could have been them, too. You all come from me, as well as him. And it comes from her, my mother."

Sunny closed her eyes. "Mama, please, tell me about Grandmother."

Her mother looked at her soup and sighed. "Your auntie Chinwe told me you were asking about her." She looked at Sunny. "Are you sure you want to know?"

"Yes."

"Once I tell you, I can't—pretend I didn't say anything," she pleaded.

"It's okay. Please, Mama."

Her mother picked a piece of chicken out of her soup and nibbled on it. "I have two younger sisters, as you know," she said. "I'm not sure how my mother and father met, but my mother became pregnant with me while she was very young. My father refused to leave her. He loved her very much."

She paused and took a spoonful of soup.

"My parents weren't married," she finally said. "I don't know why—none of us ever knew why. I just tell your father that they were. If he had known, he would have never..." She looked at her hands, ashamed. "My mother was a strange woman. She loved us dearly and taught us to be smart and independent and educated. She watched us closely, as if she was looking for something, but I don't know what. Whatever it was, she didn't find it. Not in me or my siblings. I think she would have found it in you.

"I am not stupid. I can see between lines." She paused. "Weeks ago, I was passing your room one night and I saw—I saw a pile of metal things that I once found lying in my mother's bedroom when she was alive."

Sunny put her hand over her mouth, shocked. Her mother shook her head and waved a hand at her. "It's okay," she sighed. "Everyone thought that your grandmother was leaving at night to run around with other men, but there were other reasons. My father was just a coincidence. My sister once saw Mama disappear, right into thin air. We all knew that there was something strange about Mama."

"What do you think she was doing?"

She shrugged. "I have no idea. Why don't you tell me?"

"I—I can't," Sunny said.

She nodded. "That was what my mother used to say."

A silence fell between them.

"I trust you," her mother said, reaching forward to take her hands. This brought tears to Sunny's eyes, especially after the garbage her father had just spewed.

"Mama, you can trust me. I swear it," she said.

"I know."

"What of Dad?" she said finally, hopelessly.

She smiled sadly. "Some things are inevitable. But you're suffering for her dishonesty. He may not know that my parents were never married, but he knows of your grandmother's reputation. Men always blame the woman when a child dissatisfies him. In this case, he is right—in more ways than one."

"Does he hate me?" she asked.

Her mother paused. "We moved back to Nigeria because of you. I had this strong feeling that something bad was going to happen to you in the United States, and I told your father this. He didn't want to move here."

Sunny frowned. "So that's why he agreed? Because he thought your feeling was right?" Her father had moved back to Nigeria because of her? She found it hard to get her mind around this idea.

Her mother nodded. "But I was wrong. It wasn't that something bad would have happened to you in New York. It was that something needed to happen to you here in Nigeria."

Her mother got up and gave Sunny a tight hug.

"I love you, Mama," Sunny whispered.

"I love you, too," she said. "But be careful. Be very, very careful." She held her face in her hands. "Today is the day my mother was killed."

Sunny froze.

"Yes," her mother said. "And that day, it...was raining, too. It happened in my father's *obi*, behind the house."

Timing, Sunny thought. *The scholars had said it was all a question of timing.*

When she returned to her room, she found a wooden box on her bed. A ghost hopper sat on top of it. She quickly closed her door. This must have been the box her auntie told her about. It was made of thin wood. It was cheap. The moment she touched it, it flipped open. Inside were a hand-written letter and a sheet of Nsibidi symbols. The letter said:

Dear child of my child,

If you are able to read this then you were able to open the box which means you have manifested my spirit's touch. Welcome. Oh, welcome, welcome, welcome! I left this box with my oldest child. It was charmed with juju that would make her keep it safe and secret until the time came to pass it on. She has done well, for the juju would only work if she wanted it to, if she believed in me. This is good.

I am Ozoemena Nimm, but most called me Ozo. I am of the warrior folk of the Nimm clan, born to Mgbafo of the warrior Efuru Nimm and Odili of the ghost people.

I will get to the point. I was a rebellious child. I did not like being told what to do. So I went out and found a Lamb man and gave him children. I did not realise that to do this would lead me to a double life. A Leopard is not to tell a Lamb what she is, for Lambs fear Leopards by nature. I did not realise that my actions would lead you to a double life, too. And for this I am sorry. Only after I gave birth and went to live with the father of my children did I realise the mistake I'd made.

I was born with black, black, black skin. And my ability was not only invisibility, it was the ability to go back and forth between the wilderness and the physical world. I only learned this after I reached third level. What is your ability? I feel strongly that it will be like mine. If it is, then there is more history in you than you yet know. As I was, you have been busy.

There is something coming. This is all I can say. Not soon but eventually. Maybe you know about this already. Don't fear it, if you do. There is more than you realise.

Know that I love you. Know that I wish you well. Know that I have confidence in you because I have confidence in myself. I am incredible. Make Leopard friends so that you will not be alone and forgive the blindness of your parents and siblings. It is not their fault. It is up to you to be mature.

I must go. I hear my husband calling. I want to seal this box tonight for I feel strongly that something bad will happen to me soon. Take care of yourself and remember what is important.

Sincerely, Your ancestor, Ozo.

It was as if Sunny had just gotten a glimpse of her own soul.

Now she knew why her grandmother wasn't married. Like Chichi's mother, she too was Nimm, though Chichi's mother was some sort of royalty and her grandmother was a warrior. What did that mean? And did this make her Nimm, too? Did that mean she couldn't marry? Was she a warrior?

She looked at the sheet of Nsibidi symbols. It was all too sophisticated for her to understand—yet. She put it back in the box with the letter. She blinked and took the letter and Nsibidi sheet back out. There was one more thing in the box, an old black-and-white photograph of an unsmiling very dark-skinned woman holding a large knife across her chest.

"Grandma," she whispered. As the old blind woman at the council meeting had said, Sunny looked nothing like her. But what did that matter? She smiled to herself and carefully put the picture back in the box.

CHAPTER TWENTY-TWO
HEADLESS AND HEADLINES

The next morning, her wasp artist had built a man made out of something like sawdust with a hat of chewed up leaves. The man was plump and looked suspiciously like Black Hat. When Della saw Sunny looking at it, it flew to the dust man's head and hovered next to it batting its wings. The head blew away. Sunny laughed hard and clapped and said, "Well done! Looks just like him!" The wasp buzzed its wings with glee and flew out the window.

She grabbed the day's paper and unrolled it with shaking hands. The headline read:

Children Returned Safely To Their Parents

ABA, Nigeria (AFP)—A Three-year-old girl and a two-year old-boy, believed to be the children recently kidnapped by ritual killer Black Hat Otokoto, have been safely returned to their parents. They were found wandering the streets by two young men during yesterday's storms. The two men declined to give their names.

"They were angels sent from God," the mother of the boy said. "If you are out there and reading this, know that you have saved my life as you have saved my son's and I am eternally thankful." The parents of the girl declined an interview, but were also deeply thankful and relieved.

Further down the page was a photo of Black Hat's fuel station. And that headline read:

Fuel Station Goes Up In Flames

After Being Struck Twice By Lightning

EPILOGUE

Sunny sat down for her first class after the rains. She felt odd. She glanced over and met Orlu's eyes. They smiled at each other, as if sharing a joke. Once the teacher started talking, Sunny was surprised that she was still interested in learning normal things like algebra, literature, and biology. She could still concentrate.

During lunch, Orlu told her that Anatov would let Chichi know when they'd next meet. "He will probably give us two or three weeks to recover," he said. "But we will also be meeting with our mentors on our own."

"I think I have my work cut out for me," Sunny said.

"Of course, since Sugar Cream is your mentor, there is no doubt about that," he said, laughing. "Oh, did Chichi tell you? She and Sasha are going to prepare to pass the second level."

"I thought you had to be sixteen or seventeen for that."

"Well, who knows how old Chichi is? Sasha is early, but after what they just went through, he might as well have gained two years."

She nodded.

"You don't always have to be that age," he said. "It is just recommended. But if you don't pass, you will suffer, so you see why it is best to wait?"

"Yeah," she said. "So you don't think you're ready?"

Orlu shrugged.

"You're afraid to fail?"

"What of you? How many people can say they faced Ekwensu and lived? Not even the scholars can say that. And you have friends in the wilderness."

"Oh, please, I don't even remember what the second level is called."

"*Mbawkwa,*" Orlu said, as the bell rang.

"Feels weird, doesn't it?" she said to Orlu as they walked back in.

"You will get used to it," he said. "Having two lives is better than having no life at all."

"True." And she laughed.

ACKNOWLEDGEMENTS

Thanks to my editor at Penguin (United States), Sharyn November, for daring to taste pepper soup (literally and metaphorically). Thanks to my editor at Cassava Republic (Nigeria), Chinelo Onwualu, for seeing that a novel about witches and juju could be great fun. To my mother, for telling me about *tungwas* and my father for showing me how masquerades dance. To my sisters Ifeoma and Ngozi, for finding the original title of this novel (Akata Witch) hilarious. To my brother Emezie, for exposing me to pro-wrestling and naming my character Miknikstic. To my daughter, Anyaugo, nephew, Dika, and niece, Obi-Wan, who are constant reminders that the meaning of the word 'akata' runs deep. To Nollywood director and actor, Tchidi Chikere, for helping with all the Pidgin English portions of the book. To author Tobias Buckell and blogger Uche Ogbuji for the much needed help with the soccer/football terminology. And lastly, to Naija for being Naija. One love.